JUBAL

JUBAL

Norman Daniels

NEW ENGLISH LIBRARY
TIMES MIRROR

First published in the United States of America by Paperback Library, January 1970

*

FIRST NEL PAPERBACK EDITION OCTOBER 1973

*

NEL Books are published by
New English Library Limited from Barnard's Inn, Holborn, London, E.C.1.
Made and printed in Great Britain by Hunt Barnard Printing Ltd., Aylesbury, Bucks.

45001618 8

ONE

The work was backbreakingly hard, but he was the man for it. Riding atop the high seat of the beer wagon, he made husky, thickset Paddy O'Brien seem diminutive by comparison. When the horses pulled up along the muddy streets of St Louis, he'd hop down, remove the gate in the stake wagon, roll a full barrel of beer to one shoulder, curl a long, muscular, bronze arm around it, and make his way into the saloon.

His name was Jubal. If he had another, he didn't know it, because his folks were dead. He was nineteen, tall for his age, big, full-chested, brawny. He had high cheek-bones and a straight nose with little flaring of the nostrils. His lips were somewhat thicker than those of a white man, but not to any exaggerated extent. His eyes were a deep soft brown. His hair was wooly and jet black.

Somewhere in his family background there was probably a trace of Arab blood, but he was mostly Negro. His skin wasn't coal or blue-black. It was a brown shade, much like bronze.

He was naked to the waist because this was hard work under a hot sun. His pants were skintight and sweat-soaked, and they bulged with a manhood even looser pants could not have successfully concealed.

The tan-colored girl in a polka dot cotton dress worked in the kitchen of the saloon where she prepared the free lunches and sometimes entertained men who didn't mind a skin darker than their own. As Jubal went by, easing the barrel of beer through the doorway, she made a pass at his crotch, barely touching him.

'Man,' she said in admiration, 'is you as big as you look?'

Jubal stopped, peering down at her, fascinated by the smooth, shiny black hair which hung in a thick braid down her back. He couldn't resist reaching out and touching it, letting his fingers move lightly along its silky fineness.

'How come your hair's not wooly?' he asked.

' 'Cause my mama was white, that's why.' She used the tips of her fingers to make light, slow circular motions as they moved up his inner thighs to his crotch where they encircled and hefted the weight of his testicles.

'Them's mighty big balls,' she said, her fingers once again starting their slow, caressing movements. 'I juice up jes' feelin' of 'em. You want me spread my legs for you?'

Jubal stood with the barrel on his shoulder, his right hand

supporting it while his left tried to shoo her away. Any more of this and he'd quite likely drop the barrel and be fired while he was still floundering around in the suds. She arched her body and started a slow forward and backward motion while her pursed lips made sucking sounds. Jubal grabbed her right breast, squeezed it so tightly he expected to hear her scream. Instead, a low moan of delight escaped her throat and her hips started a rapid undulation.

'You that hungry for it, let go of my balls and let me set this barrel down.'

When her hands continued manipulating him, Jubal slapped them away. He continued on to the cellar where he deposited the heavy burden so gently it made only a whisper of sound as it hit the dirt floor. He ran back up the stairs. The girl was waiting for him, as he knew she would be, also angry, as he'd expected her to be.

'What you so uppity 'bout, nigger? Or are you only made to pleasure men?'

He grabbed her by the shoulders, his hands moved down, began kneading her buttocks. Oh Lord, he thought, she is nice. Good arms and legs, hard, young breasts impudently mounding the dress, a right pretty face and utterly available. And that hair. He wanted to undo that braid and run his fingers through it.

He spoke in a gentle voice, but there was a warning in it. 'You say that again and I'll paddle your ass so you won't sit down for a week.'

'If there ain't nuthin' wrong with you, big man, then what's wrong with me you don't care for what I got to offer?'

'Didn't say I didn't care for it.'

'Ever had a gal before, boy? A real gal, I mean?'

'Plenty. I had plenty of 'em, more gal than you.'

'I don't believe it. I don't think you'd know what to do if you went to bed with me, boy. I think you'd just lie there an' holler for your ma.'

He smiled thinly. 'Try me,' he invited. 'You just try me.'

'Now you talkin'. Every time you come here, I been tryin' to get your eye, but you don't even see me.'

'I saw you. I saw them big titties you got pressed up against me. You could drive a man crazy makin' them shake every step you take.'

His hands drew up the osnaburg she was wearing. She was completely naked underneath. Her legs parted willingly to let his fingers probe, separate and slip between the vaginal lips. They immediately became drenched with her juice. Her mouth sought his and she sucked first on his lower lip, then his upper, moving from one to the other and using her tongue in a manner that set his blood on fire. Her hands loosened his pants and pulled them down until his organ sprang loose from its confinement.

Jubal bent his legs so as to pierce her. She was moaning and gyrating and shaking her body so that she was in constant movement. His hands caught the osnaburg and jerked it over her head. At the same instant, she did an about-face, and, still with legs spread, bent forward, flinging her hands between her legs. She captured Jubal's penis, pressed it between her vaginal lips and started her gyrations again, her hands caressing his taut testicles.

'What you trying, woman?' Jubal gasped, now thoroughly aroused.

'Like doin' it this way. Go with me, man, go with me.'

'I want to put it in.' He was angry himself now and felt he was being made a fool of. 'You said you wanted it.'

'I do, man. I do. Tonight we'll do it your way. Now we do it mine. Don't you like what I'm doin' to you?'

'Sure do. But I don't like being called a man-pleaser.'

'Know better now. Do it my way now, man, please?' Her voice was almost a whisper, a pleading.

'What you want me do to you while we're doing it this way?'

'Squeeze my titties, man. Squeeze 'em real hard. Let's go now, man.'

Jubal went along with it. Her hands were in constant movement, mooing sounds came from her throat, even while her lips made sucking noises. His hands closed around her breasts, seeming ever more ample with her body bent forward. Their bodies moved in unison, and though he tried twice to enter her, each time she successfully eluded him, but she never let him slip free of her lips and their juices mingled. Just as he had his orgasm, her hands cupped and closed around his penis, catching his sperm.

She jumped free of him, spun around and brought her hands, still holding the liquid, to her face. She smelled of it first, then greedily lapped it up with her tongue, obviously savoring its flavor. Anger surged through him. He felt like striking her, for he hadn't been ready to break free, but his anger quickly changed to stunned surprise at what she did.

'You smells good and you tastes good. Real good, man. Got me a nice place in the roomin' house upstairs. You come see me 'bout nine tonight.'

'You let me put it in, I'll come.'

'I'll let you put it in, frontward and backward. Jest had to taste you, man. Better put your pants on. It's comin' up again.'

Jubal looked down. It was. He pulled up his pants, which had dropped to his ankles, reached down for the osnaburg and handed it to her. She managed to slip it on, even while still licking her fingers.

'Hey, Jubal!' Paddy O'Brien was yelling from the wagon,

"what the hell's keepin' you?"'

'Room 204. Don't forget. Room 204.'

'Ain't likely to.'

'Jubal, you don't get your damn ass out here in two minutes, I'm goin' to fire you.' Paddy was growing impatient.

'Coming,' Jubal called back.

He pressed her to him for a brief moment and then fled out to the wagon where he hoisted another barrel, delivered it to the basement, but he didn't see the girl this trip, nor the next four, and he knew she was busy in the saloon, setting up the lunches for the late afternoon crowd.

'Damn you,' Paddy grumbled as he clambered on to the wagon, 'I'm goin' to be late again. On account of you.'

Jubal didn't reply. He was in no position to tell Paddy that he was supposed to juggle some of those barrels too, and not merely act as a teamster. Being a free Negro didn't mean he could critise a white. Jubal didn't mind. He was paid three dollars and seventy cents for ten hours a day, six days a week and he managed to live on it. Besides, he liked being out of doors, seeing people, and meeting girls like the one with whom he intended to spend the night.

It wasn't bad work for a young, healthy, eager Negro boy in the St Louis of 1840. Better than being a slave on some plantation, driven by whips, given no freedom. He often thought about what it was like being a slave. His father and mother had been manumitted before he was born. They'd gotten out of the true South as quickly as possible and Jubal had been free from birth. As free as a person of color could be, even here in St Louis.

His parents had died two years ago, but he still occupied the two-room shack close by the river. He liked to wander down to the water and watch the barges go by, marvel at the riverboats bright with candlelight and oil lamps, paddle wheel churning the water and smoke eddying from the tall stack. He wondered what it would be like aboard one of them. He knew the boats went all the way down to New Orleans. That seemed a world away, but he could dream about it. Now and then he met a river black who told him lurid tales of savagery, of staged fights to the death between slaves, set upon one another by their white masters so money could be exchanged in betting. They spoke also of the tan-skinned women, the food, the warmth, the excitement of sexual freedom.

Tonight, Jubal smiled softly to himself, he'd have all the excitement he needed right here in St Louis. He washed carefully and rubbed on cornstarch so that his skin would smell sweet. He was proud and he would not go to a woman with the muskiness that exuded from his sweat-soaked body by day.

He wished to bring some small gift along, so he rummaged

among the minor articles his mother had left. He came upon a small mirror which shone brightly under the ministrations of some abrasive dirt gathered outside the cabin, and plenty of soap and water. She'd be vain. All of them were, and anything that catered to her vanity would be gratefully received. He hoped so, because he knew he'd want to see her again.

He put on pants as tight as those he worked in. A white shirt he had laundered himself seemed ready to split under the stress from his muscular body. He polished the shoes he'd bought secondhand. He didn't mind that they were too big for him. Unlike most big men and very much unlike most Negroes, his feet were comparatively small. Yet they gave him a fine sense of balance and allowed him to move with more than average agility.

At five minutes of nine, he climbed the outside stairway leading to the second-floor porch and the hallway along which there'd be the rooms so common in these two-story structures. They were rented out by the week. Some were good, some were not, and most were so bad they were evil. But they were good enough, he was often told, for niggers. Not to Jubal. Nothing was good enough, not even the fanciest lodgings the whites could provide for themselves. That was his idea of the difference between being free or slave.

He ran up the stairs beginning to feel the rise of his anticipation and he moved quickly down the darkened corridor. Each door had brass numerals nailed to it so it was a simple matter to find 204. He stopped before it, waited until his breathlessness died down and some of his eagerness abated. Then he ran a hand over his wool, brushed the shoulders and sleeves of his shirt and knocked. A feminine voice told him come in.

He opened the door and stepped into a darkened room.

'Close the door,' the girl in the bed said, her whispered voice a command. 'Go on, close it. You want an audience?'

'Reckon not,' Jubal said. He was mildly disappointed. He would rather have looked at her for a while, admired her and fondled her before taking her to bed. She was too eager, too anxious and she'd likely have little staying power, but if this was the way she wanted it, he wasn't complaining. The second time she'd be better, and he could then take the time to admire her.

'You want I should get straight into bed now?' he asked.

'I been lyin' here waitin' and itchin' and startin' to get hot 'nuff to cook on. What you waitin' for, man? Shuck your clothes. I'm aimin' to make you pant. You like what I did today?'

'Been thinkin' about it ever since.'

'Kinda surprised you, didn't I?' Her voice was so soft Jubal had difficulty in hearing her.

'Sure did. Never had a woman wanta eat my juice before.'
'Never had a woman suck on you?'
'Nope.'
'Ain't you ever sucked on a woman?'
'Kissed a few there. The ones ain't too musky.'
'I ain't musky, honey. Come on. Try me.'
'Aim to.'
'Think you big enuf to fill me up?'
'Ain't never had any complaints.'
'All I'll say is you sure looked like a man, felt like a man, juiced like a man, tasted like a man. Now let me see if you is. No more talkin'. I'm gettin' too impatient.'

She'd find out he was a man all right. When he gunned her, she'd yell. They all did, but once they accommodated to his size, they reacted with wild gyrations, outflung legs, hands and mouth busy everywhere they could reach and, afterwards, the places they hadn't been able to get at before.

Jubal grinned in the darkness as he raised one foot to remove a shoe. Then the other, after which he dropped his pants, then took off his shirt. He fumbled in the dark for the bed, crawled in and at once the warmth of the woman enveloped him and his arms went about her. It was good that she didn't wish to wait because he knew he could not. He moved her on her back with one deft application of hands and knees. He flung himself atop her, entered her, and she uttered a moan and clung to him. It was better than he expected. This was a girl he wanted to see often. She smelled good and she was able to handle his enormity with ease.

It was so satisfying. It made up for the backbreaking work he was compelled to do in order to eat and live. It was recompense for the abuse he took because his skin wasn't white. He'd known girls before, but none like this. It was going to be a great night and there'd be many afterwards.

Her hands moved slowly down the length of his body, teasing and exploring, and his maleness responded. His hands moved up to touch the silkiness of her hair and he let his fingers entwine around it. He wished she'd stroke his body with it. He'd ask her to later. His face rested against her breast and his mouth sought her nipple. It was soft, but he worried it with his tongue and felt it grow hard. He sucked on it gently until her whispered 'Hurt me' caused him to bite on it while his hands moved down to her buttocks. He caught bits of flesh between his fingers, moving along the areas and pinching hard. He knew he was bruising her, but it was what she wanted, for she responded with passionate moans and slow thrusts of her body which quickened as his mouth found hers and their lips and tongues mingled. She caught his upper lip between her teeth and bit hard. The taste of his own blood made him want to penetrate her, hurt her the way she had him.

He raised himself and moved between her legs. Her body arched and she reached for his penis, using both hands to guide his organ into her. Their bodies began a slow rhythmic movement that increased with their passion until her scream of ecstasy broke off in midair to signify her climax.

Even then, she held him close, keeping his now-limp organ inside her. Her hands caressed his buttocks and her thighs still jerked spasmodically. It seemed to Jubal that sweat also suctioned their bodies together and he liked the feeling. Her mouth, against his ear, whispered obscenities – words and expressions he'd, up till now, heard only men use. He liked hearing her say them. It made their act more complete. He always imagined a white whore would talk this way. Jubal wished the night could last forever.

He was too engrossed to hear the click of the door latch, but when the room filled with yellow light, he gave a grunt of anger and exasperation and sat up in bed. Two white men were in the room. One held a lamp, the other a very large pistol.

'Git up outen there,' the one with the gun said. 'Git up, you black bastid, or I'll spill you all over that bed.'

Jubal glanced over at the pillow, but the girl had pulled the gray sheet over her head as befitted her modesty. He began to reach for his pants, still on the floor.

'I said git up outen there,' the man with the gun repeated. 'I ain't sayin' it again.'

Jubal slowly slid out of bed. He was buck-naked, but he didn't mind that. What he did resent was the fact that these men were going to take his place in the bed and the girl would be raped. It happened all the time. There wasn't much he could do about it either, so long as one of them handled a gun. Even if they weren't armed, he'd be expected to stand aside.

The one with the lamp stared at him. 'Boy, you shore are a big one. If I was equipped like that, I'd peddle it up and down the street and get rich.'

'What you gen'men want?' Jubal asked. 'I ain't done nuthin' bad, 'cept bed down with a gal who wanted me to.'

'I can see why she wanted to,' the one with the lamp grinned broadly. 'But, black boy, you know better'n that.'

Jubal knew he was in trouble. He didn't know how deeply nor what kind, but when this happened, it was best to act like a no-account nigger. No one paid much attention to them and regarded them as too stupid to do anything deliberately wrong.

'Don't know whut you talkin' 'bout, masta,' he said.

'Reckon you do. There's just one way to treat a nigger who rapes a white gal.'

Jubal stared at him. 'Ain't no white gal heah, masta, and they sure wasn't no rape. You jest ask. . . . '

His mouth opened and his eyes bugged. The girl now sitting up in bed was white as talcum powder. This wasn't the girl he'd met. He'd never seen this one before. He was so stunned he couldn't speak.

'Hang him.' she said coolly. 'Take him out so the law can hang him. I been raped and I'll swear to it in court. Get him out of here!'

Her eyes lingered on his crotch. Jubal disregarded the gun and picked up his pants. He slipped into them, drew on his shirt.

'Reckon ain't much I can say, this gal says I raped her. You gen'men the law?'

The one who seemed to be in charge set the lamp down on the rickety dresser. 'This gal you raped is my sister. I ought to shoot you down. But I'm willin' to make a bargain with you. What's your name?'

'Jubal, suh. Jes' Jubal.'

'You a free nigger?'

'Yes, suh, I'se free.'

'Then I reckon it ain't so bad.' He glanced at the girl now sitting on the edge of the bed, showing no embarrassment in her nudity. They weren't even being clever about this.

'How much I got to pay, suh, for rapin' your sister?'

The white man looked at his partner. 'What you think, Wiley?'

'See no reason not to turn him over for hangin'. Too good for a black rapist, you ask me.'

'Sister,' the other man addressed the girl, 'did he hurt you?'

'Never felt nothing I didn't like,' she said. 'Be a shame to hang a man like him.' She giggled. 'He's plenty hung right now.'

'That's what's givin' me an idea,' the white man mused. 'Black boy, you got five hundrud dollahs?'

'No, suh, ain't got five dollahs, suh,' Jabal replied promptly.

'Then you'll have to do what we tell you or we'll turn you over to the law. They'll hang you tomorrow.'

'After they cuts off your balls,' the man named Wiley added.

Jubal gave a groan of anguish. It was all pretense. They were trying to scare him for purposes of their own. This whole thing had been set up to get him in this position. He had no idea why, but he had an idea he was going to find out soon enough.

Jubal prided himself on believing he was better educated than either of these men, or the harlot who sat there on the bed wearing nothing but a silly grin. But knowledge and brains were more of a hazard at this moment than an asset. First of all, if these men believed he was smart, they'd simply shoot him and say they caught him in bed with the girl. If he managed to get himself before the bar of justice, he'd find out that justice was dispensed to this whore, not to the black boy involved with her.

Even if he was wholly guiltless and had not even been in the room, the white men would be believed and his word worthless.

Jubal gave a slow nod of his head. 'Reckon I does whut you tells me, suh.'

'My name's Sedella. You call me Mister Sedella, y'hear? Now you're comin' with us. You're goin' to do some travelin', boy. Walk out behind Mister Wiley and ahead of me. If you make a break for it, I swear I'll shoot you dead.'

Jubal moved out, descended the stairs. On the street he discovered that Wiley had put the gun in his pocket, but kept a hand around it. Jubal waited for further orders.

Wiley said, 'Better tell him what we got in mind so's he don't get no fancy ideas.'

Sedella grinned. 'Boy, after I had a good look at your equipment, I got this here idea. Mister Wiley an' me, we're headin' down the river a piece. By riverboat. You ever wanted to ride a riverboat, boy?'

'Sure did,' Jubal admitted truthfully. 'Sure did, suh.'

'You're going to get the chance. We'll give you a fine stateroom. You've never seen anythin' like it in your life. What we ask in return for this ain't nothin' you'll be agin. Fact is, we may have to kinda hold you back some. Ain't goin' to tell you 'zactly what it is now, but no man, black or white, will ever be so pleasured again. Now walk ahead of us. We'll tell you where to go.'

Jubal obediently did as he was told. He considered trying to run for it, but gave up because there was an open meanness in the eyes of these men. They'd have no hesitation in shooting. They instructed him when to turn and when they entered dark and narrow streets near the riverfront, Jubal began to wonder if they simply meant to kill him and throw him into the water. He believed nothing they had told him. There'd be no riverboat, no fine stateroom.

As they neared the docks, he saw that there wasn't even a sidewheeler in port. Now Wiley went on ahead, and disappeared among the low dirty-looking sheds and warehouses for a few moments. When he reappeared, he signaled by waving and Sedella ordered Jubal to move faster.

They brought him into a small shed, so low they had to crouch upon entering. It smelled as if it had housed sheep or poultry. But Jubal, looking about in the murky gloom broken only by the light from a slender candle which Wiley lit, saw the heavy planks bolted to the walls and the chains attached to the planks. This was a slave pen, though he couldn't believe it because they were outlawed here.

'You goin' to be shackled,' Sedella said, ' 'cause we don't trust you none.'

'No, suh,' Jubal protested. 'Don't want no spancels on me. I is a free nigger. I waits. I don't run, suh.'

'Every nigger runs, he gets the chance. You sure ain't no different.'

Jubal sensed violence about to break around him, and he felt fear rise in him. He decided he must stop being docile and take his chances.

'Ain't goin' to be spanceled,' he insisted.

He began to swing a big fist at Sedella, forgetting, in his desperation, that he couldn't see Wiley and that meant the second man was behind him.

Wiley had picked up a length of wood to be used as a club. He struck Jubal on the head, a skull-crushing blow to most men. Jubal fell to his knees. He tried to get up. The club swung down on him again. This time he fell forward and lay still.

TWO

He was uncomfortable. That was the first sensation he experienced. He wanted to put his hands down by his sides, but they wouldn't obey. He felt as if he had no arms. He opened his eyes and memory came back with a discouraging rush. He was in total darkness, but the smell of the place told him he was in the same shed where he'd been struck and knocked out.

He was seated on the dirt floor and his arms were held above his head by handcuffs attached to a chain which, in turn, was fastened to the heavy plank. He gave an experimental tug to the chain, but it made his wrists and hands ache so much, he gave up the idea of breaking loose.

Jubal knew what was happening to him. First, the tan-colored girl had seduced him, as she'd likely done to many others. He'd gone to her room and, in the darkness, bedded down with a white prostitute whose virtue was then saved by her so-called brother and a friend. It was all a lie, but Jubal would never be in any position to prove it.

He'd be put aboard some stinking scow that would be sent down the river to one of the southern ports and there he'd be let out and sold as an escaped slave. It was being done all the time. Many unscrupulous white men made six or seven thousand a year at this work. Sometimes the blacks they sent down were escapees, but many were not. Wiley and Sedella were paid on an average of three hundred dollars for each black they brought to market. He'd been warned to beware of these men who sometimes befriended a black until they were ready to ship him downriver. Often they got him drunk so he'd put up no resistance. The pair Jubal had met were not given to such refinements. A blow from a club cost nothing.

He had to make the most of his situation, but he quickly resolved that he'd break for it the first opportunity that came his way. So he rested and fought the pain caused by keeping his arms raised for seven or eight hours.

It was afternoon when they came for him, slipping into the shed quietly. To Jubal, it was now apparent they used the shed often. Wiley remained outside at the door while Sedella crouched down before Jubal.

'I'm right sorry we had to do this,' he said. 'Now we're goin' to make it up to you. If I take off the spancels, will you promise to behave?'

'Yes, suh,' Jubal lied. He'd break this man's back if he got the opportunity.

The cuffs were removed from his wrists and his arms dropped like dead weights. He couldn't have lifted them if he exerted every ounce of strength he had left.

Sedella lit the cheap candle stuck on a block of wood by its own wax. 'We promised you a fine cabin on a fine riverboat. That's where we're goin' now. Think I'm lyin' 'bout that, Jubal?'

'Didn't say you was, suh.'

'You'll find out I ain't. Only one good thing you got to do for us, and if you handle it real good, you got a steady job.'

'Yes, suh.'

'The best job any nigger ever had.'

'Yes, suh,' Jubal repeated stupidly, wondering what further trickery they were up to.

'Know what we've hired you for?'

'No, suh.'

'Screwin'.'

Jubal wrinkled his face. 'Yes, suh?'

'Don't blame you none for not figurin' what I mean. Wiley and me, we pick up escaped slaves and send 'em back. We get paid for some of 'em like they was a regular coffle offered for sale. Now we gets us quite a lot of nigger gals. Real young an' full of spunk. We sells 'em and they fetches a good price, but – if they's pregnant, they fetch more. Your job is to get 'em knocked up.'

'You mean . . . I beds down with gals you brings to me?'

'How's that for work, eh? It'll make up for the sore head you got when Wiley bashed you one. You goin' to behave now, Jubal, since you understands what we saved your black hide for?'

'Yes, suh, I understands real good.'

'Think you can knock 'em up? Maybe ten, twelve of 'em, on the trip south?'

'You bring 'em,' Jubal said, 'an' see.'

'All right then. Can you get up?'

'I kin try. . . . ' Jubal managed to rise, but not with the use of his arms. They were still numb and limp. He preceded Sedella out of the shed. Wiley signaled he was to follow them. Now, where there'd been no riverboat last night, a gaudy, wonderful, beautiful sidewheeler was at the dock. Negroes were swarming up and down her gangplank, laden with supplies and cargo. On the dock, passengers were already gathering to board later when the river gang's work was finished. Jubal was going aboard with the cargo and he still envisioned a stinking hold where he'd be spanceled again and brought south to be sold. He would never believe the word of a white man again.

They led him across deck and down a companionway to a cabin on the passenger deck. It was large, comfortable, ornate. There was a rug on the floor, heavy furniture of very good quality, properly placed. There were fragile curtains on the windows looking out over a private deck and drapes that could be drawn by night. There was a large and inviting bed, wash basin, slop pail, towels, everything a gentleman could desire.

The walls were papered in magenta, and in an even row along three walls, small, framed pictures hung. There must have been fifty of them. Some were duplicates, none looked expensive.

'This is where you make us rich with that equipment you got between your legs, Jubal,' Sedella said. 'We'll send the wenches in soon as the boat sails. We want each one seeded every night. Think you can do it?'

'I kin do it,' Jubal promised, still sorely puzzled because they seemed to be keeping their word.

'Good. If you step outen this cabin, you gets shot and dumped overboard. This is a first-class cabin an' niggers ain't allowed, but we wanted you to be happy and comfortable so we made a deal with the captain. We feeds you good, all you kin eat.'

'Knows you got to be fed good to do this kind of work,' Wiley added with a lewd laugh. 'We'd give you raw oysters they was in season – an' we could get some.'

'Yes, suh,' Jubal said meekly.

'If you handle this right and you knock up half of the wenches, you got yourself a steady job,' Sedella promised.

'An' if any of them wenches fights you,' Wiley said, 'you rape 'em, hear me?'

'Yes, suh, I rapes 'em,' Jubal replied. This was the craziest business he ever heard of, but it did make some sense. It was true that pregnant wenches brought better prices, and if he could start the pregnancy of these girls while they were on board, there'd be that much less of a wait in a slave pen before they began to show.

'They all looks like you, Jubal,' Sedella roared and slapped his thigh at the joke. 'Even the li'l gals, they looks like you. Tell you what. For every li'l sucker you turn out, we'll give you one silver dollah. How's that?'

'Likes it, suh. Real good, suh.'

'Like I said – some of the gals don't like bein' bred, but you breeds 'em. Every one. Knock 'em down if you have to, an' mount 'em if they hollers they goddamn heads off. You kin rest now.'

'An' you better,' Wiley said, 'because you'll need all the sap you got.'

They left him in the cabin, not handcuffed. Free as the air, except that he had an idea that if he tried to escape, they'd be waiting for that too. Besides, it seemed as if they were going to keep their word. If they had no such intentions, there'd be little point in providing him with a stateroom like this. In fact, even if he was supposed to earn his keep by raping one wench after another, it seemed strange he would be allowed to do it under such luxurious conditions. He still wouldn't believe it until the first wench was herded into the room.

Wiley drew the draperies and warned Jubal against opening them. 'White passengers sees you here, they goin' to feed you to the river bottom. Mister Sedella an' me, we are kindly folk and we aim to please you 'cause you sure enough goin' to please us.'

'Sweahs I does,' Jubal said as cheerfully as he could manage.

They left him then, taking the precaution of locking the door. Presently he heard the gay laughter and the light voices of the white passengers as they came aboard. The ship began to throb as the engine was tested. The loading was completed and, after a few more minutes, the whistle hooted dismally half a dozen times as the boat began to move out into the river.

Jubal had never been aboard a boat. He wanted to see what it was like so he risked opening the draperies enough to peek out. The dock was rapidly dropping away. It was a strange sensation to be carried like this, to see the shore receding until the boat turned its prow downstream. Now the riverbank slid by with frightening speed. Jubal couldn't get over it. He was living in luxury, aboard a fine ship in a fine cabin. Perhaps they'd string him up in the next hour or two, but at least he'd lived this much. A strange excitement gripped him. He was almost glad he'd been literally kidnapped and brought here against his will.

Later in the afternoon, Wiley appeared with a bucket full of food. It was carelessly mixed together, but there was ham, greens, boiled potatoes, turnips and carrots. Enough for two men. There was a fat chunk of white bread too, one end of it smeared with lard. Jubal realised that he hadn't eaten in many hours, but he'd been too confused and excited to think of food. Now the tangy aroma of it made him ravenous and he sat down on the edge of the bed and dug into the bucket with the bent fork provided for him.

'After you eats, you lays down an' gets some sleep,' Wiley said. 'You have to stay awake all night and be fresh for every wench we send in.'

'I'll serve 'em, suh. I'll knock 'em up fast as you sends 'em in, suh.'

'Good. It'll take four days this trip and every night you goin' to be real busy. Days you stays in this cabin an' sleeps. Nothin' else, you understand?'

'Yes, suh. Reckon ain't goin' to feel much like goin' anyplace I spends every night rapin' wenches, suh. Why you so good to me, Masta Wiley, suh?'

'That's easy. Me and Sedella like you, Jubal. You're the kind of boy we been lookin' for. You got everything in the world to make you a hell of a fine stud.'

'Yes, suh,' Jubal agreed heartily. 'I takes good keer of 'em.'

He finished the food, stuffing himself in the process, and afterwards he felt sleepy, so he lay down on the bed and dozed off. He wasn't sure how long he'd been asleep, but it had been daylight when he lay down and now it was night.

Someone was at the door. It swung open and light streamed in. Wiley entered with an oil lamp in each hand. Sedella followed with two more. They placed these about the room for maximum light.

'We'll bring in the first wench in five minutes,' Sedella said. 'You keeps these lamps burnin' full all night. That way we sees you ain't sleepin'. When you finish with a wench, you knock on the door an' push her out. We'll send another'n in right fast.'

'I'm waitin',' Jubal said.

The door closed and was again locked. He stood in the middle of the room and peeled off his shirt, removed his shoes, let his pants drop. He kicked them over to a corner of the room. They were really going to make him a stud. For a nineteen-year-old boy, that wasn't so bad. Better than riding the beer wagon and doing Paddy O'Brien's work for him. Better than hanging around the dirty nigger slums and sleeping alone in the old shack where he'd been born.

The door opened and a girl was roughly pushed in. She hurtled across the cabin until Jubal grabbed her. She was no more than fifteen, a skinny little thing, but full of savage spirit. She knew what she'd been brought here for and she fought him furiously. She clawed at his face until the blood ran. She kicked him, aiming for his crotch as well as his ankles, but her bare feet made little impression. Her nails, however, did.

Jubal's hands enclosed her waist. He picked her up and, holding her as far away from him as possible, spun her halfway around. When he caught her, her back was to him. Still in that position, his arms crossed as he turned her so that her head was toward the floor. Her osnaburg fell over his arms. All the time she was screaming for him to let her go. He threw her lightly into the air and grasped her groin. The dress was now held on only by her arms clasped about her shoulders. Her legs still kicked out, trying to find a target, but he still held her away from him. Holding her only by the thumb and last two fingers of each hand, he let his remaining fingers move back and forth lightly along her pubic hair. His grip on her moved down still further and he pulled her legs apart. His fingers again went to work and her screams lessened and became tortured sobs as he succeeded in arousing her. He brought her close to him, let her head touch the floor and moved his penis along her vagina a few times, then raised her again. This time her arms dropped and the osnaburg slipped over her head. He believed he had her now and, still holding her in a hanging position, he carried her over to the bed, laying her gently the length of it. He was about to join her when her leg thrust out in a savage kick meant for his groin. He moved in time to avoid it and struck her a savage blow across the face. She cried out in pain and made no further attempt to fight him.

Her rebelliousness made him more desirous than ever.

'Why you fightin' me, gal?' he asked, using the lingo of his people. He had been betrayed by one of his own already, and he had no idea if another might be sent in to spy on him. If so, they'd have nothing to report except he was a stupid black doing what he was told.

The only reply to his question was a look of hate.

'You pure?' he asked, feeling a twinge of pity for this she devil.

When she made no answer, he spread her legs and used an exploring finger. It entered her without resistance. He kept it there.

'Why you fightin' me, gal? When you been had before? An' how many times?'

'Yesterday for the first time. By them.' She motioned with her head toward the door. 'Many times as they was good for.'

'I gotta take you, gal,' he said softly. 'You want it be rape, it be rape. You want it be good, I'll make it good. You say.'

While he spoke, his free hand moved lightly along her thigh, up to her waist and over her stomach in slow, circular motions. Gradually, her mouth softened and parted. The hate left her eyes and they gentled, reminding Jubal of a puppy dog's. Her arm raised, stilled in midair for a few moments. Jubal wondered if he was once again going to feel the sharpness of her nails, but he was rewarded by her soft palm touching his cheek and her fingertips moving slowly down as they traced the line of his cheekbone.

'Take me. Take me kindly.'

Jubal smiled at her trusting innocence. He removed his finger so that he would have both hands free to arouse her further. He bent down and kissed her on the mouth. Lightly first, then, as he felt her passion mounting, his lips parted and he sucked her tongue into his mouth. Shortly, she was doing some exploring of her own. Soon her body began to writhe; her legs spread and her back arched. She was ready.

Jubal eased himself between her legs and entered her. She whimpered at first, for he was big, but she didn't protest. She was as eager as he. It wasn't easy, for she was small and tight and new at this. But he was patient and as her juices flowed, it made the act easier and more pleasureful and when finally they reached their peak, she was crying out for more.

When it was over, she wanted to linger, but he knew he had to satisfy many more wenches before the night was over, so he picked up her osnaburg, helped her into it and brought her over to the door. Once again, those eyes, still innocent and trusting, regarded him with longing. He wished he could do something for her, help her escape the life she was headed for, but he quickly thrust the thought from his head. Best for him not to think. He knocked on the door and when it opened, he pushed her through it, feeling relief when it shut behind her. He didn't want any more like her, he told himself. It made him feel ashamed and he had no cause to, for he wasn't doing this because he wanted to. Not to someone like her.

He was glad when the door opened again because he had no more time to think. A woman ten years older came in. She was husky and well aware of what was expected of her.

She had a flabby stomach, ill-concealed under the cheap dress which she pulled off and threw on the floor, all the time eyeing Jubal's tumefying artillery.

'Admires that, I do,' she said. 'Wants it so's I gits knocked up and has me a sucker. Big one . . . biggest man chile in the worl' come outen me. That whut I wants an' yo' looks like the one who kin give it to me.'

'Whut fo' yo' want a son big as that?' Jubal asked.

She headed for the bed and the smile on her wide black face died. 'So's he'll git so big ain't nobody kin hurt him an' he kin kill all them white mastas an' overseers. Kill 'em all.'

Jubal lay beside her, trying to work up interest. She made it easy, pleasuring him with her hands and bouncing around on the bed, eluding him as he tried to enter her. Finally he tired of the game, anchored her with his body and got it over with. She was a lot of woman, and he knew that if he didn't have others to satisfy this night, he might have found her more enjoyable. Or maybe the first one had spoiled it for him. He'd expected to get a lot of pleasure out of this. After she slipped into her dress, he led her to the door and knocked. The lock turned, the woman left.

She was followed by a skinny girl who was equally as eager and was all hands and mouth. She made him forget the first girl and he found his desire as strong as he'd imagined it would be when he'd first heard what was expected of him. After that, there were six presented to him for service before his wind and stamina started to give out. He looked down at his penis, wondering how much longer he could perform. He was surprised it hadn't withered. And still they came. The next two, though he greeted them without enthusiasm, were young and heated, and their performance was good. But when the second one got off the bed, Jubal didn't. His wind and stamina had finally given out. He told her to knock on the door. She did, and as she left, another entered.

He sighed as he eased himself on to the side of the bed, greeted her with a grin, then lay back again.

'Rest yourself,' he told her. 'I'm tuckered.'

'Yo' gonna rape me?' she asked.

'Soon's I kin,' Jubal sighed. 'You bettah not fight me, woman, 'cause I ain't got much strength left and I'll have to whup you good so's you stop fightin', an' I kin knock you up.'

She was looking at him with interest. So far the wenches had been strictly run-of-the-mill. Most of them were very young, inexperienced, and not attractive. But this one looked good to him. She was probably eighteen, with small, firm breasts showing through the thin material of the dress. She looked strong too, and she had delicate features, a small mouth and nose. She was blacker than he, but there was an air of superiority about her.

'You want me to blow out the lamps?' she asked.

'Don't you touch 'em. Masta told me, wants this done in plenty of light.'

She nodded. 'Figured that. You sure is big. Maybe I ain't goin' to be pleasured by a man so big.'

'You gets raped if it pleasures you or not,' Jubal said grimly. 'You knows that.'

She sat down beside him, slid her dress down over her shoulders and placed his hand on one of her breasts. 'Reckon they no use fightin' a big man like you.'

He pushed her down on the bed and lay next to her. She wrapped her arms around him and placed her mouth close to his ear.

'You a goddamn niggah stallion,' she whispered, 'an' you just as dumb.'

'What you talkin' 'bout?' he asked.

'Keep you voice down. Don' you knows they's white folk watchin' us? They been watchin' you rapin' all night long.

They pays five dollahs to look through peek holes where the li'l pictures hides 'em so you can't see.'

Jubal's erection softened immediately while a brutally intense rage flowed over his body. He swore softly, but he didn't move away from her.

'You sure about that?' he asked. In his fury, he forgot that he must talk like a black, never betray his learning. 'I've heard of this before, but I thought it was all lies.'

'Saw 'em my own se'f,' she said. 'Mistah Wiley and Mistah Sedella, they been takin' runaways back and stealin' free slaves, and puttin' on these shows fo' the white passengers. They gettin' rich and all we wenches gettin' is knocked up.'

'I swear I'll kill them,' Jubal said. 'I'll not do their bidding another time.'

'You talks mighty good fo' a niggah,' the girl said. 'You educated, boy? You talk like white folks.'

'Sometimes I talks that way,' he said, lapsing into a soft drawl. 'When I gets mad, I fo'gets I'se black. Finds it helps sometimes.'

'You sure is black, not mattah which way you talks, boy. Now you listen to me. Knows these white men, I does. Heerd 'bout 'em more'n once. We's all goin' on the vendue table we gits to N'awleans.'

'Me too?'

'Man, with you shoulders and whut you got pushin' 'gainst me right now, you'll bring two thousand easy.'

'But I'm free. I was born free,' he said.

'Kin you prove it? Kin you stand on the vendue table and tell the white folks you is a free man – and show 'em the proof?'

'I got papers someplace,' he said.

'You think they gives you a chance to git 'em? When you is wuth two, maybe high as three thousand dollahs? Man, you crazy.'

'What I goin' to do?' he asked desperately.

'Right now, with all them eyes watchin', I know whut you better do.'

'No,' he said. 'Goddamn if I do.'

'Boy, they comes in heah in five minutes and the folks whut paid five dollahs to see you rape me gets they money's wuth when them two slave traders whups you to death. They'll cut you to pieces slow an' easy. There won't be 'nuff left to throw over the side.'

'You trying to scare me?'

'I'm tellin' you the truth. What's your name?'

'Jubal.'

'Mine's Malvena. I runned away, but I sure didn't get far.'

'What they do to you now?'

'Breed me and work me till I drops. They got twelve boys

chained in the hold. They run too, and they goin' back to git hung, or whupped till they dies, while every slave on the plantation they run from watches it done. Jubal, they do the same to you. Only way you kin live is to show 'em you is the best stud they evah seen. Maybe a good man will buy you. Maybe he let you jes' piddle 'round' an' knock up his wenches. But if you let's 'em know you is smart, or you tells 'em you knows you is puttin' on a show to make 'em money, they kills you diad.'

They both stiffened as the lock turned and the door opened wide. Wiley stuck his head in. 'You raped this wench yet?'

'Not yet, suh,' Jubal replied.

'You got no more juice?'

'I got it, suh,' Jubal replied. 'Jus' restin' a bit.'

'You rested long enough. Start rapin'.'

'Yes, suh.'

The door slammed shut and the key turned. Jubal was angry. His hand, on the girl's thigh, tightened until she cried out in pain.

'Sorry,' he whispered. 'Thought it was the white man's neck I had in my hand.'

'You start thinkin' that way, you get in trouble sure,' she told him, her mouth close to his ear. 'We better start puttin' on a show so them white folks gets their money's worth. Lie on your back. I knows how to stir 'em up.'

Jubal did as he was told, grateful for the opportunity to rest a little. He liked this wench. She wasn't stupid or innocent, and he could learn from her. If they put on a good show and the white bastards like it, maybe they'd send her back.

She pushed Jubal's legs apart, knelt between them, let her hands slither up his legs. Then she bent forward so her breasts hung down and she started to talk softly in a way to arouse him. But with no other sound in the room or beyond, her words carried to those on the other side of the wall.

'I hears from the wenches you is a real fuckin' man. A real screwin' man. That when you puts your pecker inside, you makes them scream real loud.'

'What else you think a cock's for, woman?' Jubal asked, entering the game. His hands reached for her nipples, started a slow pulling, circular motion on them.

She wiggled her buttocks appreciatively. 'You ever screw a titty?'

'Never did.'

' 'Bout time, don't you think?'

'Reckon.'

She moved up in the bed, supported herself on her elbows, taking care that their action was visible from all angles of the room. She grasped Jubal's penis, circled it lightly around her nipples until the area was moist from his sperm. Her other hand held the breast so that the penis wouldn't stray from its target.

'Pleasure yourself, man. I'll keep your pecker in the right place.'

'Woman, you is good.'

'Had lots of practice.'

Jubal's hands moved up the inside of her thighs. He straightened two fingers of one hand and entered her.

'Close your legs, man, while I spread mine.'

Carefully, they changed positions. The wench toyed with his genitals as she started to raise and lower herself gently, pleasuring herself at the same time she did him. He was amazed at her dexterity. Then he started his own thrusting, for the hardness of her nipple had fully aroused him. As he watched his penis disappear into the full roundness of her breasts, his thrusting quickened and he forgot they were putting on a show. Their shouts and moans mingled, filling the room with sensual sounds and it wasn't until someone outside, apparently carried away by what he was viewing, uttered a bacchanalian cry, that he remembered. But he didn't care. This wench liked what she was doing and he liked it too and their figures blurred in a frenzy of movement. When they'd completed the act, she lay on her back, pushed Jubal's legs apart with her feet and wriggled up until their buttocks touched. She felt for his limp penis, sandwiched it between her vaginal lips and let her fingers caress it.

'Won't do no good,' Jubal said. 'Jest ain't got no more juice.'

'Too bad,' she said. 'You like screwin' my titty?'

'Sure did.'

She chuckled. 'My titty stiff from your juice dryin' on it.'

'Make you think of me till you wash it off.'

'Won't wash it off – leastwise, not tonight.'

The key, turning in the lock, brought them back to reality. Jubal reluctantly freed his penis, flung his leg over the wench's still-reclining form, and got to his feet. He picked up her dress and tossed it to her. Still in a reclining position, she slipped it over her head, deliberately making her movements seductive. She arched her body and slowly drew the dress down, letting her fingers move enticingly along her body till they reached her groin. She pleasured herself for a full minute, caressing her pubic hair, spreading her vaginal lips and lazily moving a fingertip along them, all the time making mewing sounds. Almost reluctantly, with body still arched, she pulled the dress down and slid to the side of the bed.

Jubal watched, hiding his amusement, knowing she was doing it for the benefit of the hidden audience. He liked her and hoped she'd come back. She'd pleasured him because she wanted to. He wondered, though, if he'd get lashed for not planting a sucker in her. It didn't matter. She'd made the evening worthwhile, not only because of what they'd done, but because he'd learned what Wiley and Sedella were really up to.

She moved up to him and he pulled her close. With his mouth to her ear, he whispered for her to cry out, as if he was biting her.

She did and he said. 'Like you. Wants you back.'

'Likes you too, Jubal,' she whispered between cries. 'Prays for you, I do.'

He thrust her from him, opened the door and she stepped through. It closed behind her and he started walking toward the bed. He'd scarcely reached it when Wiley came through.

'You plant a sucked in that one?' Wiley asked.

'No, suh,' Jubal said, knowing damn well Wiley had seen what went on.

'What you do with her?' Wiley asked, not knowing his eyes still showed the effects of what he'd viewed.

Jubal told him, in detail, knowing he wanted to hear it. 'You mad, suh?'

'Not a bit, Jubal. Man's gotta pleasure himself a little. Now ain't that so?'

Jubal felt like hitting him. 'Sure has. An' that wench sure knows how to do it. Only you wants me to make suckers. I gotta makes 'em.'

'Maybe I'll send her back again. Only this time, you be sure to plant one in her.'

'I'll do it, suh, only maybe I need more time.'

'We'll see. We'll see. Rest now. Tomorrow's another busy night.'

He picked up the lamps and carried them out, locking the door behind him. In the darkness, Jubal returned to the bed and pulled a sheet over his nakedness. When the ship was silent, except for the creaking engine below, he crept across the room and moved several of the small pictures.

Malvena was right. There were peek holes, so placed that the edges of the frames kept them from being easily spotted from inside the room and blending well with the design of the magenta wallpaper. Jubal seethed with rage, but most of it came from his helplessness. There wasn't a thing he could do about it and, for him, the worst was probably yet to come.

THREE

He was being shaken roughly and his eyes opened to a drapery-shaded cabin, but there was enough light to make him close his eyes again without seeing who was being so rough about awakening him. A fist slammed against the side of his cheek. He sat up quickly.

Wiley stood over the bed. 'When I wakes you, black boy, you wakes up real quick. Brought you some grub. Eat and rest. Tonight you take care o' more wenches.'

Jubal rubbed his sleepy eyes. 'Yes, suh, masta, suh. I sure knocked up some of 'em last night.'

He grinned at Wiley and tucked the bucket of food between his legs and began to eat. Wiley left without comment. Jubal finished eating, arose finally and washed. He wondered what it was like on deck, walking about, perhaps with a cane and a beaver hat and fine clothes.

Still dreaming, he went back to bed. It grew hot and stuffy in the cabin, but he didn't mind. At supper he was brought another bucket of the same kind of food. It wasn't the most appetising he'd ever tasted, but there was enough of it. A stud had to be well-fed, he reasoned, and this was no kindness on the part of Wiley or Sedella.

At night they both appeared with the lamps, turned all the way up. He was again specifically warned not to touch the lamps, to strip down and be ready for the first wench soon.

She came, one he'd never seen before. She fought him the entire time and cried just as bitterly as he pushed her out. The second was young and willing. The third and fourth were far past girlhood, but still fecund enough to provide at least one more sucker. They were submissive without protest. This was nothing new to them.

Malvena was sent in at the height of the evening. Jubal stood in the center of the room, arms folded across his chest, legs spread, his organ limp, as if awaiting her ministrations. They exchanged silent greetings with their eyes, after which she bent to grasp the edge of her dress, raising it slowly, moving her body in a lazy, seductive rhythm. She tossed the dress aside, used a finger of each hand to tease the nipples into hardness. Then, smiling provocatively, she moved over to Jubal, dropped to her knees and started to give him moist kisses along the inside of one leg from his knee up to his groin, then switching to the other. All the while her hands caressed his buttocks. The second time, when she reached his groin, she moved her head slowly back and forth against his stretched testicles. Again, using her mouth, she started at the base of his penis, letting her tongue lap its way to the fleshy tip.

He jerked involuntarily as her mouth closed around it. She made soft mewing sounds of pleasure as he thrust it deeper into her mouth, but after a few thrusts, Jubal stepped back, causing her to lose it.

'Don't you like that, man?'

'Sure do. Only can't make suckers that way. Masta say I gotta put suckers in wenches.'

'Masta right. You put a sucker in me next time. This time I want you to shoot off right in my mouth. Or ain't you man enuf to do it with the same woman twice?'

They were both playing a game and doing it well. It served two purposes. To entertain the hidden audience and fool Wiley and Sedella into thinking they were stupid blacks.

'I can do it with you five times, you got enough juice for it.'

'I got the juice. Now put it back in my mouth like the sweet fuckin' man you are.'

Jubal moved forward, thrust his penis at her. She gave a cry of delight as her thick, moist lips closed around it. Her hands caressed his testicles, his groin, his buttocks, moving ceaselessly. He started pumping, and his hands came down to hold her head, as if he feared it might slip out. But he needn't have worried, for, in some way, without stopping all she was doing, she'd managed to wind her legs around one of Jubal's. She wiggled sideways so that her lips separated. Her vaginal juices moistened his leg and now she was pleasuring herself at the same time as she made up and down motions. Their orgasms occurred at the same time, and even afterward she held on to his penis, nibbling on it with her teeth.

Finally she let it slip from her mouth and she rested her head against his organ. The sperm oozing from it made her head glisten. Some of it ran slowly down the side of her face, sliding into her still open mouth. She licked at it with her tongue, seeming to relish it.

Jubal reached down and picked her up. He carried her over to the bed, set her down to rest after that and it gave him a chance to speak in whispers without rousing suspicions.

'Any way I can get out of here?' he asked her.

'They's keys in the cap'n's cabin,' she said. 'They's all hooked with the numbers on 'em. You wants to get out, Jubal?'

'I want to look around.'

'Cap'n he gets paid good by Masta Wiley and Sedella so's they kin use this cabin with all the peepholes. Cap'n he drinks plenty whiskey every night. I kin go to his cabin. He's been horny all day, coming down to the hold where they got us chained. Fingers me and says he'd make it easy for me I come to see him. Reckon he saw us last night and it hottened him up real good.'

'Can you get the key?'

'Jubal,' she said, 'aint' nothin' to me I gets raped by that old man, but whar you goin' you gets out of here? Ain't no place to go. They gets you back sure.'

'Jus' want to get out,' he said. 'Mayhap, I get lucky, I can kill these men who are makin' us do this so's they can get rich.'

'Lets the whole crew rape me if you kin kill one o' them. I gets the key, Jubal.'

'Good. We'd better put on a show now.'

'An' you talks loud, you bettah start talkin' like a nigger.'

She leaped out of bed, ran to a corner of the room and came back, holding a low rocker without a back. She placed this in the center of the room and motioned for Jubal to sit on it.

'What you want me do?' he asked, looking down at it.

'Sit on it. We screw real good on that.'

'Sure 'nuf?' he asked, lapsing into the lingo of his people.

'It's a help. We'll rock an' screw an' rock an' screw.'

He sat down gingerly, testing his weight on it. It had a cushioned seat, but it seemed sturdy enough. Malvena spread her legs, straddled him and was about to seat herself when he pulled her close, pushed his mouth into her moist interior and forced his tongue its full length inside her. She writhed and moaned and gyrated and her hands moved up to squeeze her breasts as if she had to feel pain with her pleasure.

Just as she was about to have an orgasm, Jubal pushed her back. She almost fell, but he quickly caught her, pulled her down and pressed his tumescence into her. It was just as she said. Rocking made it easier. It seemed as if every part of their bodies rubbed against one another. She bit his ear and Jubal's teeth cut into the flesh of her shoulder. Blood ran from both. Their cries mingled and dwindled only with their passion. When the act had been completed, she was supported only by Jubal's propped-up knees. Her head fell back. His lay on her bloodied shoulder.

'Don't forget your promise,' he whispered.

'I won't.' She spoke without moving her lips.

He got up then, half carried her to the bed. He reached for her dress, then went to the door to knock. Malvena slipped into the dress and, as when she entered, their eyes revealed their mutual satisfaction, for they treasured the idea they'd put something over on the unseen audience.

After Malvena left, Wiley came in to remove the lamps. He grinned lewdly at Jubal.

'Believe I put a sucker in her this time, suh,' Jubal said, with the proper meekness.

'You looks like you did. Looks like you put a whole passel

of 'em in the wench. That's all for tonight.'

He didn't add that the show had had such an effect on the audience, some of them had moved their hands down to their groins to relieve themselves. One lady, with an extra long-handled parasol, had anchored its tip to the deck and used it as the wench had used Jubal's leg.

After the door had closed behind Wiley, Jubal moved wearily to the bed. He felt exhausted. It hadn't all been faked. He must have lain there an hour before he arose and parted the drapes enough to see out and watch the dim outline of the shore slip by. It was cooler by night and he breathed in the moist air hungrily. He wanted to sit quietly here and plan, but he didn't know what to plan. He was a prisoner with nowhere to go. He hated Wiley and Sedella. Wiley the most, for he was sadistic and cruel.

At this moment, Jubal was a slave and this he knew very well, but certainly he'd be given an opportunity to prove he was a free man. No one could deny him that right. He moved away from the window and threw himself face down on the bed. Despair coursed through him. for he knew he wouldn't be given such a chance. He would never be free again. The fact his parents had gone north so he might be born there meant nothing. His skin was black and blacks were slaves.

Slow anger took the place of despair. Some of it was directed at himself for being so helpless, but most was meant for Wiley and Sedella. There was a killing rage in Jubal. An important one, but it would grow, and someday the opportunity would come. For the moment, he had to think of escape. There was one chance. If Malvena managed to steal the key from the Captain's cabin, he might slip overside, swim ashore and somehow make his way back to St Louis, where he was a free man. He had to manage that or be condemned for the rest of his life to obey a white master, bow to him, submit to his whip and never speak a word in self-defense. He didn't think he could live under those conditions.

He went to sleep finally, and the following day was a repetition of the first two with the exception of Malvena not being presented to him. Apparently he'd run through all the wenches aboard, for these were repeats, but picked for their tender years and the way they'd fought him.

By the time he'd wrestled the last of them on to the bed, he was exhausted. Sedella and Wiley came for the lamps and Sedella stayed behind for a few moments.

'Kinda slowin' up, ain't you, boy?'

'Yes, suh, reckon so, but I took 'em as they come, suh. They fights me, it takes longer, thass all, suh.'

'We'll send you that good-lookin' one tomorrow night. It'll be the last night before we get to N'awleans, so you make goddamn sure you get her knocked up real good. She'll fetch a fancy price.'

'Does my best, suh.' Jubal looked up eagerly. 'Suh, how many you reckon I knocked up? I gits a silvah dollah for each one. Thass whut you told me, suh.'

'You fix up the good-lookin' one and I'll make it two dollahs,' Sedella said. What he really meant was that they should put on a good show, but he couldn't say so out-right because, so far as he knew, Jubal was totally ignorant of the fact that he was performing publicly each night.

He was locked in again. He alternately dozed and lay half awake, disconsolately contemplating his future if he didn't escape. At least he had a chance. Malvena would be brought to him and she might have the key. It was, in fact, the only chance that would come his way. He knew better than to believe Wiley and Sedella would allow him to return north with them until they had accumulated another coffle of wenches for him to serve. He was young and strong. They could get two thousand for him, Malvena had said, and Jubal believed it.

It was midafternoon when the key rattled in the door and Sedella walked in. He closed the door quickly and put his back against it.

'Get yo'self washed,' he ordered. 'Don't want you stinkin' any. An' when I brings in this lady, you does what she says or I'll whup the black skin right off you.'

'Yes, suh, masta, suh.' Jubal leaped out of bed, poured water in the wash basin and drenched himself, using soap and more water. He dried himself on a towel he'd used since he came aboard.

Sedella stepped closer to him and audibly sniffed. 'Reckon you don't stink none now. I be back.'

He locked the door after him. Jubal shrugged. He had no idea of why Sedella was bringing a lady. The word implied she'd be white. He put on his shirt, now soiled. but it was all he had. He pulled on the pants, but left his feet bare. He sat down on the edge of the bed to wait.

It was an hour before Sedella returned. He unlocked the door, looked in, motioned that Jubal was to stand away from the door so he wouldn't be seen, and then Sedella hissed and beckoned to someone down the corridor.

The woman who entered was not more than thirty. An undoubtedly beautiful and self-assured woman with blue eyes and light brown hair whose side ringlets escaped the brimmed bonnet she wore. Her dress was full-skirted and rustled softly with her slightest movement. Its color matched her eyes and complimented the fairness of her skin. She carried a parasol of the same shiny material as her dress. It was ruffled at the edges and, at the point, it had a large pompon ruffle.

She regarded Jubal through eyes shrouded by a strange desire. She made him feel uncomfortable and nervous. He backed away a few steps.

'Stand still,' she ordered coldly. She turned her lovely face toward Sedella. 'You may go, sir.'

'Yes, ma'am, but ain't there somethin' you fo'got, ma'am?'

She slipped a hand in her pocket and drew out a bill. Sedella snatched it and backed out of the cabin, grinning lewdly and bowing at the same time.

She coolly looked Jubal up and down. 'Come here,' she ordered.

He took several tentative steps in her direction. He'd had no cause to fear a female before, black or white, but he was frightened and wary.

'That's close enough.' She extended her parasol and touched his chest with the tip of it as if to hold him back.

'Shuck down,' she commanded.

'Ma'am?' He couldn't believe his ears.

'Take your clothes off, nigger. All of them. Now! Unless you want me to order you lashed until you're half dead.'

'Shuck down?' He still didn't believe it.

'Strip!' she half shouted at him. 'Stop wasting time!'

He unbuttoned his shirt and let it fall to the floor. He opened his trousers, wriggled slightly and they fell to his knees. Her parasol flicked out to indicate he was to rid himself of the pants completely.

When he stepped out of them, she riveted her gaze on the crotch. Jubal, too terrified to even think straight, gave no reaction. She raised the parasol, moving the tip of the pompon lightly along his organ. She kept prodding gently until the stimulation gave him a reaction. He wondered what he'd do if she ordered him to go to bed with her. He was beginning to tremble and there was sweat on his forehead.

A sensuous smile touched her lips and her eyes narrowed as she regarded his erection. She continued moving the parasol, caressing his groin with the soft, silky material, stroking his testicles with it. Once she jabbed him between the legs with the parasol to indicate he was to separate them.

Then she set the sunshade on the bed while she proceeded to remove one of her white silk gloves. She picked up the parasol, slipped one of the fingers of the glove over its tipped end and, extending it, moved it back and forth in front of Jubal's nose. A spicy fragrance emanated from it, exciting his senses even further. Then she resumed her play with the parasol, letting the silky finger move along his penis, teasing the fleshy tip with it until his hips started jerking. He wanted to stop and then he didn't because he knew she wouldn't leave until she'd succeeded in making him have an orgasm. When it came, it soaked the glove and he broke out in a sweat, expecting to be struck with the parasol or, at least, cursed.

Instead, looking quite satisfied, she calmly removed the sodden glove, slipped it on, walked to the door, opened it and went out. Sedella must have been waiting because the key turned promptly. Jubal didn't move for a few seconds and then he sat down on the edge of the bed. He'd never felt so ashamed and debased in his life. He swore to himself that if the opportunity ever arose where he could kill that woman, whoever she was, he would do it. There was no thought of rape in his mind. She was too dirty for that. Then he slowly turned his face toward the pillow and wept. He hadn't cried since he was two or three. There'd never been reason to. Now he did, and he felt alone, tormented, whipped by the lash that sparked from that woman's eyes. Degraded by the desire she showed and the fact that she would not let it go beyond desire.

He wanted to break something, to kill someone. Yet he wept instead and there was more anger in the tears than sorrow.

By the time Sedella returned with the pail of food that would be his supper, Jubal was himself again. Meek, cooperative, respectful and showing no anger.

'You evah see anythin' like that before, Jubal? Woman who wants to admire a man's balls. What good it do her? Paid me just to look at you. Reckon she's crazy?'

'Don't know, masta, suh.'

'If you did, you know better than to say so,' Sedella growled. 'This is the last night. You better get that good-lookin' wench knocked up, y'hear? Don't care a good damn 'bout the others, but you fix her up or I swear I'll have your hide.'

'Does the best I kin, masta, suh.'

'Well – I got to admit that's pretty good.'

'Masta, suh, kin I ask somethin'?'

Sedella gave a curt nod of assent.

'Does I get to go back to St Louis with you and Masta Wiley, suh? So I kin ride down this heah river again and have me all the wenches I wants to knock up?'

'One silvah dollah for each one that gets a sucker,' Sedella lied. 'That's the deal an' we expects you to earn it.'

'Yes, suh, I sure craves to.'

Sedella grinned and went out. Jubal ate everything. There was no telling when he'd eat again. He had deliberately forced all thoughts of the strange white woman who'd visited him out of his mind because the memory of her was too disconcerting.

By the time the lamps were placed and the first wench sent in, Jubal was feeling himself again, but thoroughly angry and completely desperate. From now on, he'd look for a chance to escape.

Malvena was sent in late. Jubal guessed that the main part of the peep show wasn't held until a maximum audience was ready. By this time they'd perfected the performance and they enjoyed it, especially when they pretended to be exhausted and lay side by side, whispering and plotting.

'I stole the key,' she said. 'When I gets to go, I'll hide it under the doily on the bureau.'

'Where you got it?'

'Pinned in my dress.'

'The cap'n good as me?' he asked with a grin.

'He hung 'zactly like a peanut,' she giggled. 'Didn't do me no more harm than a boy baby. Old man like him. Jubal, whut you aimin' to do?'

'Run. Going overboard if I get the chance. You want to come?'

She shook her head. 'Reckon not. I cain't swim nohow, an' I be too skeered. You run, Jubal. Run far an' run north.'

'Aims to,' he said. 'Kinda wish I didn't have to. Means you can't be my woman any more and I love you, Malvena. I hope you're knocked up so's you can remember me.'

She fondled him and snuggled closer to him, their naked bodies glistening with perspiration, for the cabin was stifling by now.

'Takes a mightly forgetful woman to disremember what you is like, Jubal. Goin' to miss you real bad.'

'Reckon we got one more time left in us?' he asked. 'We got folks watchin' an' I reckon they be real disappointed we stop now.'

'I'm ready,' she whispered hoarsely. 'I been ready all the time, Jubal.'

After she left, there was but one more, an anticlimax, for Jubal was dead tired. Before Sedella came in with Wiley for the lamps, Jubal slipped the key from the bureau and palmed it.

'You were mighty good tonight,' Sedella said. 'You sure are some stud.'

Jubal couldn't resist the temptation. 'Suh, kin I asks a question?'

'Go ahead.'

'How do you know I so good?'

Sedella almost answered honestly and caught himself just in time. 'We kin tell by the way the wenches walk and act. You sure wore 'em out. You got to be good to do that.'

'Yes, suh, I wears 'em out fine,' Jubal said.

They left, turning the lock. Jubal threw himself on the bed as if in a state of sheer exhaustion. They might be watching him and there were the peepholes for their convenience. He dozed lightly until he judged it must be about three in the morning. The ship had grown very quiet. The engine throbbed, now and then he heard a crewman sing out, but that was all. Jubal slipped off the bed, put on his shirt and pants and went to the door. He listened for a few moments before he slipped the key into the lock. Turning it, he opened the door a crack. There was no one outside.

He closed the door behind him, put the key in his pocket and ran lightly up the stairs. All he had to do now was cross the deck, leap over the rail and swim ashore. There'd be a hue and cry go up, but he didn't doubt that he could evade any posse they might send for him. At least he'd be free.

'Nigger!' a voice said harshly.

Jubal whirled about. Sedella, a pistol in his hand, was moving toward him. Jubal gave a great sigh of resignation. They'd kill him now. What's more, when they found he had a key, they'd discover it was missing from the captain's cabin. They'd quickly guess that Malvena must have stolen it and passed it on to him. That meant they'd kill her too.

'What you doin' on deck?' Sedella said softly. At least he wasn't shouting to draw others to the scene.

Jubal spoke, using the only excuse he could think of. 'Suh, I was sent to find you, suh.'

'You what? You were locked in that cabin. What the hell do you mean?'

'The lady . . . the one who came this afternoon. . . .'

Sedella's antagonism expired on the wave of greed which now afflicted him. 'She come to you?'

'She in the cabin now, suh. She say she wants to buy me.'

'Well now, think of that,' Sedella said. He stuffed the pistol under his belt. 'Wants to buy you, Jubal, how'd you like to service that fine lady whenever she wants you?'

'Real fine, suh. She sure is a good-lookin' woman.'

'Let's find out what she's got to say.' Suspicion entered his crafty little mind again. 'How she get in the cabin?'

'With a key, suh. Way she said, she got it from the cap'n, suh.'

'Which means she paid him and it shows me how much she wants you. Jubal, no nigger will have ever sold for more than I'm going to get for your black balls. Come on.'

Sedella went into the room first, as Jubal knew he would. He looked around for the woman, suddenly realised he'd been tricked and reached for the gun. Jubal kicked the door shut, pinned Sedella's gun arm, gave it a sharp twist and broke it. Sedella opened his mouth to scream in pain, but two powerful black hands were around his throat and two thick thumbs crushing his windpipe. Jubal thrust Sedella's head under his arm, grasped the top of the head firmly, gave his body a hard twist. Bone snapped and Sedella went limp. Jubal let go of him and he fell to the floor, his stomach against the rug, his face turned to the ceiling. Jubal had broken his neck.

With distaste, Jubal picked up the dead man and after a quick look into the corridor, carried him to the deck. There was no one aboard. Of course, he might be seen from the wheelhouse, but he had to take that chance. He moved agilely across the deck, lifted Sedella's body over the rail, let it slide down until he was able to grasp only the wrists of the dead man. He hung over the rail, lowering the corpse as much as possible so it would slide into the water noiselessly. He let go. There was a minute splash and the river closed around Sedella.

Jubal was sure he'd not been seen. He hurried back to the cabin, closed the door, locked it from inside, opened the cabin window and threw the key as hard as possible. It cleared the veranda rail and fell into the river. He closed the window, undressed and got into bed.

It was too late for escape now. They'd find Sedella's body soon enough. If they discovered Jubal missing at about the same time, he'd be more than suspected of the murder. He'd be blamed for it and hung as quickly as they could find a rope. It had been a choice between slavery and death. Slavery might, one day, provide him with another chance to escape. Death was too final.

Jubal pulled the grimy sheet over him and fell asleep. It was the first good night's sleep he'd had aboard the ship.

FOUR

A sharp pain awakened him. He sat up with a shout of agony. Wiley stood over him with a short whip in his hand. It had cut open Jubal's cheek and the blood was running down it to drop off his jowls and stain the sheet.

'What you do that for?' he asked. 'I ain't done nuthin', suh.'

'Get up outen there an' face the wall,' Wiley said.

Jubal felt his first note of worry. Maybe they'd found Sedella's body by now, saw that he had a crushed windpipe and a broken neck, and guessed a powerful man like Jubal must have done it. A black man had been hung on much less evidence than that. He faced the wall and stood naked while Wiley searched the bed, Jubal's clothes, every cranny in the cabin. He was looking for the key, but he wasn't going to find it, and Jubal realised he'd been smart in throwing it overboard, and in not escaping.

'Bend over,' Wiley said. 'Spread your cheeks.'

For a moment Jubal thought he was going to make a physical examination, but he cut Jubal with the whip over his bare buttocks and told him to straighten up.

'What for you hit me, masta, suh? I tells you I ain't done nuthin', but whut you tol' me.'

'When did you see Sedella last?'

'Masta Sedella, suh? When you an' him went out with the lamps, suh. Ain't seen him this mornin', suh.'

'Neither has anybody else. Get dressed.'

Wiley returned in a few minutes with handcuffs, which he slipped over Jubal's wrists. He forced him out on deck. The ship had docked. Jubal hadn't even been aware of it, for he'd been too busy worrying about Wiley. Passengers were disembarking, being led to carriages by happy friends and relatives.

Jubal was kept waiting on deck, under a burning hot sun, until the slaves were brought up from below, all spanceled and secured to a long chain. Wiley added Jubal to the chain and they were marched off the boat to the dock where a man on horseback, armed with a whip, herded them along the gutter to the slave jail.

It consisted of a large yard, surrounded by a high wooden fence and entered through a gate over which an arched sign read:

MANNING & WOLFSON, AUCTIONEERS

They slogged their way across the yard to a low building, where each window was barred. Two other men waited for them in the corridor. Their chains were removed, the spancels unlocked and they were herded to a cell and locked in. Two men for each dark, narrow and dismal cubicle.

There was nothing to sit down on, nowhere to sleep. There were only a rickety stool and a slop pail. Jubal's hopes had grown lower and lower, along the short route to the pens. When the door slammed shut, they were at the lowest ebb he'd ever known in his life.

'You is shorely troubled,' the other occupant of the cell said sympathetically. 'Best you jes' set an' thank the Lord you is still alive.'

Jubal sat down beside the man and looked at him for the first time. He was old – perhaps fifty-five. His hair had turned gray, his jet-black face was seared in the lines of age, and he had but a few teeth left. His hands were huge and toughened by field work. Only his eyes betrayed the fact that he was at peace with himself.

'You call this living?' Jubal asked, forgetting to use the dialect again. 'This isn't fit for a pig, and from here we get sold like hogs.'

'Keep yo' voice down, boy. You talks like you white. Kin you read an' write?'

'I been up to ninth grade,' Jubal confided. He'd instantly liked this old man and trusted him. He would be a friend. For how long was doubtful, but while they were together, Jubal would be grateful for his company and a share of his experiences as a slave.

'How old you be?'

'Nineteen. I was born free. My mammy and pappy were manumitted years ago.'

'Then how you come heah, son? Whar you from?'

'St Louis. I was stolen, that's what. Two men just took me. Said they'd give me a job and put me to work being a stud for a coffle of wenches they had aboard the riverboat.'

The old man chuckled. 'From St Louis to N'awleans fo' five nights runnin' time. You been knockin' up wenches all that time you mighty lucky. I been in the hold. Near died, it so damn hot. An' they fo'gits to give us water an' all the food we got was slops. Sho' wishes I was beddin' down with all them wenches, son.'

'But I'm free. Now I'm locked up like a slave. What can I say to make them understand they can't do this to me?'

The old man touched Jubal's lips gently. 'Whut you doin', son, is talkin' you se'f into a grave. Us niggers, we don't git no schoolin'. We knows too much, they gits skeered o' us. Son, they finds out you kin read and write, they gonna cut your throat sho'. You heed an old man an' act like a po' nigger, don't know nuthin', and you gits along. You big and strong. You wuth plenty money. They take good keer o' a buck like you. But let them see you smart as they is and they kills you daid. Sweahs it.'

Jubal nodded. 'I know, I'll try.'

'You do more'n jes' try, son, or you got a mighty little time to live. Won't be so bad. Buck like you, they'll give you wenches so's you kin make suckers. Maybe you sees a chance to run. But they hangs runners down heah, son. They strings 'em up soon's they caught. You goin' to run, you gots to be mighty sho' you got a place to run to.'

'I'll find one,' Jubal said. 'How long they keep us here?'

'We goes on the vendue table tomorrow, likely. Evah been sold? No – you said you was born free. Ain't goin' to be easy fo' you, son. All you kin do is don't think 'bout it. Jes' do like you told.'

Someone was stamping down the corridor. Wiley peered through the barred door and signaled a man at his side. The door was unlocked. Wiley motioned Jubal to step out.

Jubal felt the first wave of elation. They were going to let him continue to serve as a stud. At least the life was easy. He wouldn't mind that and the opportunities for escape would be much better.

'You fixin' to let me knock up mo' wenches?' Jubal asked hopefully.

'Sure are,' Wiley grinned crookedly. 'We goin' to take good keer o' you, Jubal. Step into this room.'

Jubal entered a long room illuminated by two fat candles. A huge buck, stripped to the waist, stood against the further wall. He gripped a long, wide leather strap in his hand and he sized Jubal up with a cold eye.

Driven into the cement floor were four iron rings, each provided with a handcuff. Jubal suddenly realised what this meant. He began to turn. Wiley hit him on the head with the butt of his pistol. Jubal fell to his knees. Wiley kicked him in the face, making his senses reel wildly. Before he knew it, he was lying face down on the cold floor, his wrists and ankles in irons and he was spreadeagled for the torture he knew was about to come.

Wiley stood over him. 'You killed Sedella, didn't you, you goddamn black bahstid?'

'Ain't seed Mastah Sedella, suh,' Jubal managed. 'Ain't seed him since last night, suh.'

'You're a liar. You killed him. Where'd you get a key? Or did Sedella come to see you and you killed him 'fore he could yell?'

'Mastah, suh, I din' kill nobody. I din' see Mastah Sedella since you an' him come get the lamps.'

Wiley stepped back and signaled. The huge black stepped up, raised the lash and brought it down against Jubal's back. It cut through his thin shirt. It didn't bite into his flesh nor draw any blood, but the pain was as excruciating as though it had been equipped with brass studs. The lash fell half a dozen times before Wiley called a halt.

'You killed Sedella,' he accused Jubal. 'You busted his arm an' you busted his neck. We found the body.'

'Ain't seed Mastah Sedella.' Jubal braced himself for the lash. It came, a dozen times before the big buck stepped back. Wiley put a foot against Jubal's neck and then applied all his weight on it. Jubal choked and groaned and thought he was then about to die, but the pressure was released finally, though not without Wiley kicking him alongside his head.

'I'm askin' you once more, you damn nigger, and then I lets you be whipped until you're daid. After that we cut you up and feed you to the hawgs. Now you tell me you killed Sedella.'

'Ain't seed him. . . . ' Jubal moaned. 'Sweahs I ain't seed him. . . . '

He bit his lip as the flat strap moved down to his buttocks. It fell again and again, until he was one living mass of pain, so that the final lashes had little or no sting. He felt the blackness coming up, felt the contents of his stomach reach his throat and his mouth. He vomited violently and tasted blood. The whipping stopped and someone threw a bucket of water on him. He let himself go limp and lapsed into a merciful unconsciousness.

They were applying salt packs to the lacerations and the sting of them awakened him. They were trying to bring down the swelling so that he'd be fit to place on the vendue table tomorrow. But he hadn't spoken. Wiley had gotten nothing out of him. He could take a whipping. He could endure it and live, therefore they couldn't humiliate him completely. He'd always have one spark of his dignity left so he might defy them, openly or secretly.

The big buck seized his wrists, twisted him on his back and then dragged him down the corridor to the cell. He was dumped inside and the door clanged shut.

The old man helped him sit up and he examined his back carefully in the dim light, clucking his tongue as he did so.

'Seen 'em worse than this, son. They used a snake, you'd be bleedin' and dyin' likely. Used a strap so you wouldn't get cut much. White folks don't pay high fo' niggers cut up by a snake 'cause they knows a whuppin' means the nigger is ornery an' mean. Now you jes' sit back. Pretty soon the misery won't be so bad. Whut they whup you fo'?'

'Says I killed a man.'

'Did you?'

'That's whut they asked me,' Jubal evaded the question.

'Yo' keeps answerin' 'em that way too an' you be all right. Knows how you feels. Been cut with the strap my own se'f. Pain din' last. You feel kinda sick, you close you eyes and try to sleep. That helps.'

Sleep! At a time like this, Jubal thought; when his mind was so filled with hate that there wasn't room for anything else, not even the thought of sleep. He let himself sag to the floor, where he turned on his belly. The old man had water. He dripped some of it on the swollen flesh and began a gentle massage. It made Jubal cry out with pain at first, but then he began to feel better, and after a while he did sleep.

That was the only escape left for him, he thought, as he dozed off. The old man was right. Make the best of it and wait. Maybe forever, but keep away from the whip. Jubal had just one plan now. To give as little as he got. To scheme and use his educated brain to seek a way out. There'd be one. He'd find it.

Jubal could hear someone crooning, a low, bass voice that was as soothing to the nerves as the gentle massage had been to the body. The pain seemed to have left him and the despair. He was a man. That much he'd proven to himself. They'd never get the best of him, never drive him into a black abyss from which there'd be no escape. He felt a rocking motion and realised the old man had his head cradled in his lap while he rocked back and forth. That was another thing – so long as there were men like this old one, Jubal had friends.

He let himself drift off into the welcome world of sleep.

When he awoke, the fire swept over his body again and he groaned. His eyelids seemed to be swollen shut and when he gently rubbed them, he felt a granular substance and realised these were tears, long since dried.

He sat up quickly. The inside of the cell was almost totally dark. Someone was snoring loudly. That would be the old man. Jubal wondered how long he'd been asleep.

His body ached and his mouth was bone dry. He peered about for a bucket of water and found one. The water tasted as if it was covered with a layer of scum, but he drank it anyway and then poured some of it over his head.

'How you feel, son?' The old man had been watching him. Jubal didn't even realise the snoring had stopped.

'Like I been lashed good.'

'Cain't see how else you'd feel, seein' that's whut happened to you. Feel dizzy or sick to your stummick?'

'Reckon not.'

'Crawl oveh heah, son. Got some talkin' to do 'fore they comes fo' us.'

'What they going to do to us?' Jubal asked.

'Sell us. Whut you think, boy? Sell us like they sell they cows an' they sheep an' they hawgs. We stand up theah an' they 'spects us. Then they bids an' who bids most gits us.'

'That's all there is to it?'

'Thass the beginnin'. Only the beginnin'. Now wants to warn you, son. I 'members you talks like a white man.'

'Yes. I can read and write and do sums.'

'First thing you do, fo'git every damn thing you learnt. You talks an' acts like a po' nigger, they treats you like one. You gits uppity and starts talkin' like a white man an' you goin' to scare hell outen them white folks.'

'Because I talk like them?' he asked incredulously.

'Because you a nigger and you ain't got no right to talk like them. Niggers ain't smart. Once they is, the masta gets rid o' them fast as he kin. Don't want no uppity niggers 'round.'

'Why not? If I'm smart, I can do things better'n a no-account nigger.'

'They don' want you doin' anythin' bettah, son. Only whut they tells you. You jes' keeps up with the rest of 'em in the fields an' you gits food. Ain't much good, but they's plenty and you don't starve. You gits a cabin. If it ain't so tight, you kin make it so. You gits a wench. What mo' kin a man ask fo?'

Jubal groaned. 'What more? Old man. . . . '

'My name's Drill.'

'Drill, then. There's plenty more. There's a real house and a woman you take for yourself, because you want to take her.

There's white bread and good meat, there's whiskey and gin and wine. There's money in your palm every payday. That's what there is, Drill. That and more.'

The old man sighed. 'Nevah did have any o' that. Nevah will, so far's I goes. They ain't such things. I asks only that some kind man buys me an' makes me a houseman. Or maybe gits me a high hat and let's me drive a purty coach. I sure ain't good fo' field work no mo' an' I sure ain't got no sap lef' to knock up a wench.'

'My mammy and pappy were seventeen when they were manumitted,' Jubal explained. 'They went north and I was born in St Louis. I went to school and got my learning. Got me a job. Three dollars and seventy cents a week. Don't buy much, but it's pay for working. My mammy and pappy died and left me a little cabin all paid for, so I got along.'

'How'd they git you down heah, you bein' free an' all?'

'They got a tan gal to go to bed with me, only when I went to her room, it was dark and the gal in bed turned out to be white. She says I raped her. Mr Wiley and Mr Sedella came in and seems like the white gal I raped was a sister to one. That's what they said. Next thing they got me aboard the riverboat and they gives me a stateroom and I gets to work knocking up as many wenches as I can. That ain't all – Mr Wiley and Mr Sedella gets white folks to pay to peek into the cabin while I knocking up them gals. Some of 'em fights me, so I whales 'em real good 'fore I spreads 'em on the bed. The white folks got their money's worth.'

'Heered tell o' worse way o' gettin' heah.' The old man's lips parted in a wry grin.

'Says I gets me a silver dollar for each wench I knocks up, but reckon they didn't mean it.'

'Son, they's a auction this afternoon, so they ain't much time. Now you heed whut I say, 'cause I an old man an' I knows whut I talkin' 'bout.'

'Reckon so,' Jubal conceded.

'You gits bought by a cane planter, you goin' to bust you back in no time. Man don' live more'n six-seven years cuttin' cane. So pray it ain't no sugar cane farmer buys you.'

'Drill, what would happen if I stood up there at the sale and told everybody I was free?'

'Tonight you'd be floatin' in the rivah, boy. Far as these gen'men in N'awleans be, they ain't no such thing as a free nigger. An' they see's to it they ain't no such thing as a smart nigger.'

'Reckon I talks noways splendiferous, old Drill. Talks like a nigger, I does.'

Drill laughed softly. 'An' don' you fo'get it. You a slave now, son. They works you to death in no time, you lets 'em, so you keeps your eyes an' ears open and you looks fo' any chance to get away with sumthin'. You cuts cane fast when they's lookin' an' slow when they ain't. You does the bes' you kin and you keeps your faith in yourse'f. Long's you got that, you ain't so bad off.'

'Got somethin' else, old Drill. Better'n the white folks got. I'se worth plenty o' money an' they ain't aimin' to kill me they got no mighty big reason to. But they ain't worth a thing to me, an' if I kills them, I don't lose nuthin'. Thass the way it's gotta be, old Drill. I'se worth money, they ain't.'

FIVE

The man who came for Jubal wasn't Wiley, but a hulking, pot-bellied creature with one eye patch-covered, a broken nose and an incredibly slow wit. He did, however, hold a heavy club, which made up for any other lack, because he looked as if he'd enjoy using it.

Jubal was pushed, via the end of the club, out of the compound, through the gates, across several city streets and then down to the river. There he removed his clothes, wincing as he did so because the welts were still sore. He was given a tin can of crude paste soap and told to wash.

He waded into the dirty river, but welcomed it because the water was soothing to his bruised skin. He soaped himself well, ducked to rinse, came out of the water and was handed his old clothes to dry himself with. This done, the hulk of a man threw him a thin white shirt and a pair of old pants that almost burst as he struggled into them.

'You busts them trogs, boy,' Potbelly warned, 'an I bust you haid with this heah club. Walk easy now . . . you got so much hangin' 'tween yo' laigs ain't no pants goin' to hold up, seems like.'

Jubal didn't say anything. He walked back to the compound, but he wasn't locked up. Instead he joined a group of six others, seated on a bench waiting to be called into the auction room.

Only one of the group interested Jubal, for she was a lithe, young-breasted wench of about eighteen or nineteen. Rangy, hot-eyed, with straight black hair and the nose of an Arab, not a Negro. Jubal sat down beside her.

'Wishes you a good masta,' he said by way of greeting.

She smiled. 'That's nice of you. Wishes you the same.'

'Name's Jubal.'

'Likes that name, I do. Jubal. Mine's Calinda. Whut farm you off'n?'

'Masta died.' Jubal evaded the question skillfully. 'Everythin' he got gits sold.'

'My masta shinin' up to me and gettin' fixed to rape me, so mist'iss sold me to the first trader come by. Don' mind none. White masta gits mighty drunk 'fore he comes rapin'.' She let her eyes drift up and down his body. 'You sure goin' to fetch a mighty price. Reckon two thousand. Maybe more.'

'Reckon so,' he said without further comment on the subject.

'We gits bought by the same masta, you kin come see me any time you wants, Jubal.'

Jubal nodded. To himself, he hoped the same thing, for she was desirable to such an extent that he felt a driving urge for her despite his ache-filled body and the horrifying fact that he was about to be sold.

They were summoned with the sweep of a short whip in the hands of a man dressed all in white – dirty white, for the coat and trousers looked as if they'd been slept in for days, and the white shoes were so filthy they looked more brown. As Calinda was the only female to be offered in this batch, she was brought to the small platform before which thirty or forty men sat on benches, chewed tobacco and spat noisily on the floor, and on one another's boots.

The auctioneer buttoned his white coat and went to work. He passed his hands down over Calinda's breasts so they'd be well outlined under the thin cotton dress and the nipples would stand out.

'Tittied up real good. She's sixteen, pure as they kin be. All ready fo' breedin'. Strong, good lines. Yas suh, Mista Turner, suh?'

The man named Turner was thin, hawk-nosed, with small, greenish eyes now glittering with a desire for this girl.

'Claims the right to examine her, suh. 'Fore I bids.'

'Now, Mistah Turner, suh,' the auctioneer grinned. 'I ain't agin you examinin' this heah gal, but you sees her right now and it ain't like buyin' no pig in a poke, suh. This heah ain't no pig, as you can plainly see, and she ain't wearin' no poke.' He suddenly grasped the hem of Calinda's skirt and pulled it higher than her head. 'Leastwise,' he went on with a lascivious wink and laugh, 'that sho' don't look like no poke.'

'All Mister Turner wants to do,' a voice from the audience said, 'is poke around some. I say the gentleman pays for the privilege. He can see what he's getting right now. I bids five hundred dollahs.'

Jubal watched and listened and sweated to keep from groaning. He'd heard of the vendue table before, but nobody had told him it was this bad.

The auctioneer dropped Calinda's dress and went to work. The bid went up, fifty dollars at a time, to nine hundred. Turner dropped out at five hundred and fifty. The man who bought Calinda kept raising the bid in a lazy, indifferent voice, but he topped everyone.

'Mistah Thibault, suh,' the auctioneer bowed. 'This hea gal's now you propitty, suh. You claims her any time you wants. You stayin' in our fair city fo' the night, we boards her fo' two bits, suh.'

'Have her sit on the bench,' Thibault said. 'Bring up that big buck next.'

The auctioneer pointed to Jubal. 'Him, suh?'

'Yes – him!'

Jubal walked on to the platform. Thibault arose slowly and began moving toward him, but Turner, who'd lost out on the girl, was faster. He climbed on to the stage.

'This heah a likely lookin' niggah,' he said. 'Reckon I'll buy him.'

'Well now. . . . ' The auctioneer glanced at Thibault, who merely nodded.

Turner was too busy to notice. He faced Jubal, put his hands to Jubal's neck and squeezed hard. Then he passed his hands down over his chest and sides, feeling for lumps and scars.

'Wants him to shuck down,' he said.

The auctioneer jabbed Jubal with the end of his whip. 'You heard the gen'mun.'

Jubal peeled off his shirt. Turner squirmed around behind him. 'Whupped! Them's fresh marks. Got us a bad nigger heah. Ain't wuth much he needs whuppin'.'

'Mistah Turner,' Thibault said from the audience, 'you wants to buy this buck, you start bidding or I will.'

Turner glared at the older man. 'Mistah Thibault, with all due respect to your age and your wisdom, I got me a right to see whut this buck is like. Then I starts the biddin'.'

'Oh, go ahead,' Thibault gave in.

Turner motioned toward Jubal. 'I tol' you shuck down. Now you aimin' to do it or you want a taste o' the whip?'

Jubal slowly untied the rope around his waist and let his pants drop. There were a few astonished grunts from the men close enough to observe him and make obscene catcalls. Turner grinned and used the end of his cane to move Jubal's testicles experimentally. Then he hefted them in the palm of one hand and nodded.

'Biggest I seed in years. 'Members a big buck named Lukey, back four five yeahs ago, hung like this, but not as heavy. Turn 'round, niggah, and bend oveh.'

Jubal's teeth made grinding noises only he could hear. He turned, he bent. Fingers spread his buttocks, a finger was rammed against his rectum.

'No piles,' Turner said. 'Straighten up, niggah, and turn 'round to face me.'

Jubal obeyed. Turner fingered his neck again, then grabbed his lower jaw and forced his mouth open. With the same finger he tested his teeth, even grasped a couple, shook them to see if they were loose.

'He'll do,' Turner said. 'I bids.'

'Two thousand,' Thibault said from the bench.

Turner whirled about. 'Suh, you be good 'nuff to let a man bid.'

'Top two thousand,' Thibault said.

'Two thousand an' fifty,' Turner shouted.

'Three thousand,' Thibault said.

'Three? Mastah Thibault, you clear outa you mind, suh? This heah buck's been whupped – looks like yest-dy by his lumps. You can see plain, he's ornery, but he's strong an' he cuts cane, so I wants him.'

'Top three thousand,' Thibault said.

Turner's thin face assumed a crafty look. 'Five thousand, suh.'

Jubal's impression was that both these men were crazy.

Thibault said, 'My bid is three thousand. So far. You bid five. I wants to see your gold, suh. Right now.'

'You questionin' my honah, suh?' Turner shouted.

'You haven't got five thousand,' Thibault said. 'You bid that much so I'd drop out and then you'd admit it and hope to get him for two after I leave this auction. I'm not leaving until you get up five thousand and you have until the auction closes to do it or I claim this man for three thousand. That's how it is.'

Turner jumped down from the stage and strode out, slashing at the end of each bench with his cane, muttering his rage, but confessing by his silence and retreat that Thibault was right.

'Looks like you bought yourse'f a right strong boy,' the auctioneer said.

Thibault mounted the platform. He motioned to Jubal 'Pick up your pants and put your shirt back on.'

Jubal said nothing, but he obeyed. At least this man seemed to have enough compassion to realise that even a slave might possess some degree of modesty.

'You a Coromantee?' Thibault asked.

'Yes, suh.'

'Pure?'

'Yes, suh.'

'Where you from, boy?'

'He's from Major Sedgewick's plantation up no'th,' the auctioneer put in hastily. 'Major died and all his stock been sold.'

The auctioneer was covering for Wiley and Sedella's kidnapping. Jubal didn't say anything.

'Never thought much of the Major's stock,' Thibault said.

'This heah boy's an exception, suh,' the auctioneer said smoothly.

'Reckon he is. All right, boy – sit down beside the wench. Now, let's get on with this. Where's the two runners?'

'In the jail, suh,' the auctioneer said. 'You pays the reward of three hundrud dollahs and they's yours again.'

'I'll tend to it soon. Lock these two up for a while.'

'Yes, suh, an' in the same cell, you wants, suh? Might be you'll be breedin' fo' they gits to you plantation, Mistah Thibault.'

'I don't give a damn what you do as long as they're here when I'm ready to take them.'

Thibault looked Jubal straight in the eye and Jubal looked back, not dropping his gaze as he knew he was supposed to do. With this man, he couldn't. He didn't know why, but he had to face him.

Thibault was a tall, well-built man of about fifty, with graying hair, and blue eyes that were getting steadily colder as Jubal met them. He had a well-shaped mouth and he was undoubtedly handsome, but he was no fool. Turner had been an idiot. Had his bid been high, Jubal would have been planning to run even now. But with Thibault, there'd be no running, not if he wanted to live. There'd be no lashing either, unless he richly deserved it.

Thibault gave one emphatic nod of his head and turned away. Jubal's lips parted in the slightest trace of a smile. He hadn't lowered his eyes. That much he'd won.

Two boys, about fourteen, were led on to the vendue table as Jubal was jabbed off it with the auctioneer's whip. Jubal sat down beside Calinda.

'Knows that man Thibault?' he asked.

'Knows of him, I do. Nevah seed him befo'.'

'What's said 'bout him, Calinda?'

'He's mean as a man kin be, but he's fair. Sure rather have him fo' my mastah than that dried up ol' whore-masta' whut lifted my dress.'

'I meets Mistah Turner some dark night, Calinda, I kills him.'

'You talks too much, Jubal.'

'I kills him fo' whut he done to you.'

'You kills him you hangs, an' I ain't worth that.'

'Wouldn't kill him anybody see me do it. I means kill him if I gets away with it.'

'That's bettah.'

'He got a big plantation? Thibault, I mean.'

'Sugar crop. Heerd he got seven hundrud an' fifty niggers workin' the place.'

'That ain't small. Well, looks like we'll be together like we said. I ain't sorry.'

'I ain't neither,' she said with a grin. 'Mistah Turner wasn't the on'y one who saw whut you got hangin' 'tween you laigs. Hopes I get to be you wench, I does.'

'I hopes so too.'

The burly man with the whip approached and herded them through the compound to a cell. He slammed the door behind them and locked it. They sat down on the welcome coolness of the dirt floor in the dimly lighted cubicle.

'You feels horny, Jubal, we kin do like the man said.'

He gave her a wide grin. 'Feels horny I'm with you, but got the aches so bad I ain't fit right now.'

'Whut they whup you fo', Jubal?'

'Nevah did get to tell me,' he said.

'Heerd you killed a white man.'

'I killed a white man I'd be kickin' my heels offen the ground under some tree 'bout now.'

She snuggled closer to him and he let his big arm drape around her shoulders. 'Why I git a feelin' you ain't jes' a po' nigger don' know nuthin'?'

'Cain't answer that 'cause it all I am. Jes' a po' nigger who's goin' to be set out cuttin' cane. Wants to know mo' about Mistah Thibault. He got a wife?'

'Wife and son. Miz Thibault kinda quiet. Sure is a handsome lookin' woman too. The son 'bout your age, Jubal. He like his pa – stalkin' roun' lettin' us folks know he the mastah heah. Heered he don' mind usin' a whip.'

Jubal eyed her lazily. 'How you know so much 'bout him?'

She smiled, a small twisting of her lips. ' 'Cause I was upstairs maid fo' him an' his mist'iss.'

Jubal was interested now. 'You were a Thibault slave?'

'Sho' was. Mist'iss, she sold me. Masta, he come slewin' 'round me an' mist'iss up and sells me 'fore he knows whut happened.'

'He a rapin' man?' Jubal sighed.

'Mighty fussy who he rapes. You wants to hear whut he done one night in my cabin?'

Jubal closed his eyes. 'Ain't got nuthin' else to do.'

'Had me a buck. Wasn't much good. I spread my laigs fo' him one, two times a week, he tuckered out so he cain't work good. Mastah Thibault, he say why I don't birth no suckers, an' I tells him he lookin' at the most unsatisfied wench on his plantation. So he fingers me some an' say I tittied up real good and mayhap he rapes me. Suits me good. Masta rapes you an' he takes keer o' you, so I jes' waits. Long time, nothin' happened. Then the buck livin' with me got sent to take keer o' the boilers in the sugar mill. Keeps him wukkin' all night. Masta he waitin' till I makin' baids one mawnin' an' he kinda whisper I git myse'f clean and smell good, he comin' that night.'

Jubal opened one eye. He was far more interested than he pretended to be. If his new master had a weakness, Jubal wanted to know all about it.

'You reckon masta git hisse'f all clean an' smell good fo' he comes rapin' you?'

She gave a loud and raucous laugh. 'Reckon they thinks they smell good all the time.'

'He did come?'

'You know whut he did? Brought me a bottle of cologne. He took off my clothes. Whut I got on. Jes' my dress. He rubbed the cologne all ovah me till I stink good. Then he sits on my baid and I sits on his lap facin' him and he diddles 'round. Nevah saw a man so horny. Thinks he got six han's fo' he got me wigglin'. Been raped by white masta befo' Mist' Thibault, but wasn't much. Jes' set me on my back, git on top, squeeze my titties some, bust in me fo' a minute an' its ovah. Nevah even got started myse'f. But Mist' Thibault, he sho' got me squirmin' and beggin' and fightin'. Mo' he gits, crazier he gits. But he got nothin' to rape me with. Nothin' but a li'l white worm whut stays soft. Wasn't no rape. Sure 'nuff no rape.'

Jubal said, 'Ain't no white man got whut I got. Ain't no white man kin pleasure you like I kin.'

She slipped her hand beneath his trousers and grasped him tightly. 'Mist' Thibault, he ain't big as yo,' Jubal. Been horny my own se'f since Mist' Turner made yo' shuck down.'

'Reckon Mist'iss Thibault sold you 'cause she found out masta tried to rape you?'

'Reckon. Wants to be raped now, Jubal. Wants it bad.' She suddenly maneuvered her body over his, at the same time tearing madly at his trousers. She got them down to his hips and buried her face against him, until he secured a handful of her hair, lifted her up, arose himself and struck her across the face. She staggered across the room and sat down heavily.

'When they's rapin' to be done, I does it,' Jubal said angrily.

She bent her head and began to cry. He strode over to her, knelt, pulled her legs out straight, whipped up the dress and then removed his trousers. He straddled her, taking his time. He rubbed his face against the hardness of her small breasts until she was heaving and panting and moaning for him. She gave one brief little cry as he entered her, but if the pain lasted, she gave no heed to it for she squirmed and rotated, clawed at him, bit his cheek, screeched once and lay back, heaving great gusts of air in and out of her lungs.

Jubal slipped into his pants again. 'Reckon you kin say you been raped, Calinda. You wants mo', it'll be here when you is ready fo' it. An' I wants it.'

She studied him sleepily. 'Firs' you busts me in the face and then you rapes me. Thinks you crazy, Jubal, but sho' likes the way you is crazy. Reckon they keep us locked heah fo' a week, I don' mind none.'

'Reckon we could make the time go by,' he said with a grin.

She arched her naked body upwards toward him. 'No sense wastin' time, Jubal. I ready if you are.'

He grinned and shook his head. 'Ain't goin'to let you wear me down none. Whut's masta's son like? He come whorin' 'round too?'

She turned on her side. 'Don' rightly know, Jubal. Fo' his daddy rapes me, I kind o' pushed 'gainst him one day in his bedroom. Nuthin' much. Jes' let my laig git in the way an' nex' thing I knows, I sho' on the bed.'

'Sho' nuff?' Jubal asked. 'He a rapin' man too?'

'He done whut you done, Jubal. He bust me good so's I fell on the bed an' then he walked out. I was a mind to run away that night. Way I figured, next day I was goin' to be whupped. But nothin' happened. Seed him three-four times the next day an' he jes' look at me, but he don't say nothin'.'

'Reckon he hung right?'

'Sho felt like it.'

'You seed 'em cuttin' cane befo'?' Jubal abruptly changed the subject.

'Cut some myse'f when frost gits at the crop.'

'How's it done?'

She drew up her knees to her chin, still stark naked. 'Why you ask?'

' 'Cause I gettin' sent to cut cane sure. Wants to know whut to do.'

'Yo' come down from Major Sedgewick's plantation, you sho' knows how.'

'Didn't come down from there. Man who sold me said that 'cause he don' know whar I comes from and don' want to say it.'

'Whar you from then, Jubal?'

'Been hoein' cotton befo' now.'

'Whar you come from?' she repeated.

He knew how to make her forget her demands for an answer. He yanked her legs down, crawled upon her and pressed his lips against hers in a brutal kiss. She squirmed beneath him, wrapped her legs scissor-fashion around his body and clung with a strength that surprised him. This time he rammed her so hard she shivered and yelled, but clung even harder. Twice he satisfied her, and she made a healthy attempt for a third, but failed and fell asleep before he was free of her.

He'd have to be careful with this wench. She'd lain with too many white masters, and obviously she hadn't suffered for it because her back was free of any whip scars. She was well fed, healthy, extremely well versed in how to satisfy a man, black or white.

A girl like that might talk at the wrong time. To the wrong people. Jubal would need a story to tell everyone that would be easily believed. He lay back to think of one and fell asleep too.

SIX

Murphy Thibault made his way from the auction yard to his bank, where he arranged to pay for the slaves he'd bought. He'd attended four auctions since he'd been in New Orleans and there was a sizeable coffle waiting for him when he began the day-long journey back to his plantation.

He removed his hat from time to time as he passed women he knew, mostly by sight and not name. The socialising at Briarfield Plantation was done by Ann, his wife. The less of it Thibault had to endure, the better he liked it.

From the bank he went to his favorite cafe on Basin Street, a resplendent palace done in bright red with gold leaf trim. The Negro who took charge of carriages was dressed in red and gold; the arched entranceway was of gold leaf. Within, rugs, table linen, uniforms and even china service was the same shade of red. Thibault didn't care for the decor, but he did like the elegant food and fine drink.

Sartorially, Thibault was quite correct in a frock coat, mouse-gray trousers of suitable tightness, a large white scarf, gray gloves and a gold-headed cane. His hair, definitely graying at the temples, gave him a distinguished appearance. He wore neither mustache, beard or sideburns, which set him apart. He was a lavish spender, and wherever he went, he was greeted with a mixture of friendliness touched by a good measure of greed.

He was seated at the best table in the cafe, a captain and three waiters hovering about him, paying no further attention to other diners at nearby tables.

Thibault ordered his usual double whiskey, which he drank neat, and was provided with a refill without his being required to ask for it. He ate oysters in cracked ice, a dozen and a half, in a sauce that invariably brought tears to his eyes, but he enjoyed the spicy heat of the condiments. He ate a double steak with fried potatoes and a side order of fried eggs. He disdained dessert, unless his third and fourth double whiskey could be considered a dessert. He drank an entire pot of strong chicory coffee laced with brandy. He spoke to no one and his obvious desire for privacy was respected. At about nine o'clock, he drifted into a gambling casino, lost a hundred dollars in ten minutes and gave up, finding no pleasure in it.

Pierre Devol stopped him as he was leaving. 'Good evening, Mr Thibault. I have a proposition for you if you will honor me by having a drink.'

'What's happened, you got a new horse?' Murphy asked. He didn't especially like this fawning, smirking man.

Devol was a notorious gambler, a ladies' man and a fashion plate, now wearing a cream-colored coat and fitted trousers of a deep gold color. His weskit was a pale green and the scarf-neckcloth was tan, with an emerald pin. If he'd been asked to describe the man's appearance, Thibault would have used the word flamboyant.

'My dear sir,' Devol said, 'horse racing is too tame for New Orleans of today. I refer to the new buck you bought this morning.'

They had drifted into the bar where Thibault was served brandy without asking for it. 'What about my new buck?' he asked.

'Looks to me like a fighting man, sir. Got me a big buck too, never been beaten. Got so I can't get any opposition. They take one look at my boy and refuse to risk theirs.'

'What makes you think I want to risk mine? I just paid a lot of money for him.'

'I'd be willing to give you fair odds. Say, two to one. I'd expect you to lay five thousand on the line, sir, and you may name any date for the fight you wish.'

'I'll think about it.'

'My boy's fighting tonight, you want to size him up. Mr Thibault. I ain't trying to get you into something you can't handle.'

'Where's the fight?'

'In the Vienna Parlor of Ida Meeker's place.'

Thibault nodded. 'Might be there, sir.'

'Midnight's when it begins. Nothing barred and the loser gets dragged away. We don't stop the fight till one of them niggers is dead.'

Thibault finished the rest of his drink, tipped his hat and walked out. He was going to Ida Meeker's place anyway and he wondered if Devol could have known he almost always paid Ida a visit when he came to New Orleans. It didn't matter. He didn't give a damn who knew it.

Ida's place on Basin Street had been the home of a French nobleman at one time. A two-story frame, gabled house of sixteen spacious rooms, it was exactly right for the purpose Ida put to it. There was an ample veranda and an ornate double door with stained glass windows.

Inside was her famous Vienna Parlor, normally dominated by a piano set upon a small stage and backdropped with red velvet drapes. The furniture was massive, man-sized, and overstuffed. The rug, a ruby shade, was thick and soft, the animal skins spread on it were real and one was careful not to trip over the lion's head or the bear's gaping jaws.

Tonight, however, the piano had been removed and so had all of the furniture and rugs. There were simply four bare walls in a room spacious enough to be a small theater or meeting hall. Thibault's footsteps made hollow sounds as he strode across it.

The amber-colored maid trotted along behind him, still trying to get him to surrender his hat and cane, without much success. Ida Meeker greeted him in the doorway of the next room – the French Parlor. She was still a handsome woman, bleached, well-corseted and hearty.

'Murphy,' she called out. 'Murphy Thibault! Risen from the dead. Where you been?'

'Busy,' he said. He hugged her and slapped her ample fanny before he accepted a drink from the liveried slave who had quickly prepared it the instant Thibault entered the establishment. 'You look well, my dear, or should I say, my sweet colleen?'

'Certainly could be either with a name like yours.'

'It's a damned curse, Ida.'

'What's wrong with it? Your mother was Irish, your father was French. Damn sight better'n Ida Meeker.'

He finished the drink. 'If I was called Ida Meeker, I wouldn't be here now, would I?'

'I don't know. Might be you'd be here working for me. Ever give any thought to that?'

'It's an interesting idea. I understand you're having a fight tonight.'

She shrugged her ample shoulders. 'I don't like 'em, but they pay so damn good I can't turn 'em down. Why men can stand there and watch one buck nigger kill another is more than I can figure out. I know just one good thing about it, the bloodier the fight, the more men stay all night with my girls. What's there in watching a man killed that gives another man a hard-on?'

Thibault laughed. 'I don't know. The primitive instinct, I suppose. This going to be a good one?'

'If you like blood.'

'Pierre Devol's boy worth watching?'

'Murphy, by the time that fight starts, you won't be able to fit another person in the room. Devol collects a hundred dollars from each admission. They flock to see his boy because he always wins, and he always does it in the most brutal way he can.'

'Not much opposition, eh?'

'Take tonight. Devol's boy is in prime condition. They're going to pit against him a buck fresh from cutting cane. He'll be wore out before he even starts. His master bets on him – five to one, I think – but he never has to pay off. He gets some of the money Devol takes in. Enough to make it worth his sacrifice of the buck. Myself, I'd give five thousand if it was Devol who got killed in the ring.'

'Some day,' Thibault said, 'a buck'll come along who'll bust Devol's boy to little pieces.'

'That'll be the day a hell of a lot of money changes hands.'

He nodded. 'I'm ready now.'

'Any particular gal, Murphy?'

'You know I always want Carmen. She knows what to do.'

'Yes. Why you do it, Murphy? Why can't you just go upstairs and fuck that girl like a normal man? Hell, you're normal. I should know. You were my best customer when I worked for Blanche Grosso. You changed. The girls don't like it. Neither do I.'

'I'm aware of that. I pay extra, don't I?'

She nodded. 'All right. Whatever you say. My place and my girls are always yours.'

'Save me room at ringside for the fight,' he said.

'Yes. Shall I send up more whiskey?'

'Carmen likes to send for it.'

He walked slowly up the wide, formal staircase to the bedrooms on the second floor. He used the one at the far end of the hall and when he walked in, Carmen gave him a cool nod of her small head.

'Evenin', Mr Thibault,' she said.

She was raven-haired with a swarthy complexion in which there might possibly be a trace of tar, though her features were Caucasian and nobody ever questioned her about antecedents. There was a discreet knock on the door. She opened it just far enough to accept the small whip passed to her. She laid this across the bureau.

It was a large room featuring an oversized bed of ornately carved mahogany. The window was heavily and artistically draped. There were two comfortable chairs, a small stand on which rested a blue and white pitcher and wash basin. There was a mound of towels beside it.

A chandelier, its facets glittering in the candlelight, gave surprising illumination. Everything here was sedate, dignified and scrupulously clean.

'Like before, Mr Thibault?' Carmen asked.

He sat down on the edge of the bed. 'Just like before, Carmen.'

She nodded and moved over to stand before him. He touched

the calf of one leg and she raised her foot so he might remove the shoe. He took off the other one. She turned around so he might get at the hooks and eyes and buttons, until her dress slithered to the floor. She stepped out of it.

He unlaced the black corset, a garment Carmen never wore until she was told that Murphy Thibault was here. Beneath this she wore nothing. She turned around, stark-naked, to face him. His hands reached up to caress her breasts until the nipples were hard and pink. Then he stood up and quietly removed all his clothes. Carmen took possession of each garment and carefully hung it up. He stood before her now, both of them naked.

'I could try again,' she said. 'I'd be mighty glad to try, Mr Thibault. French way or anything you fancy.'

'No,' he said harshly. 'Get to work.

He lay face down across the bed. She picked up the whip and lashed his back with it.

'Harder,' he growled. 'What the hell's the matter with you tonight? Hurt me! Goddamnit, hurt me!'

She brought the whip down smartly across his buttocks. Not a sound escaped him. She stepped back and began to wield the whip harder and harder, while her pretty face began to contort into lines of savagery. The more she used the whip, the better she liked it. All the genuine reluctance and sympathy she had for him when it began disappeared. That was why he wanted her most of the time. And that was why she never refused, for she enjoyed punishing a man who would not respond to her varied store of tricks.

A series of great sobs shook his strong body. He groaned and jerked with each lash of the whip. She didn't stop until her arm was so tired she couldn't raise it again. Then she hurled the whip into a far corner, cried out in sympathy as her nature again reversed itself. She flung herself on the bed beside him. He turned to face her. She drew him close and kissed him. She caressed him, used every wile she knew. It never worked. A once glorious manhood, renowned in bagnios like this, was forever gone.

'It's no use,' he said in a hollow voice. 'No use at all.'

She moved away from him, exhausted by her own frantic efforts. She slid off the bed, poured water into the basin, carried it back and began to wash him carefully, tenderly. The welts stood like small peaks and contacts with the towels made him wince. Each time he did, Carmen spoke soothingly to him. Then, as if she couldn't stand it any longer, she crawled down and buried her face against his hairy softness. She fondled his penis, his testicles, kissed them, did her best to french him, and finally gave up, more in sorrow than anger.

He lay back finally, and rested while Carmen pulled a velvet cord beside the door. When a slave answered promptly, she gave him Thibault's trousers, coat, shirt and shoes. In twenty minutes they'd be returned, pressed and sponged and the shoes shined.

Carmen began to dress. 'Will you stay for the fight, Mr Thibault?' she asked.

'Yes. Devol saw me buy a good-looking boy this afternoon and wants to challenge me.'

'Devol's nigger is the strongest man I ever saw,' Carmen said. 'They say he can tear a man's arm or leg clean off.'

'I heard that too. I'm not risking my boy yet. I don't even know if he can fight or even has the heart for it. I don't like these fights much, but I don't stand away from a challenge either.'

A maid knocked and entered with a silver service of steaming coffee and a decanter of fine brandy. Carmen took a dollar bill from the money she'd removed from Thibault's clothes and gave it to the maid.

While Thibault dressed, painfully heeding the welts on his back, she poured the coffee and the brandy. They sat down at a small table.

'Mr Thibault,' she said, 'can I say something personal?'

'You know you can.'

'Mr Thibault, when the day happens you feel you can get a hard-on, please come to me.'

'That's a promise,' he said.

'Now, I don't mind so much – what you make me do.'

'I warned you long ago, we don't talk about that,' he said harshly.

'Yes, Mr Thibault. Saw your son Shawn last week. He's bigger'n you are.'

'I hope,' he said, 'you refer to the size of his body. As a whole, that is, and not one particular part of it.'

She laughed. 'He ain't been here yet. Girl who gets him is going to get something. Mmmmm. . . .'

'There's plenty of stud in him.' Thibault went to the door, opened it and listened. He closed it again. 'Lot's of noise down there, so the fight must be near ready to begin.'

He stood before the mirror, set his hat carefully on his head so the graying temples would show well. He grasped his cane and smiled.

'Ready for them now, Carmen,' he said. 'You'll find the usual, plus a little more, under the pillow, and thank you very much.'

She held the door for him. After he left, she lifted the pillow and picked up the five double eagles. They were a sizable weight in her hand. She dropped them into a bureau drawer and began to freshen up. As soon as the fight was over, she'd be busy. There were already two reservations.

Downstairs, the Vienna Room was packed, but a liveried slave was waiting especially for Thibault and had a place for him. Thibault found himself beside Devol again.

'Well, well,' Devol said, 'first time I ever seen you at one of my fightin' matches, sir. Am I to assume you took me seriously when I challenged your new boy?'

'I don't know one damn thing about my new boy,' Thibault said. 'Maybe he can't even lift his feet off the floor. But I want to see what this seven-day wonder of yours is like.'

'Want to make a small bet? Say a hundred dollahs of your money, sir, to win a thousand of mine if my boy gets whipped?'

'Might make it a little more interesting,' Thibault agreed, and he handed over a hundred dollars, accepting in return a slip of paper from Devol, attesting to the transaction.

The challenger came into the ring then, led by his owner, a small, wizened man Thibault recognised as an impoverished rice grower in the Delta. He held by the hand, a hulking brute of a man, blue-black, with a coarse face, massive shoulders and hands. He looked like a pygmy leading a giant.

Thibault knew this type of Negro. A Gaboon, stupid, cheaply purchased, sometimes very strong, but unable to make any use of his strength because he lacked the intelligence to utilise it. A Gaboon made a fine physical appearance, except for the vacant face. They lived but a short time, were subject to almost any disease, which they often got, five times as often as other slaves.

Devol's boy entered the ring next. He wore a bright red shirt and tight pants ripped off at the knee. He was a magnificent specimen, standing well over six feet without a shred of fat. He'd been trained, carefully fed, nurtured, just as the owner of a prize race horse spends a great deal of money keeping his horse in trim. If this buck lasted long enough, it was possible Devol might become a rich man from his work.

There were no preliminaries except that some of the new members of the audience screamed for their bets back after a glimpse of Devol's boy. No one paid any attention to them.

The auctioneer who'd sold Jubal stepped into the middle of the cleared space. He had on the same white suit, a trifle dirtier by now.

'We's 'bout ready, gen'men. Niggers, shuck down.'

The two fighters stripped to the buff. Thibault saw that there were a score of women present and they were busy inspecting far more than the fighting prowess of these huge men.

'Go to it!' The actioneer leaped nimbly aside as the two blacks leaped towards one another.

'Kill him, Lib!' Devol yelled encouragement.

Thibault guessed this boy's name was Liberty. The other hulking brute bore the name Jonah, and Thibault wryly guessed his luck was going to be even worse than that of his namesake.

Apparently Lib had standing orders not to end the fight too

soon, for he absorbed half a dozen punches with ease, pulling away from them so they looked and sounded far worse than they really were. He made a couple of weak passes at Jonah, toying with him and obviously enjoying it. The crowd quickly began to mutter in dissatisfaction.

Lib gave everyone a wide, toothy grin. He leaped at his opponent, neatly tripped him and when the big man crashed to the floor, Lib drove his thumb into Jonah's right eye socket, pushing the eyeball out until it hung by its bloody muscles.

Jonah screeched in agony, but he was either courageous enough – which Thibault doubted – or he knew that if he didn't kill Lib right now, he himself was going to be killed. Jonah was back on his feet, floundering around, apparently not able to see– until Lib moved in a little too close.

Jonah was on him like an ungainly cat. Before Lib could parry the attack, Jonah's teeth buried themselves in Lib's neck. Lib howled as blood spurted and Devol gasped in fear that Lib's jugular might have been severed.

He wasn't even sure it hadn't been, even when Lib broke the vise-like bite by grasping Jonah's jaw and breaking it with a snap that could be heard above the heavy breathing of the audience.

Jonah's knees buckled as pain rendered him weak and helpless. Lib glanced at Devol. Thibault saw Devol give a slight nod of the head.

Lib promptly knocked Jonah down with a blow to his already fractured jaw and Jonah fell backwards. Lib bent down, used both hands to grasp Jonah's penis and testicles. He set his feet firmly on Jonah's thighs and pulled.

Jonah screamed once and then died a moment later as blood gushed out from between his legs. Lib yanked Jonah's mouth wide open and stuffed it with what he'd torn free from the man's crotch.

Thibault walked away slowly. There was a lump in his gut and a dizziness in his head. He didn't see Devol's sneer. All he wanted was to get out of there.

The fresh air turned his stomach even more. Suddenly the welts on his back began to ache. Somewhat unsteadily, he headed for the nearest cafe where he intended to drink himself into a near state of unconsciousness.

It was always bad after he left Ida's place, and Carmen's unholy ministrations, but the bloody brutality of the fight hit him even harder.

Yet he knew he shouldn't feel this way and he really wasn't like this back on the plantation. He had a bloody job to do when he returned and he wouldn't shrink from it, but this combination of gore and lust seemed too much.

After the first drink, he got hold of himself. Five minutes

later, he walked quite briskly along Canal Street. He turned, without hesitating, on to an iron grilled stairway leading to the second floor of a neat, modest house with a balcony and more iron grilled work in the railing. He walked to the door, midway along this balcony, and knocked.

A girl of about eighteen, in a dazzlingly clean white dress, which made her golden skin glow all the more, stepped out to meet him.

'Hello, Marcy,' he said. 'You look wonderful.'

'That's how I feel – when you come to see me, Mr Thibault. Won't you please come in?'

SEVEN

The procession consisted of Murphy Thibault's fringed carriage in the lead, followed by two heavy wagons, loaded with supplies. In the first one, four wenches were allowed to sit on sacks of wheat and salt, unfettered, and able to enjoy the journey. In the second wagon, chained to iron rings bolted to the bed of the wagon, were two slaves, their eyes rolling in constant terror, sometimes shaking so much it was visible even above the jouncing of the wagon.

Behind the second wagon trudged the coffle. Thibault had bought thirty bucks, half a dozen stripling boys and one old man – Drill. All the men were handcuffed and attached to long chains so they marched two by two, and they kept up with the speed of the wagons or they were dragged. The red dust had long since fouled them. As Jubal discovered, there simply wasn't any sense trying to keep it from entering the mouth, nose, ears and eyes. It was just there, with every breath, and covered him before the first ten minutes were up.

Jubal was one of the last two in the coffle. Just ahead of him was Drill, and Jubal watched the old man in case he stumbled from exhaustion. Drill never stumbled, never slackened his steps. He walked as a wooden doll might, stiff-legged, and his head often dropped so low that his chin rested against his chest, but he kept up.

When the procession stopped for the night in a small town, some ten miles from Thibault's plantation, the coffle was herded into three jail cells made into slave pens for the night. It didn't matter that there was barely enough room to lie down, so long as one could get off his feet.

Jubal pushed and shoved his way to Drill's side. The old man stared at him blankly for a moment. 'Why, effen it ain't

Jubal,' he exclaimed happily. The poor old man's exhaustion had been so complete during the trek that he hadn't even known Jubal walked directly behind him.

'Reckon we got much further, Drill?' Jubal asked.

'Starts at sunup, gits theah 'bout noon. Makes it fine, I does. Don' you fret none 'bout me.'

'Ain't frettin'. Masta, he looked a little peaked this mornin'.'

Drill showed his toothless gums. 'Masta looks like that ev'y time he comes back f'm N'Awleans. He cuts loose. He sho' do.'

The cell door was unlocked and two white men handed over a wash bucket full of bits of ham fat, greens, turnips and carrots. The communal table was set. The men dug in with their hands, shoving the food into eager mouths to quell huge appetites brought on by twenty miles of walking.

Jubal made room for Drill at the bucket. Drill ate, but Jubal couldn't bring himself to dip into the mess. He drank some of the tepid water that served as a beverage and let it go at that. He'd had a double breakfast anyway. Calinda, too scared and worried to eat, had given him hers.

Drill fell asleep as soon as his belly was full. Jubal stayed beside him all night, seeing that he had enough room so his old bones wouldn't grow too cramped. No one argued with Jubal. Those who were about to, changed their minds after a careful look into his eyes.

At dawn they were rousted out, given tin cups of hot water into which grain had been sparsely sprinkled. Jubal drank his, chewing slowly on what solid substance he was able to filter out of the water with his teeth.

When they were lined up for chaining, Jubal managed to arrange it so that Drill became his partner. The two slaves in the front wagon had apparently spent the night there because they were sleeping when the procession began to roll.

Thibault had come by, on a morning inspection, making sure none of the spancels were too tight, looking for any signs of illness or weakness. He'd paused beside Drill, but he addressed Jubal.

'Old man able to walk?'

'He doin' fine, masta, suh,' Jubal said.

'He stumbles, you sing out and we'll put him in the wagon with the wenches.'

'Yes, suh, masta, suh.'

After Thibaut moved on, Drill cleared his throat and spat on the ground. 'Puts me in with the wenches! I ain't rid in no wagon yit, an' don' aim to. Got plenty juice lef' in me.'

'Sure you have.'

The wagons creaked and groaned as they began to roll. The coffle moved, and the balance of the journey had begun. The day grew hotter than it had been all year. Jubal estimated the temperature must be a hundred or better, and the dust was getting worse. Now it seemed to eat into the membranes of the nostrils and mouth and throat. The coffle plodded on. There was no use complaining. Unless a man dropped in his tracks, he stayed with the coffle, and if he dropped, he was sometimes sent to the slave pens in New Orleans, with his owner getting credit for a slave too weak to work and therefore turned back.

In the carriage, Thibault mopped his face and neck repeatedly and wished the journey were over.

The road ran between the sugar cane fields and Drill pointed them out. The stalks were tall and looked tough. Then they turned through an arched gate by which Briarfield Plantation was entered. The curved archway over the gate had the name burned into it.

Jubal saw the row upon row of little slave cabins. Hundreds of them, he thought. There were barracks for the unmated slaves. Sheds dotted the plantation. Well to the rear were the mill buildings where a steam boiler was housed. Many of the things Jubal saw were alien to him, but he asked no questions of Drill or anyone else. If he was supposed to have come from another cane plantation, that suited him.

The mansion was like nothing Jubal had ever seen. There were the usual white pillars, but more numerous, taller and more deeply fluted than the average. The porch wound itself around three sides of the house and was decorated by rows of cane-bottom chairs and rockers. The door was double size, mounted with a massive brass knocker and an oversize brass knob.

Behind the mansion was the spring house. A shaded walk led to the necessary house. There were toolsheds, barns and stables. Jubal had never imagined a plantation operation as large as this.

The procession stopped. The coffle dragged itself off the road to the green grass where every man sank wearily and gratefully down to rest. Jubal kept his eyes on the house. He wanted to see the others who lived here. Thibault's wife and son, especially.

When the door opened, a duplicate of Thibault came barreling out. He was taller than his father, heavier too; but they were remarkably alike in looks. He wore a white shirt, open at the neck, white linen riding pants tucked into black boots. On his head was a large, flat, floppy hat.

He embraced his father and shook his hand several times. He walked to the tailgate of the second wagon and stood regarding the two chained slaves with utter contempt. They groveled and spoke in pleading voices. Jubal couldn't make out the words.

The boy inspected the wenches and he had an eye for

shapely figures emphasised by the clinging dresses they wore. He marched back to where the coffle rested and the slaves all stood up, tired, but respectful.

Thibualt, meantime, had walked slowly, almost casually, toward the mansion. As he neared it, a woman came out to greet him. A dignified, slim, aristocratic-looking woman suffered being taken into Thibault's arms for a second or two. Then they walked on inside. Whatever else he'd find out about this plantation, Jubal knew now that the master and his mistress abided one another and little more than that. It made an interesting beginning.

Then young Thibault was facing them. He saw Drill and came at once toward the old man.

'Drill,' he exclaimed with obvious pleasure. 'You old black scalawag. How'd you get in this coffle?'

'Done was sold, masta, suh,' Drill said meekly. 'Yo' pappy bought me and I heah. Like comin' home, masta, suh.'

Shawn Thibault stepped back, raised his head and bellowed for someone named Mason. A burly man in white shirt and pants came hurrying from the nearest barn. He was soft-looking, nearly bald, with small, mean eyes and a mouth utterly devoid of any trace of humor.

'Yes, Mist' Shawn,' he said, breathless from his rapid approach.

'Take the spancels off Drill. You remember Drill? He was houseman and butler at the Correau place.'

Mason nodded coldly. 'Remembers him all right.'

'Take him to the kitchen and see that he gets fed proper. I mean no slops. You understand, Mr Mason?'

'I heard you.'

'Drill, what would you like to do here? Houseman, butler, anything you want. . . .'

'Loves hawses, I does,' Drill said. 'Masta, suh, kin I be coachman?'

'Of course. You taught me to ride and damned well too. I'll tell Daddy you're the new coachman. Mason, whoever handles the coach now, send him to the fields. And Drill eats with the cook.'

'Thanks yo', I does,' Drill said.

Shawn wasn't listening. His eyes were on Jubal and he looked him up and down carefully.

'Coromantee?' he asked just as his father had.

'Yes, suh, masta, suh.'

'Blooded too. Likely lookin' buck. Make a fine field hand with those muscles.'

Field hand! Jubal kept his lips from curling in contempt. If he was assigned to field work, it wouldn't be for long. He'd think of some way out of it. They were no smarter than he.

Besides, he had a definite advantage because they would believe him to be slow and stupid, completely uneducated and therefore harmless.

Shawn walked away, followed by Mason. Drill, freed of his spancels, rubbed his wrists and gave Jubal a toothless grin.

'Kinda fo'got to tell me you knows this heah masta real good,' Jubal chided.

'Son, nevah tells nothin' to nobody. Nothin'! To nobody!'

'I'm glad you got yourself a good job, Drill.'

'Glad too. Field work kill me daid.'

Jubal shook his chains. 'Why they keep us spanceled like this? We's home, ain't we?'

Drill's face clouded. 'They's somethin' to be done. Looks 'round and you sees all the slaves comin' from the fields, from the mills, and the cabins and barns.'

It was true. A small army of men, women and children were converging toward the house. Streaming in from all directions, they gradually formed a solid mass and they began to sing. It was a chant, not a song, for there was little melody to it and the words were garbled so that Jubal understood little of what was being sung and missed entirely the meaning of it.

Murphy Thibault appeared on the porch. He was holding a short whip. He stopped at the head of the steps and looked down at the crowd of blacks.

His wife emerged. She moved beside him and grasped his arm. He shook himself free of her with an angry gesture. He walked down the steps and she turned and almost ran back into the house. Before she reached the door, another woman stepped out to comfort her. They both disappeared inside, while Murphy Thibault strode down the road to a cleared space beneath a stark, leafless tree that stood silhouetted against the sky like a weird skeleton.

Mason freed the two frightened slaves from the wagon bed. He lashed them with his whip and pushed them ahead of him until they fell at Thibault's feet.

'Fetch the snake.' Mason ordered a slave, who scurried to the barn and returned with the rawhide whip. Jubal didn't know it at the time, but a rawhide was only used on a slave whose value was entirely gone. Or would be, at the conclusion of the whipping.

'Whut they goin' to do?' Jubal asked.

Drill said, 'Them's runners. Run all the way to the No'th, but git caught and brought back.'

'Goin' to be whupped,' Jubal decided.'

'Till they near daid.'

'Don' make no sense. whup a man like that.'

'Don't effen you' wants to wuk him after.'

'Well, don't they?'

Drill shook his head. 'Runners gets whupped and then gets hung. While we all watch 'cause us runs we gets the same.'

'Lawd,' Jubal groaned. 'Nevah knew anythin' like this befo'.'

Drill gave him a wise look. 'Whar you from, boy? You ain't heered runners gets hung?'

'Heered it,' Jubal lied, 'but nevah saw it.'

'Well, watch an' see, an' you gets hankerin' to run, 'member whut you sees.'

'You sound like it's right to do this,' Jubal said.

'Yes, suh. it's right. We's slaves. We do like we tol' and we gets taken care of. We runs and we get hung. They don't hang runners, ev'y nigger starts runnin'. Whar we goin'? Whut we goin' to do we get there? Bettah we eats the food they gives us, we takes the wenches we gets to knock up, an' we wuks fo' them. 'Cause thass all we kin do, Jubal. All we kin do.'

Jubal watched as the two slaves were herded beneath the tree. Shawn Thibault made nooses out of two lengths of rope and they were thrown over a limb. Two other lengths of rope were tied under the arms of each slave. The ends of these were also thrown over the limb.

One of the doomed men shrieked in terror. The other one knelt before Murphy Thibault and silently implored him. Thibault struck him across the face with the stock of his whip. He stepped back. Four bucks, appointed to the task, moved up. Two of them grasped the ropes ending in nooses around the necks of the slaves. They tightened them, but didn't pull the men up.

The other two bucks used more muscle and hauled the pair upwards until they were suspended by the ropes beneath their arms. Mason used a long, dangerous-looking knife to slash at the ropes holding up the trousers of each man. He ripped their shirts off their backs and signaled. They were hauled higher, but not so high Mason couldn't swing the snake.

It hissed and wound around one man. He screamed. The whip lashed at the other and his yells were added to those of the first victim. The whip fell again and again, drawn back slowly, extending the time and agony as much as possible.

Blood ran down the backs and sides of each swaying man to drip off their feet and form small pools on the ground where a swarm of flies came down to drink their fill.

The hundreds of blacks looked on. Their chanting had stopped. They were silent. There was horror in that intense silence. Jubal thought, 'There are enough slaves here to take over the plantation and kill every white on it. There wouldn't even be any severe losses because the whites are not armed.'

But then, as Drill had said, where would they all go? They'd be hunted down, found eventually, treated as this pair was being treated. Nowhere to go, that was the weak point of the situation. Nowhere to hide. . . .

Jubal's thoughts suddenly faded to be replaced by harsh, genuine and frightening surprise. The woman who'd helped Mrs Thibault back into the house was walking rapidly towards Murphy Thibault. She carried a parasol with a ruffled tip. The last time he'd seen this woman she was teasing an erection out of him by using the ruffled parasol, tipped with her glove, between his legs and on his penis.

Drill was talking. At first, Jubal wasn't aware of what the old man said, but then it made sense clearly.

'Them two done mo' than run, Jubal. They white, they gets 'zactly whut these two gettin' right now.'

'Whut . . . they do?' Jubal asked.

'Fo' they runs, they rapes Miss Pauline.'

Jubal didn't hear the dying screams of the slaves or the angry hiss of the whip still being wielded by Mason in tired fashion.

'Miss Pauline – she the lady whut talkin' to Masta Thibault now?'

Drill nodded. 'How'd you know that, Jubal? Sho' is Miss Pauline. Right nice lady too. Sister to Mist'iss Thibault.'

Jubal turned his attention back to the doomed blacks. The whipping was over. Both men were still conscious, but barely so. Mason stepped up, swung the big knife and slashed the shoulder rope of one. His body dropped, the noose around his neck tightened. Two of the big bucks hauled him up, kicking and clawing at his throat, the whip lacerations forgotten in this new sense of choking and strangling.

The second runaway went jerking upwards too, and they were both held there until all struggling had ceased and there was no question but that they were dead. Murphy Thibault turned away wearily. 'Bury them,' he said to no one in particular, but Mason took the order as his to carry out. He summoned four bucks and told them to carry the bodies into the woods, dig graves and cover them well.

Murphy Thibault took the arm of Pauline Noyan and led her along the row of stolid-faced blacks. They came opposite Jubal, and Pauline saw him. For one instant their eyes met, clashed, and that was all. In her eyes, he saw a spark of intense hatred.

In his, she saw contempt. That was worse than hatred.

EIGHT

Mason lined up the coffle and marched them down to the brook which ran through the plantation. This time Jubal was given a bar of crude yellow soap, which was better than the paste usually given a slave, for the paste was almost all lye and irritated the skin. He was also given time to strip, wade into the brook, sit down in the cold, stimulating water and really clean himself.

There were new trogs too, heavier and better quality than those given him at the slave auction. Jubal had already looked about enough to realise that conditions on this plantation were not too bad. The slaves seemed content, some of them were comfortably fat and there were hordes of squalling young ones underfoot wherever a man moved. This, too, was a good indication that things were tolerable, for if they were not, too many babies were born dead of work-worn mothers. Here were hordes of little ones running about in obvious good health.

Jubal and the others were allowed to dry themselves by lolling in the hot afternoon sun. Nobody had much to say. The example of the two executed slaves was still too fresh in their minds. Jubal did wonder what had happened to Calinda. It didn't look as if he was going to get her and there was a seething anger in him because he wanted her. Still, as a slave, he had absolutely nothing to say in the matter.

Dressed in clean clothes, well-washed, Jubal felt better. He was marched with the others to one of the long buildings, a barracoon, he learned later. Inside were pallets built to the walls and covered with mattresses stuffed with corn husks. There was a wooden floor, a stove for heating, a bench on which were basins, buckets, and a huge jug of drinking water. The outhouses were as far away from the dwellings as possible, well into the deep woods fringing the area.

All of this wasn't much, according to the standards Jubal was used to as a free black man in St Louis, but everything was clean. Mason had announced there'd be no work for today, but with the dawn, every man was to be on his feet, dressed and ready for field work.

Jubal missed Drill. He'd spoken to several of the men in the coffle, but they were still too frightened to say much or show any friendliness. Jubal lay down on his mattress and closed his eyes. He fell asleep instantly.

There was noisy chatter in the barracoon when he woke up. The food had been brought by wenches carrying it in huge buckets. Unlike the slave jails, the men weren't expected to eat out of the communal pot with their fingers. Each was provided with a tin plate, spoon, knife, fork and an enameled cup.

One of the wenches was Calinda. When she entered the barracoon, she had the container of hot food balanced on her head with both hands raised to hold it steady. This pulled her dress upwards and tight, so that her nipples showed through, and so did an ample length of fine leg.

Before she had a chance to put down the heavy burden, a husky buck whom Jubal hadn't seen before moved up to her.

'Nigger gal,' he said, 'lemme he'p you with this mess o' food. It's too heavy fo' a little gal like you. . . . '

He reached up to take the bucket and as he did so, pushed his body against hers. She took one step backwards, bent slightly and dumped the steaming hot contents of the vat on the slave's head. He yelped and floundered around in the mess on the floor, but it was too much for him. He slipped, both feet going out from beneath him and he sat down in the mixture of fat meat, greens, potatoes, turnips and yellow carrots.

Someone laughed. It was taken up. Calinda screeched her amusement. The slave arose carefully, and almost fell down again, but he made it. He swung a punch at Calinda and she went hurdling backwards a dozen feet before she fell. The slave rushed to her, pulled his foot back for a kick to the face when Jubal seized him by both shoulders, yanked him back, and hit him in the stomach.

The slave grunted in pain, but he was big and he was tougher than Jubal expected. It was a strength developed by cultivating and harvesting sugar cane, but Jubal didn't know that then. He did know that when a solid punch landed against his own chest it sent all the wind whooshing out of his lungs.

Two brawny arms wrapped themselves about him before he could recover. Massive muscles came into play and Jubal felt his ribs bending, his lungs compressed to a point where they couldn't breathe in the air he needed.

Jubal managed to land two short, chopping punches to the back of the slave's head. This rattled him some, and Jubal finally broke free, but at the moment he was no match for this powerful man. Not until his lungs could breathe again and his muscles come out of their spasm.

The big buck was bent double, arms thrust halfway their length, hands opened so the fingers were like talons. There was the look of the kill on his wide face. The nostrils of a monstrous nose all but exhaled smoke and flame.

'I's killin' you, nigger,' he said. 'I is about to twist you haid clear off your body. Ain't goin' to break no mo' bones, 'ceptin' you neck. Then I goes slooin' 'roun' this heah wench an' I rapes her until she ain't good fo' any man no mo'. But you be daid, nigger, an' you don't care none.'

'Stop talkin',' Jubal jeeered. 'Fo' you gits that wench, yo' sho' got to bust my neck.'

The slave eyed him malevolently. 'I is Poley an' I kin whup any man in the worl'. I is Poley, the fightin' man.'

'Talkin' man,' Jubal said briefly and scornfully.

Poley roared in rage and charged. His arms were spread wide to seize Jubal in another embrace, and this one would leave him a broken, half-dead man. Jubal nimbly moved aside and as Poley flashed on by, he hit him squarely in the face with a massive fist. Blood spurted from a broken nose.

Poley was half blinded by the punch. He skidded to a stop before crashing into the onlookers, whirled about and met two fists rapping home one blow after another with such speed and force that Poley lost all control and dropped his arms while he began screaming in pain. Jubal had him backed into a corner and ready for the final blow, but a roaring voice from the doorway made Jubal check the punch.

Murphy Thibault strode into the barracks, flushed with anger, and marched up to the cringing Poley.

'That buck beat you up?' He pointed to Jubal.

'Yas, suh, masta, suh, he beats me.'

'What for?'

'Don' know, masta, suh. Jes' beat me.'

Thibault turned to Jubal. 'What was the fight about, boy?'

'Masta, suh, the wench spilled that bucket o' food over him, but wasn't her fault but his. He was rubbin' her while she held that big bucket on her haid.'

'That true?' Thibault demanded of Poley.

'Naw, suh, ain't the truth, suh. He jes' hit me, thass all.'

Calinda, still shaken by the bloody fight, stepped forward. 'Masta, suh, kin I say somethin'?'

Thibault assented with a nod.

'Masta, suh, this heah nigger say he goin' to rape me 'til I near die, suh. An' he pull the bucket off'n my haid, he did. Tryin' to finger me while I bringin' in the food.'

Thibault faced two other men. 'That true? Did he finger her and say he was going to rape her, and that's why the Coromantee hit him?'

Neither slave answered, simply stood there tongue-tied in terror. Their eyes slid fearfully in Poley's direction.

Thibault said, 'All right, it was the truth. Wench, find yourself a cabin and stay there. Poley, you goin' to taste the cat. March yourself down to the whipping shed and wait. You,' he motioned to Jubal, 'go with him. You two young hotheads like to hit one another so much, we'll let you use the cat on one another. Both of you – git!'

They marched out of the barracoon and walked side by side toward the sheds. 'Don' know whut's the whuppin' shed, Poley,'

Jubal said mournfully.

'Shows you.'

'You a pretty good fightin' man. Reckon you jes' about busted me in half.'

'Wish I had, 'cause I ain't feelin' good you gets through with me. I busted up some too, ain't I?'

'Well, your nose kinda twisted some. Got yourself a fat lip. Yes, sir, sure a fat lip, and you wasn't black as sin, reckon you have a bad lookin' eye theah.'

Poley glanced at him out of the unswollen eye. 'You layin' it on heavy, boy?'

'Whut you aimin' to do?'

'You snaps the cat jes' fo' it lands. Makes a big noise, but don't hurt much.'

'I try it, if you do.'

'Reckon we does it that way. First lash you gots to make good so's they don' know 'bout the rest of 'em. Sting me good, Jubal, an' then kinda hold it back some.'

'You thinkin' on rapin' that wench?'

'New wench, I thinks she anybody's. You wants her, they's plenty lef' fo' me.'

They entered the shed and removed their shirts. There was a tall bench in the center of the room. Jubal bent over it. Poley took down the cat, a short whip with half a dozen leather strands, each ending in a small knot calculated to raise good-sized welts, but without breaking the skin too much.

For more serious infractions there was a long, ten-inch-wide strap that could be swung with considerable force and could inflict enough pain to make a big man faint. The final instrument of punishment was the snake, a braided, slender length of leather. With this, a man could be slowly cut to shreds. Twenty lashes would put a man to bed for an agonising week or more. Thirty could all but cripple him, and fifty was a lethal dose. That was what had been used on the two executed runners.

Thibault and his son walked into the shed to supervise the punishment. 'Ten each,' he said to Poley. 'Have at it.'

Poley made the first one count. Jubal emitted a yelp of pain. He was surprised at the hurt it inflicted. The other nine cracked like the report of a rifle. They stung, but nothing like the first one.

Jubal groaned as he straightened up and changed places with Poley, who braced himself for the first blow. Jubal landed it across his shoulders, raising a big welt. Then it occurred to Jubal that he didn't know how to snap a whip to make a maximum amount of noise and a minimum of pain. He tried it, but Poley screeched and another big welt popped up. Jubal didn't get the knack of it until the seventh lash, and by then Poley was reduced to a whimpering, quivering mass of black flesh.

At Thibault's count of ten, Jubal hung the whip on the pegs provided for it and quietly walked out. Poley stumbled after him. Shawn began to laugh. Thibault stared at him, suddenly realised what the laughter was for and doubled up with it.

'The biggest buck didn't know how to swing the whip right,' Shawn howled. 'Poley sure went easy on him, but the other didn't know how to handle it and Poley got himself cut up good. Funniest thing I ever did see, Pa.'

'Don't mind none. Poley had it comin'. He's been a fresh nigger lately. Shawn, did you notice the muscles on that other'n? Jubal?'

'Reckon. Sure noticed 'em. Looks like a fightin' man to me.'

'What I been thinking. Set him working the cane fields tomorrow to toughen him up. Mayhap we'll pit him against that bull Mr Devol got fighting for him.'

'Pa, he better be mighty good, comes to that.'

'We'll see. But toughen him up anyway.'

'Yes Pa.'

'How's your ma feel 'bout my hangin' them two runners? Ain't fired up 'nuff nerve to see her since.'

'You know how she feels. Whole goddamn plantation be free she had her way.'

'Don't know what ails her, son. Her pa owned five hundred slaves and whupped half of 'em just for the sport. It ain't like she's from the No'th and ain't used to niggers. She says they're human. Now, son, ain't no doctor'll take care o' them. They has to get treated by a vet. Now ain't that proof they're animals?'

'Reckon,' Shawn said, hoping his voice didn't betray any of his doubt.

'You reckon we ask a preachin' man to marry two of 'em, he does it? Hell, no – no more'n he'd marry a cow an' a bull, or a mare and a stallion. O' course they're animals. And you treat 'em like they are or they don't know what in hell you're doing. They works hard, you feeds 'em good. They gets sulky, you whip 'em. They runs, you hang 'em.'

'Womenfolk just don't understand,' Shawn said.

'Pauline does. She won't miss no whipping or no hanging she can help it. They're sisters, son. Your ma and your aunt, and they no more like one another than we are like one of these here niggers.'

'Been thinking on that, Pa.'

'On what? Thinking on what? They ain't alike?'

'Some, but mostly 'bout Pauline. Them two bucks went running and you offered a reward like it's always done. Then you got word they'd been caught. That's when Pauline says they raped her. Why didn't she say that before, Pa? Ain't the kind of thing a woman will hold back. I don't think.'

'You question her word, son?'

'Hell, no, but just seems funny to me. You ask them two niggers 'bout it?'

'Didn't have time. Just hung 'em to get it over with. Now why'd she say they raped her if it wasn't so?'

'Last three boys who ran and got sent back – you whupped 'em good, but you didn't hang 'em.'

'You saying your Aunt Pauline likes to see a man hung?'

'No, Pa, never said that. Just wondering is all. Just wondering.'

They walked back to the manor house, not even looking at Jubal and Poley, who were both stripped to the waist with their bare backs to the sun so the rays would soothe the sting of the lash.

Jubal looked serene enough, but Poley was scowling darkly.

'I eveh gets to whup you, Jubal, I sho' givin' it to you good.'

'Tol' you, nevah used a whup befo'. Done the best I could.'

'Sho' hate to get whupped when you was mad at me.'

'Stay 'way from Calinda,' Jubal said pleasantly. 'I'll evermore kill you, you goes slooin' 'round.'

'They set you fo' cane field work, you ain't takin' care o' no gal, Jubal. You ain't able to get it up any higher'n a peanut.'

'Means that?'

Poley grinned. 'Means it. Hardest work in the worl', harvestin' cane. Ain't no easier they sets you to wuk in the mill either.'

'Then you don't have to worry none if Calinda stays with me, 'cause if I'm no good, she'll sure 'nuff look for you, Poley.'

'I'll be waitin',' Poley said cheerfully.

They ambled back to the barracoon, stretched out on their mattresses and went to sleep. Neither doubted that this would be one of the last days they'd be free of heavy work and they were taking advantage of it.

Someone was shaking him. Jubal stirred, tried to wake up. The shaking continued until he was annoyed enough to open his eyes. A boy about fourteen, in a pale green coat, was urging him to get up.

'Whut?' Jubal asked. 'Whut you wake me fo'?'

'Mist'iss say you run fo' whuppin' shed now.'

'Mist'iss? Whuppin' shed?'

'She say you sloth 'roun' an' you gits whaled good.'

Jubal nodded, got out of bed and headed for the door. He covered the ground to the whipping shed in fast time. When he opened the door, it was dark within – and silent.

He hesitated, not knowing if the boy was playing a trick on him, perhaps at the behest of Poley.

'Close the door,' a woman's voice said. As he did so, a small candle was lit. The woman held the flame closer to her face. Jubal groaned. Here was someone who knew he hadn't come from a ranch just north. This was Miss Pauline with the inquisitive parasol, and the uncontrollable desire to see a man stripped naked and shamed.

'I'm telling you once, Jubal. If you ever say you saw me before, or if you speak to me as if I did know you, I'll tell my brother-in-law that you tried to rape me. He'll hang you for sure if I do that.'

'Mist'iss, ma'am, ain't nevah seed you befo' in my whole life.'

'Remember that,' she warned.

'Come from Major Sedgewick farm no'th, mist'iss.'

'Good. If anybody says you didn't, I'll tell them I saw you there. That's all.'

'I thanks you, mist'iss, ma'am. Sho' ain't nevah seed you befo'.'

She blew out the candle and held the door for him. He was mildly surprised that she didn't reach for his crotch and fondle him.

He ran back to the barracoon, slumped on his mattress, shuddered once at the remembrance of her threat, and then fell asleep.

NINE

A sugar cane plantation depends on the vagaries of the weather for a substantial crop – or no crop at all. An early frost can bankrupt any plantation owner, a hurricane can sweep a year's work away in two minutes. But if the weather held, if there were no hurricanes, if the growing season was warm to hot, most of the time, then the plantation owner could make more profit than if he grew cotton or tobacco.

Once, indigo had been the main crop here, but it was produced so cheaply abroad that it no longer paid a man to raise it. Sugar was a wonderful substitute for indigo, even if everything had to be just right, and a sugar house was expensive to build.

The cane grows fast and tall. In late November or early December the growth is ready for harvest, the stalks as filled with syrupy goodness as they ever would be. First, a crop of seedlings is cut and laid in compact piles for later planting. Then the slaves go in with heavy knives. They use four strokes for each plant. The first slices off the leaves to the right, the second slice denudes it on the left. The third frees it from the earth with one slash and the fourth tops it. Then the stalk of cane is placed in a cart that follows the workers. From there it is hauled to the mill to be fed by gravity into rollers where it is shredded and squeezed. Then the extracted juice is boiled and finally rectified several times until it becomes crystals and ready for the hogsheads.

In the early spring the first harvested stalks are taken to the fields where deep furrows have been dug. The stalks are laid, lengthwise, into the trenches and covered up with a plow. In the spring, shoots grow from the eyes of the stalks at the joints, and break into the sunlight.

During the growing season the plants are carefully tended. Most of the work consists of hoeing, and Jubal discovered that this mild-looking labor can become painful and very tiring. The rows were almost a mile long. He worked from sunrise to sunset with only a short pause at noon for food and drink. It was plain food, fried hominy and meat scraps greasy enough to be sustaining for the rest of the day, sometimes drenched in molasses.

For two weeks, Jubal crawled into his bunk nightly, groaned if spoken to, and went to sleep. Gradually, however, he began to toughen up. His back didn't feel as if it had been split down the middle about noon time, and his knees didn't threaten to buckle. He knew he'd lost weight and his muscles had got so firm he was proud of them.

He approached the barracoon two weeks and three days after he arrived at Briarfield, and the boy in the pale green coat was waiting for him.

'Jubal, you gits to go to you own cabin,' he said. 'Wench waitin', and you bettah knock her up fas'.'

'I goin' to knock in you haid, you talks to me like that,' Jubal warned. 'Whut cabin?'

The boy ran ahead of him, tantalising him by going up to a closed door and when Jubal took a long breath and prepared to step in and meet his woman, the boy would shriek with laughter and scamper to another.

He knew when Jubal was heartily sick of the game and next time he led him to a brand-new cabin, the last in this particular row of them. He pointed to the door, turned and ran as if for his life. Jubal growled his anger, pushed open the door. A woman was bending over the fire. There was the aroma of fresh bread in the cabin and something that smelled like good meat from a pot over the embers.

The woman straightened up and turned around. 'You is home, Jubal,' Calinda said.

'You is my wench?' He couldn't believe it.

'Reckon. You mad, Jubal?'

'Mad? Whut you sayin', woman? You is the on'y one heah I craved.'

'Mist'iss Pauline tol' masta you an' me birth good healthy suckers.'

'We's sho' goin' to do that, Calinda. We sho' is, but why Mist'iss Pauline pick me?'

Calinda properly lowered her eyes. 'Asked her fo' you, I did.'

'You crazy. Nobody asks Mist'iss. . . .'

'I is her maid now. I waits on her all day, but when I gets to this cabin an' you is waitin' fo' me, I don' mind whut they make me do. Jubal, wants to be raped.'

'You got food cookin'.'

'I's so hot I's cookin', Jubal. Vittles kin wait. I cain't. Been thinkin' all day 'bout this.'

He grabbed her in a fury of passion. He slipped her dress over her shoulders, then forced it down so she could step out of it. There was a wide mattress on the floor. She held him tightly, bent backwards, spread her legs for him. Her body swayed and jerked.

He eased her down, took time to remove his shirt and pants and then he fell on top of her. Their eagerness made it quick, but completely satisfying – and exhausting. She'd been good before, in the slave jail, but now she was superb. She could arch upwards so that he filled her entirely and she could create for him a second erection almost immediately after the first time. They forgot the food and devoted themselves to the more important task of satisfying their appetites for sex.

It shortly became a contest to see who could keep going the longest and it was Jubal who finally lay back, unable to move a muscle except those controlling the laughter of pleasure in his throat. She hovered over him, letting her breasts touch his face, groaning when his teeth closed around them. She crawled down the length of his body, buried her face in his softened manhood. She bit him lightly, rubbed him, offered her body again, but he could only shake his head slowly.

'You is gettin' old,' she chided him. 'Tomorrow I gets me a young buck who kin pleasure me. . . .'

'You do an' I kills you both,' Jubal said happily.

'You kills me if I messes 'roun'?'

'Daid,' he said.

'Reckon you pleasure me 'nuff,' she said, laughing.

Then she remembered the food and jumped up. So the stark-naked buck was served a well-burned dinner by a stark-naked wench, and before it was half over, they were on the mattress again. She rotated and writhed and it was an hour before they both fell back, this time exhausted to the point of sleep.

Jubal awoke just as dawn was breaking and lay quietly, regarding the sleeping girl beside him. His hand moved to her thigh and slid up to lightly stroke her pubic hair. She moaned slightly and her lips parted as did her legs and his fingers continued their exploring, slipping into the moist area, finding the now-hardened tip of the clitoris, grasping it and pulling on it gently. His other hand moved the covering from their bodies and he watched her hips start a slow pushing motion while the nipples of her breasts hardened. He bent down and moved his tongue slowly along one of them.

He thought he heard her say, 'Mist'iss, ma'am,' as her legs spread wider. Then her eyes opened and she saw Jubal.

'I Jubal, not your mist'iss,' he said. 'You mist'iss finger you like I doin'?'

She looked frightened, but her voice was a vigorous denial. 'Frightened me, you did, Jubal. Thought I was sleepin' on the floor by my mist'ress's bed and she wake me.'

'She do things to you like I doin' now?' he asked, his voice more curious than demanding. 'That how she wake you?'

'No, Jubal, no I swears it.'

Her arms raised, slid around his neck and pulled him down. She sucked his tongue inside her mouth and rolled hers around it, at the same time moving her lips against his. Jubal changed his position so that he was between her legs. His hands shifted to her buttocks and he kneaded the firm flesh. Her hands moved down to his penis, captured it and guided its tip along the now well-moistened area of her vagina.

He pulled his tongue free and looked straight into her eyes. 'You good, Calinda. You pleasure Mist'iss Pauline like you pleasure me?'

'You talk crazy, Jubal. Don't pleasure no woman.'

'No black woman, maybe. But if a white woman tells you to pleasure her, you better, or she find a reason to send you to the whippin' shed.'

'Miss Pauline a lady, Jubal.'

Calinda now moved her body up and down, letting the tip of his penis enter and leave her warm interior. He found it more difficult to concentrate and he had a feeling Calinda meant it to be that way. He also had more than a suspicion she was pleasuring Miss Pauline, but she would never admit it any more than he'd tell what Miss Pauline had done to him. He wasn't angry. A slave had no choice. He plunged his penis into the warm juicy depth of her with such vehemence that she cried out. He didn't apologise. He wanted to hurt her, and though Calinda bore the violence of his act, it was really directed toward the system they were forced to live with.

He completed the sexual act, thrusting and stabbing, his hands squeezing Calinda's buttocks so hard that her cries were a mixture of moans and sobs. When finally he'd spent himself, he let his weight rest on her until his breath had resumed a normalcy. Then he arose, slipped into his clothes and left the shack.

Calinda lay limp and spent. He'd never hurt her like that before. Her hand moved down to her pelvic bone which had borne the brunt of his thrusts, but even touching the area made her wince. She knew he hadn't believed her and he'd taken out his resentment by giving her more pain than pleasure. She wondered what she'd said before she became fully awakened. If it had been something pertaining to her pleasuring Miss Pauline, she'd never admit it.

She arose with difficulty, slipped on her dress and left the cabin, heading for the house. Jubal had left without breakfast and she had no desire to linger and make some for herself.

She opened the door to Miss Pauline's room and closed it softly, not certain her mistress was awake. As she'd been ordered to do on the first day she'd entered this room, she turned the key, locking it. She wondered if Miss Pauline would want her to take off her dress today. That was the next thing she did after entering the room. She serviced Miss Pauline without her dress and much of the time her mistress lay on the bed, completely disrobed, legs spread and a pillow under her buttocks.

Calinda moved silently over to the bed and sat on the floor, wincing as her bruised buttocks protested its hardness. The figure hadn't moved, but that didn't mean she wasn't aware of Calinda's presence. Somehow, Calinda feared this woman, who had shown nothing but kindness. Calinda liked pleasuring her, though. Her skin was so soft and white and when they were in bed together, Calinda even forgot she was black, for Miss Pauline kissed her and Miss Pauline's tongue explored Calinda's mouth, sucked her breasts, demanding Calinda do the same to her. In a seated position, with legs spread, their juices mingled as they moved in a rocking motion, while Miss Pauline said things that excited Calinda. Miss Pauline made Calinda repeat them as they rocked faster and faster to their climax, their legs twined round each other, each grasping the other's breasts and squeezing and rolling them in a circular motion.

Calinda bathed Miss Pauline every day, afterward stroking fragrant liquid over her body, then applying powder and smoothening it over her soft flesh. Sometimes Miss Pauline reciprocated. Once she even held Calinda in her arms, told Calinda to suck on her nipple, even bite on it. When Calinda demurred, fearing she would cause pain, Miss Pauline slapped her hard across the face. Calinda bit them and was told to bite harder. She did, finding she liked hearing her mistress moan. She kept biting and her mistress kept moaning and her hand went down and she spread Calinda's legs and forced two fingers up inside her. One was wearing a ring and it hurt, but it was a beautiful hurt and Calinda's moaning matched Miss Pauline's.

Then Miss Pauline pulled her breast free, manipulated herself so that Calinda's head was between her mistress's legs.

Calinda knew what was expected of her and her tongue teased and explored, finally jutting into that hot liquid well. She used her hands to further stimulate her mistress. Nor was the slave surprised when her mistress removed her fingers and replaced them with her tongue. There were moans and cries and thumps as they rolled over and back and their buttocks hit the floor in their thrusts, which quickened with their passion, reached a peak, then subsided.

Though Miss Pauline lay prone and spent afterward, Calinda didn't remove her tongue, though slowing its rhythm as it moved deep into the receptacle, then withdrawing, though never entirely leaving the area. Calinda thought that sometimes an hour passed before her mistress told her she had enough, but though Calinda's tongue got tired, she didn't mind, for it was a lot easier than field work or polishing furniture around the house.

Never once were they disturbed, and if the other slaves knew what went on, they never even by a glance gave a hint of it. None of them wished to incur Miss Pauline's wrath or displeasure, so Calinda was favored, even in the kitchen. But she'd never tell Jubal. She remembered hearing someone say once only a dumb slave talked. And Jubal sure didn't talk. Calinda was sure he was full of secrets. Pleasuring Miss Pauline would be hers, only she'd have to be careful not to talk again when Jubal woke her up by fingering her.

'Did Jubal fuck you?' Calinda jumped, not at the word, but because she had no idea her mistress had wakened.

'Yes, mist'iss, ma'am.'

'Are you full of his juices?'

'Yes, mist'iss, ma'am.'

'Pull down the bedclothes and take off your dress. Is the door locked?'

'Yes, mist'iss, ma'am.'

'Don't ever wear your dress in this room when the door is locked.'

'No, mist'iss, ma'am.' Calinda drew off the dress, flung it in a corner.

Miss Pauline sat up. 'Straddle my legs.'

Calinda did so.

'Spread yours wide. So I can smell you.'

Calinda obeyed. Nor was she surprised when Miss Pauline spread Calinda's vaginal lips and used her tongue to taste the moiste substance oozing from the slave.

'Tastes like Jubal.'

'Ma'am?'

Miss Pauline laughed. 'I mean I imagine that's how a big buck like Jubal would taste.'

'Yes, mist'iss, ma'am.'

'You like Jubal's pecker in you?'

'Yes, mist'iss, ma'am.' Then, knowing her mistress liked this kind of talk, added, 'He real big and hard.'

'Did he make you scream?'

'Sure did, mist'iss, ma'am. Pinch my ass so hard it hurt all over. Bite my titties hard too.'

Miss Pauline's hands squeezed Calinda's buttocks, making her cry out.

'Sorry, mist'iss, ma'am. But they hurt real bad.'

'It's a nice hurt though, Calinda. It's the kind of hurt that makes your juices flow.'

'Sure does, mist'iss, ma'am. Can I ask you a question, mist'iss, ma'am?'

'You may,' Her hands still squeezed Calinda's buttocks, watching the black girl's face, knowing she was making every effort not to cry out, and pinching harder to make her do so.

'Will you still wants me to pleasure you, mist'iss, ma'am? Now that I pleasure Jubal, I mean.'

'Don't you want to pleasure me any more?'

'Oh yes, mist'iss, ma'am,' Calinda's voice was almost a whimper because the buttocks were throbbing from the unendurable pain. Her question obviously made Miss Pauline angry and she squeezed harder. 'Loves pleasurin' your beautiful white skin, smooth as a rose petal.'

The grip on the buttocks loosened. 'Then pleasure me now. You're all juiced up. You smell of Jubal. Never had you when you smelled of him before. When we finish, you'll smell of yourself and Jubal and me. Then you can give me a bath and maybe I'll give you one.'

'Thank you, mist'iss, ma'am.'

Miss Pauline spread her legs and Calinda eased her sore buttocks on to the bed, moving them into position so they touched those of her mistress. She placed her inner vaginal lips between those of her mistress, their legs entwined each other. Miss Pauline's tongue moved slowly in and out of her mouth. Calinda did the same. Their heads moved closer until their tongues met and touched and teased. Miss Pauline then closed her teeth around Calinda's tongue, bit gently, then sucked it into her mouth. Their hands fondled each other's breasts and they started their slow rocking motion. Their eyes, exchanging looks of pleasure, narrowed as their passion rose. Their organs never slipped from their position, for they'd become quite expert in the act.

Calinda always knew when her mistress's passion had reached a peak, for her hands tightened on Calinda's breasts, making her moan from the delicious pain. At the same time, she quickened her rocking to match her mistress's and when it was over, her mistress dropped back on her pillow. Calinda dropped to the foot of the bed, being careful not to lose the position, for Miss Pauline wanted to keep the feeling. Calinda, still in her lying position, moved her hands down to pet and stroke and finger her mistress as best she could without changing position.

After a night of Jubal, Calinda had been afraid she'd not be able to respond the way she knew would be expected of her. Now she had no further fear. She enjoyed it as much as her mistress. She liked pleasuring a white woman. For one scant minute, she dared to entertain the thought of why she did. She knew now that, inside, there was no difference. Only their skin was different. They liked doing the same things in the same ways. They got the same feeling and same pleasure. Her mistress gave an impatient jerk. Calinda's fingers had stilled as she lay thinking and she'd slipped from position. She quickly spread her lips and placed her mistress's between them and her fingers resumed their play. She warned herself not to think again. It might show in her face and she'd be sent to the whipping shed and Mis Pauline would get someone else to pleasure her. Calinda couldn't bear the thought of another wench's hands on this beautiful body.

Her thumb and forefinger sought the soft, fleshy part at the top of the vagina and she gently pulled on it. She was rewarded by a soft moan. This would go on all morning, Calinda thought with satisfaction. It was good, having Miss Pauline and Jubal too.

Calinda was pleased to be back at the plantation. Pleased also that Miss Pauline had selected her as her body servant. At first, she feared Mrs Thibault would object, but the only recognition she'd given of Calinda's reappearance at the plantation was a brief look of startled surprise.

Calinda knew her master had repurchased her as a gesture of defiance toward his wife. Her presence would be a constant reminder he was still master of Briarfield Plantation.

TEN

That same morning, Jubal staggered to the cane field. Now that his maleness was to be well satisfied, now that he had a cabin and all he could eat, Jubal began to think of ways to get out of this back-breaking work. Calinda, who made Miss Pauline's bed, cleaned her room, brought up her breakfast tray, bathed her and let her slim brown hands touch the white woman's body in stimulating caresses, was never tired by night, while Jubal found it less and less satisfying to crush the mattress with her. Many more days of this work and he'd be good for nothing.

Yet he could see no way out. He didn't dare confide in Calinda, though he trusted her completely. What she didn't know she couldn't whisper or tell if they got into trouble. There wouldn't always be Calinda. Jubal knew that, and when the time came for them to break up, he didn't want to be saddled with worry she might talk about him to another buck who might not be reticent about going to the master with information he could exchange for favors.

So far Jubal hadn't been near the sugar mill and he had grown very curious about it. Before long, the cane was going to be ready for harvest and Jubal knew, from the work he himself had so far done and from what others told him, harvesting was the labor that killed men. The hours were without count, days meant nothing. There was no Sunday rest. Everything gave way to the cutting of the stalk before the frost came. It was a time when Jubal would like to be away from the fields and the mill seemed to offer the best opportunity. But how to get there. How to make himself more useful than in the fields. That was work the mules could do if they had hands. Jubal felt above it and, slave or not, he had a certain pride that compelled him to use his head and better his lot.

This was a good plantation. It was in warm country. He had all he wanted to eat and a snug cabin. He had Calinda, and also a certain hold over one member of the ruling family. That could backfire easily, he knew, but at least it was something, and it had certainly gotten him Calinda. Pauline was repaying him for his silence.

He wanted more and that, he knew, was the difference between an ordinary, ignorant, plodding slave and a man who'd been free and who'd had enough schooling to know there was more to the world than work, food and pleasurable manufacture of suckers.

His chance came when Mason, the overseer, selected him at random, with half a dozen other slaves, to go to the mill proper and there clean and sharpen the plows which would soon be used to dig the deep furrows for the seed.

The mill was modern enough to have a steam-driven grinding wheel, which made the sharpening easy. Jubal handled the operation expertly.

There was a sugar boss in charge, a lanky man named John Roswell. As sugar boss, he was as completely in control of the mill as a captain who controlled his ship on the high seas. A sugar boss was hard to come by, for there were few men who knew exactly when the sugar was going to crystalise and could get the most out of the cane with the waste material – the bagasse – left as nearly dry as it could be. The bagasse consisted of what remained after the squeezing and shredding was done. Sometimes a sugar boss was judged on the amount of syrup left in this waste matter.

Roswell had one fault. It was overlooked because it didn't seem to interfere with his skill. From the first dark syrup, a potent alcoholic drink named tafia could be easily distilled and Roswell had a weakness for it. So did the slaves who worked at the mill, but they were extremely careful not to let it show. A drunken slave was instantly whipped, and then sent into the fields, something worse than the whipping.

Jubal picked up the last of the blades. He was enjoying himself. At least, this took a little brain work and he'd been feeling empty lately, with nothing to occupy his mind except Calinda. After a while, even she began to pall.

A wiry, undersized slave, with the black skin of a Gold Coast tribe, was applying oil to the roller wheels of the shredding machine. He was perched atop a wide belt which would carry the stalk when in operation. He did his best to apply the oil and grease where it was supposed to be, but he wasn't doing a very good job of it. Oil splashed down, lumps of grease splattered on the floor of the mill.

Roswell stepped into a smear of grease and he almost fell. He looked up. 'You, Rafe, get down here, you black baboon. Don' you know 'nuff not to go up theah when you drunk.'

Jubal stopped work and stared. He'd wondered what ailed the small slave with the oil can and bucket of grease. Of course he was drunk and getting drunker.

'You heered me?' Roswell yelled. 'Come down!'

Rafe began to clamber over the huge rollers, trying to descend to a point where he could easily jump to the floor, but Rafe's legs were short, the roller was very thick and without the use of his hands, which were busy holding a can of oil and a bucket of grease, he couldn't quite balance himself and he seemed to be hung up there, unable to scramble up or down.

He was in that awkward position, with the irate sugar boss yelling at him, when Mason, the overseer, walked in.

'Get down off there,' he ordered, adding his voice to that of the sugar boss.

'Cain't.' Rafe sobbed in frustration.

Perched atop the roller, he was helpless. If he dropped the can of oil, or the bucket of grease, and used only one hand, he could have balanced himself and slid off the roller, but Rafe's dull wit was further muddled by too much tafia, so all he could do was sit there and worry.

Roswell picked up a hammer from a workbench and threw it at Rafe, but missed. Mason walked towards the machine.

'I'll haul him down and tan his black ass at the same time,' he roared.

Mason climbed on to the belt, reached the roller and made a grab for Rafe, who at that moment grasped the idea he was going to be whipped, and made one final attempt to free himself. He raised one leg, threw himself off the roller and the extended foot caught Mason full in the face. It was a hard kick, and it unbalanced Mason, treading on the sagging slipper belt. He crashed down.

It looked as if he was hurt, and Jubal instinctively started away from the grinding wheel, until he realised there was nothing he could do. No slave touched a white man, even if he was injured, unless he was told to do so.

The sugar boss clambered on to the belt and tried to drag Mason off. When he found the task too difficult, he shouted for Jubal, who promptly ran to help.

There was blood on Mason's face and his arm seemed to be awkwardly twisted under him, as if it might be broken. He was unconscious. Jubal dragged him off the belt, lifted him easily and, with the sugar boss running on ahead, carried the overseer to the big house. Jubal looked behind him just before he left the sugar house. Rafe was sitting on the edge of the belt, still holding the can of oil and bucket of grease, and looking forlorn and troubled. He had a right to be, Jubal judged.

Shawn came running out to see what had happened. Pauline and Murphy Thibault were right behind him.

'Get Mason inside,' Shawn ordered. 'Follow me!'

Jubal had never seen the interior of a house as grand as this. Until now, he couldn't even have imagined it. All this gleaming furniture, the mural wallpaper in the hall along which he walked with his heavy burden, the chandelier above his head, glistening in the sunlight. There was the smell of delicate cooking from the kitchen and of polish from the furniture.

Upstairs, he was led into a bedroom where he gently deposited the unconscious overseer on the bed, but with his boots hanging off so that the white spread wouldn't be damaged. He whipped off the boots and placed them on the floor.

Someone nudged him aside. Mrs Thibault took charge. She'd wasted no time and when she entered the room, she was supplied with water, towels, bandages, and two wenches.

'What happened?' Shawn Thibault demanded.

Roswell answered him quickly, for which Jubal was glad, because the question was asked suddenly and Jubal had almost answered without thinking. Had he done so, he might have given a hint that he was educated.

'Sonabitch named Rafe . . . the little black monkey who oils the machines . . . kicked him in the face.'

'Why'd Rafe kick him?'

' 'Cause Mr Mason was trying to get Rafe down from the roller.'

'Why didn't Rafe get down himself?' Murphy Thibault asked. 'He's used to climbing around the machine.'

'He was drunk,' Roswell said. 'Reckon he been runnin' a still somewhere and turnin' out 'nuff tafia fo' hisself.'

Murphy said, 'Somebody take Rafe down to the whipping shed and spancel him. I'll have his hide later.'

Roswell turned on Jubal. 'Boy, you heard what masta said?'

'Yes, suh, masta, suh, I heered him.'

'Fetch Rafe down to the whipping shed.'

'Yes, suh.'

Jubal was glad to get out of there. The more contact he had with white folks, the greater the chance he might give himself away. Yet, he thought, as he sped back to the mill to round up Rafe, if he was going to ease the work expected of him, he'd have to do it by being in attendance at this house. If that happened, he'd be prepared for it. Not like today when he was suddenly ushered into a situation that scared him.

Rafe was on the floor of the mill, curled up and sound asleep. Jubal grasped him by the back of his shirt and by his crotch, lifted him and carried him outside.

Rafe set up shrill screaming until Jubal put him down. Then he promptly took off in the direction of the cane fields, running as fast as he could. Jubal cursed and went after him. If Rafe got away, Jubal would probably take his place in the whipping shed. Jubal's longer legs covered far more ground and he gained on the small man quickly. Rafe reached the edge of the field. All he could think of now was escape by whatever means he could find and he all but stepped on an abandoned hoe.

He grabbed it and, as Jubal rushed up, swung it. Jubal took the sharp edge alongside his neck. He felt the sting of flesh being cut, and warm blood ran down his neck.

'Kills you,' Rafe shrieked. 'Kills you daid, you takes Rafe again.'

Jubal touched his neck and was surprised at the amount of blood running down his clothes. A sudden anger came upon him. He ducked under Rafe's next pass with the hoe and seized the smaller man by the throat, lifted him off the ground and held him like that until he dropped the hoe and ceased some of his struggling.

Pacified now, half-conscious, Rafe offered no further resitance. Jubal tucked him under one arm and marched down to the whipping shed. Shawn was already there.

'What happened to you?' he asked Jubal.

'Rafe done swung on me with a hoe, masta, suh. I is all right.'

'Fasten him to the floor,' Shawn ordered, 'and then wash all that blood off so we can see how bad you're cut.'

'Yes, suh, masta, suh.' Jubal quickly fettered the slave to four handcuffs attached to rings set in the floor. Rafe was spread out, arms and legs pulled to their extreme. He lay on his stomach and he was beginning to groan.

Jubal helped himself to the water in a basin outside a slave cabin. He drenched the wound, wincing at the stinging sensation. When he returned to the shed, he found Murphy and Miss Pauline also present. Shawn brought Jubal to a window where the light was good and examined the wound.

'Ain't deep,' he said. 'Keep it clean.'

'Yes, suh, masta, suh.'

'That's all,' Murphy said.

'Wait a minute.' Shawn stopped Jubal's departure. 'Pa, come outside. Want to talk to you.'

Jubal was uneasy alone with Pauline. She approached him and he stood his ground, but all she wanted to do was examine the wound.

'Afterwards, come to the house and we'll give you something to bandage that cut with,' she said. 'Don't reckon you'll bleed to death, but you got to keep it clean.'

'Yes, mist'iss.'

She turned her back on him and walked over to prod Rafe with the narrow toe of her shoe. He groaned, so she kicked him a few times and made him groan more.

Outside the shed, Shawn was explaining to his father why he wanted Jubal to do the whipping.

'Did you get a look at him? Field work has hardened him real good. Never saw such muscles, and he toted that nigger like he weighed nothing.'

Sees he's strong and getting fit, but what's that to do with having him whup Rafe?'

'He's a fightin' man, Pa. He's big and strong and he acts smarter'n most. I want to train him.'

Murphy nodded. 'I still say whut's that to do with having him whup Rafe?'

'A fighting man's got to stand blood and plenty of it. He's got to be able to kill a man and not think about it. He's got to do as he's told and obey every time. Let him cut that nigger good. Rafe's got it coming. Make him half kill Rafe till we see he begins to enjoy it.'

Murphy nodded. 'It's a good idea. Let's get it over with.'

Rafe had managed to twist his head so he could see who stood above him. 'Masta, suh, please don't whup me. Cain't stand no whuppin', masta, suh.'

'Then you shouldn't get in trouble this way,' Murphy said unfeelingly. 'Shawn, get down the snake.'

'Masta, suh, not the snake! Don' whup old Rafe with no snake, masta, suh. Cain't stand it. Last time I near died. Please, masta, suh. Don' kill po' old Rafe.'

Shawn held out the long, thin whip to Jubal who took it

automatically. Then he realised what they meant for him to do, but he stood there, apparently ignorant of their intentions and waiting for orders.

'Whup him,' Shawn said. 'Whup him real good.'

'Else you'll find yourself on that floor being whipped,' Murphy added. 'Wants to see that ornery nigger bleed good. Open up his back so he'll ever more remember to be careful.'

Jubal walked over to the man on the floor. He reached down and ripped the thin shirt off his back. Then he pulled down his trousers to his knees. Out of the corner of his eye he saw Pauline eyeing the man. It occurred to him that if there was to be any raping done, she'd be the aggressor. She was a dangerous woman.

Rafe was howling before the snake landed its first bite. Jubal, still oozing enough blood from the neck wound to feel it trickling along his throat, had little inclination to hold back on the force of the lashes. He knew by now what was expected of him, so he put his back into the first lash. which cut Rafe almost to the ribs. His scream attested to Jubal's strength.

The second lash bit deeply in Rafe's buttocks and he screamed loader. Jubal stepped further back to get a better purchase on the whip. He swung it, saw blood well up from another cut, and Rafe's scream turned to a moan. Jubal glanced at Murphy for encouragement.

'Go ahead,' Murphy Thibault ordered. 'Give him fifty good licks. Don't take all day.'

Jubal began the rest of the whipping in methodical fashion. He hit Rafe high, then around his midsection and finally in the buttock region. He could no longer see how deeply the whip cut, because there was too much blood, and presently the flesh began to swell so that it didn't look like a human back any more, but something dragged out of a slaughterhouse.

Rafe passed into unconsciousness after the first twenty lashes, but Jubal was ordered to continue them while Murphy Thibault doused him with buckets of water. Jubal was thinking that Rafe would never get over his whipping. It seemed impossible he'd endure as much as he had.

'All right,' Murphy said finally. 'Wash him down and put him in his bunk.'

'Yes, suh, masta, sah,' Jubal said obediently.

They all filed out and returned to the plantation manse. Jubal hung up the whip after wiping the blood from it. Then he went out and got a pail of water. He sluiced this over Rafe's back and waited for him to start groaning.

He waited half an hour. It didn't matter. So long as he was here, tending Rafe, he didn't have to wield a hoe in the cane fields. When Rafe showed no signs of waking up, Jubal finally knelt beside him, turned his head and two unseeing eyes met his. Jubal emitted a low moan of his own, turned Rafe on his back and pressed an ear against the man's chest. There was no heart-beat, no sound of air going in and out of the lungs.

'He daid!' Jubal exclaimed. 'He said a whuppin' 'd kill him an' it sho' did. He daid!'

His first inclination was to run to the house and tell Murphy Thibault, but Jubal hesitated a moment. He was thinking fast and he already saw a glimmer of what he might do if things worked out properly. He straightened up and sat down on the bench, over which he'd obediently stretched himself when he'd been whipped. He wasn't dwelling on that, nor did he have hate for anybody. It was just that with his intelligence he ought to be able to outwit the white masters and somehow find for himself an easy job. One where he might even have authority, and perhaps access to kitchen food. Even what Calinda cooked any more was palling on him because of its sameness.

He knew the risk he was taking, but the gains seemed worth it. He carried Rafe's body over to the bench, slipped it into the shadows beneath it and then threw some old rags over him. He sauntered back to the fields, passing close by the big house on his way.

Trash was simply thrown into a pile outside the back door and periodically a slave would gather it all up and dispose of it. At the moment there was a fair amount and Jubal came to a stop. He looked around, made certain he was not being observed, before he bent swiftly and picked up part of a canning jar which had been broken. He took this with him, but paused long enough to bury it before he was back at the fields.

He found his hoe, attacked the rows of cane again, bringing earth closer to the stalk, tamping it loosely. He kept it up until Mason hobbled out to call them off the job.

Jubal approached him, whipping off his cap as he did to. 'Masta, suh, kin I ask a question?'

'What do you want?' Mason asked, but without his usual show of irritation. He knew Jubal had totted him to the big house and been very gentle about it.

'I chases Rafe 'cause he runs away an' when I ketches up with him, he hits at me with a hoe. Got this heah cut.'

'I heard about it,' Mason said. 'I hope you whaled the ass off him.'

'Sho did. He still squealin',' Jubal said. 'Mighty good hoe an' it lyin' out theah an' gonna rust. . . . '

'All right, fetch it and bring it to the toolshed.'

'Yes, suh,' Jubal said. That was what he wanted to hear. He brought the hoe to the toolshed and along with it the piece of broken canning jar. which he'd retrieved. Alone in the toolshed, he provided himself with a hammer and a wide, flat piece of iron. On this he placed the glass and methodically crushed it into a fine powder which he brushed into a fold of paper. He promptly crumpled this so it would fit easily into a pocket.

ELEVEN

He was moody as he ate his evening meal and Calinda noticed it. 'Been workin' too hard,' he explained. 'An' old Rafe, he got drunk and kick Masta Mason in the face and near bust his arm, so I gets to whup Rafe.'

'You whupped him real good,' she said. 'Heered Miss Pauline tellin' it to Mist'iss.'

'Had to. Masta Murphy, Masta Shawn and Mist'iss Pauline watchin' me. I don't whup him good, they does, and they whups me too.'

'Po' Rafe.'

Jubal changed the subject deftly. 'Calinda, whut niggers they got workin' 'round the big house?'

'You knows. The cooks, the maids, the houseboys.'

'Thinks I could get me a job theah?'

'Doin' what?' She cackled in amusement. 'You belongs in the field. Whut kin you do in the big house?'

Jubal thought about several things, among them slipping into Mist'iss Pauline's room some night and finding out if she'd like to tease him again.

'I jes' askin',' he explained. 'Knows Masta Murphy and young Masta Shawn, they talks 'bout me today. Don't reckon 'cause I done anythin' bad, 'cause I didn't.'

'You is dreamin'.'

'Then why they whisper?'

'Jubal, big buck like you good fo' two things. One of 'em is tendin' cane an' the otheh is makin' suckers. An' I reckon you ain't been tendin' to your duties good 'nuff.'

'Whut you mean by that?

'I ain't knocked up, is I?'

'How do I know that? Sho' been tryin' ever since we got here. Maybe I planted one in you las' night.'

'Hope so.'

Jubal had an idea. 'Rafe, he got some tafia in his bunk sho'. He ain't goin' to need it tonight. Dark now so I goes an' gets it. Maybe it helps make a sucker. Sho' won't hurt us none.'

'Sho' won't,' Calinda said. She had an appetite for the strong liquor. Some afternoons, Miss Pauline sipped it from a large glass with a wide bottom. She'd sniff and sip and sniff and sip. She told Calinda it was brandy.

One day she had Calinda undress her and spilled some of the amber liquid on her breasts, letting Calinda lick them dry. Another day, she sat, fully dressed. with her legs spread and commanded Calinda to slip her hands up under her dress and finger her while she drank. Calinda obeyed, and from time to time her mistress would let her sip from the glass, but never once did Calinda's fingers stop their probing and caressing except when she was told to place the largest fingers of each hand back to back and thrust them up inside her mistress.

By then both Calinda and her mistress were drunk and her mistress kept calling Calinda by the name of Jubal. Calinda knew then that Miss Pauline wanted Jubal in bed with her and wondered how long before she would get him there. Calinda even felt a twinge of jealousy. Not because Jubal would rape Miss Pauline, but Calinda didn't want anyone else to touch her mistress. Calinda liked doing it with Jubal, but she liked doing it with Miss Pauline even more. She even found herself regarding ten- and twelve-year old wenches in the kitchen and wondered what it would be like teaching them what Miss Pauline had taught her, though she knew better than to try.

When they were quite drunk. Miss Pauline staggered to her feet, pulled Calinda close and started rubbing against her. Calinda responded and was ordered to undress her mistress. She started to, gently as always, but was slapped for her efforts and was told to tear the garments off. Calinda did so, ripping the silken finery and tossing it aside. Miss Pauline turned her back, bent forward, grasping the foot of the bed to hold herself up. Calinda thrust her hands between her mistress's legs, reached up to her waist and ripped her pantalets to her crotch. It wasn't difficult. They'd been loosened anyway to make Calinda's fingering easier, but they both laughed heartily.

Calinda squatted between her mistress's legs, used her tongue and fingers to further arouse her. Miss Pauline looked down, her eyes lust-filled.

'Stand up and make believe you're Jubal.'

'Yes, mist'iss, ma'am.'

And the play-acting began.

'What are you doing in here, Jubal?' Miss Pauline asked.

'I comes to rape you, Miss Pauline, ma'am,' Calinda said boldly. The alcohol had robbed her of fear of reprisal. 'Love you white skin, you soft titties that shakes when you walks, you sweet juicy kunt. Gonna stick my pecker in you an' make you scream and holler.'

'Stick it in, Jubal. Stick it in all the way.'

'Want you in bed to stick it in.'

Miss Pauline lurched around to the side of the bed. flung herself in it and pushed a pillow underneath her rump. She spread her legs and started humping up and down. Calinda crawled up from the foot of the bed, used her fingers as if they were Jubal's organ and, covering Miss Pauline's body with hers, started bouncing up and down, moving her fingers in unison. All through it, Miss Pauline kept shouting Jubal's name, and afterward she clasped Calinda to her, her hold only easing after she had dropped off in a drunken stupor. Yes, Calinda had a taste for strong liquor.

Jubal slipped out of the cabin. It was still early enough so that he wasn't breaking any rules, but he had to work fast now. First he stopped by the whipping shed and made sure nobody had stumbled on to Rafe's body. Jubal touched the man's face, found it cold and stiff. He was dead all right.

He went to the barracoon where Rafe had lived his bachelor's existence, mainly because he couldn't get along with any wench, and only precipitated trouble if he was assigned to one. Rafe always kept tafia on hand and Jubal found the almost-full bottle of it.

Five minutes later, he presented it to Calinda. She squealed in delight and they sat down at the table to do some serious drinking. Calinda had dropped the crude sacking which served as a window curtain and their privacy was relatively complete. She blew out the lamp so everyone would believe they were already in bed.

After a couple of drinks, they were. Jubal was good tonight. Calinda told him so. He was as virile as the first days they'd been together, as capable as he had been in the jail. Calinda gave proportionate return to what she got.

She grew more and more wanton as the alcohol took effect. She arose from the mattress and strutted up and down the cabin, making lewd gestures, tempting him to reach out and touch her and then pulling back with a jeering laugh.

Jubal poised himself to make a flying leap next time she came by, but she suddenly threw up the burlap covering over the window so that moonlight streamed in. She stood motionless, letting its light flood her body. Jubal quietly settled back on his haunches, governed by some curious compulsion not to interfere.

Her head lifted in a listening attitude. Then, as if the cabin was suddenly filled with the beat of African drums, she began to stamp her bare feet on the floor. From somewhere out of a not-too-remote past, the jungle in her blood began to take possession of her.

She writhed seductively, arms high above her head, breasts bouncing impudently as she shook, twisted, wriggled and squirmed. Then her movements slowed and she started swaying as if under a hypnotic spell. She arched back until it seemed she must lose her balance and fall. Her long arms slowly came down to hang passively at her sides, her head was far back, to the full extent of a thin and supple neck. Her hands moved slowly up her legs to her groin. She fingered herself, still swaying and moaning softly.

Jubal, still squatted on the mattress, was fascinated by her. He felt his organ rise. He wanted to enter her, but was reluctant to end the dance. His juices were already spilling out of him, just watching.

Slowly now, Calinda straightened, bringing herself up and forward, but never letting the spell weaken. She moved even closer to him and stood there, her hips gently moving, her legs apart, hands caressing her thighs, her eyes teasing, inviting, daring.

Where this dance originated, the male would have whisked her into the jungle by now, to throw her down in the soft grass and pierce her. Jubal only had to pull her down beside him.

They rolled off the mattress more than once in their fiery passion. He gave her no rest except for the few minutes when they drank more. He kept his tongue against the neck of the bottle whenever he pretended to drink, so that she was getting most of the liquor. Before long, she showed it. She tried to pleasure him, but her head fell to one side. Her eyes glazed, then the lids dropped. Jubal waited half an hour longer, because he was in no hurry now.

Then he arose quickly, dressed and slipped out of the cabin. He made his way to the toolshed. There, he appropriated a shovel with a sharp edge, holding it tight against his body so that if he was seen the shovel might not be noticed. He headed across the fields toward a forest growth from which firewood was harvested, but he doubted they'd reach the spot he picked, for years. He stood in the moon-swept forest for a few minutes, listening. When he was certain no one roamed nearby, he dug a deep grave.

Next, he returned to the whipping shed where he picked up Rafe's stiff body. He realised he couldn't carry it this way, so he applied pressure and heard the dead man's spine crack. Now the body could be more easily toted. He dumped Rafe unceremoniously into the grave, filled it in, scattered the surplus dirt as far as possible, and after leveling off the grave, he transplanted small bushes on top of it.

Satisfied with the arrangement, he returned to the cabin. Calinda was sound asleep and didn't stir when he entered. He dropped beside her. So far, things where working as he'd planned. He thought he could manage his scheme perfectly now. Moments later, he snored.

Calinda awoke with a headache and sullenly made his breakfast, brushed away his exploring hand and left the cabin, heading for the big house to pleasure her mistress. Jubal waited until after it was time for him to join the field workers. He doubted Mason would be there this morning. He was quick to take advantage of any chance to loaf, and after being kicked in the face by Rafe, he had an excuse.

Jubal sauntered toward the big house. He could hear sounds of activity and smoke was pouring out of the kitchen chimneys. Big Harp, the three-hundred-pound chief cook, would be waddling her wide shape around the kitchen mixing her biscuits. Little Harp, fifty pounds heavier than her twin sister, would be frying ham, grits, eggs or whatever had been ordered for breakfast.

Jubal stepped close to the screen door and peered inside. Little Harp was wedged between the range and a work table, getting ready to transfer the cold grits to a frying pan in which fat was already beginning to sizzle.

The maids were busy elsewhere, so only the two cooks were present. Jubal pulled open the screen door. In the palm of his hand, held there by a tightly closed fist, was a portion of finely ground glass.

Big Harp aimed her several chins in his direction and shook her massive breasts in reproval of Jubal's presense.

'Whut you wants heah, nigger? Knows you ain't s'posed to set foot in this heah house you ain't asked.'

'Gots to see Masta Murphy,' Jubal said.

'You pesters him this time o' mawnin' an' he hides you good. Now git!'

Jubal backed away from her. Neither she nor her twin saw him dust the powdered glass into the mixture of grits. He backed away clumsily and went on out. Now it was a question of timing this just right. He let himself be seen hurrying to the barracoon where Rafe lived. Everyone had reported for work, so the building was empty. Jubal thrust what was left of the powdered glass, wrapped in the bit of paper, under Rafe's mattress.

It was time now to put the most important part of his plan to work. If he failed, if they suspected him or they found Rafe's body, he was going to be strung up on the limb of that ancient oak where he'd seen two men already executed. That was the chance he must take, but his tracks were so well-covered he felt safe.

He suddenly began running toward the plantation house. He climbed the steps, dashed across the wide porch, pushed open the front door and rushed through the house to the dining room. They were all at the table. Platters of food had been brought. Murphy Thibault was in the act of transferring a portion of fried grits to his plate.

Jubal's excited manner, the way he barged in against all rules, so stunned them, nobody said anything. Jubal reached out and brushed the plate before Murphy Thibault to the floor. Then he seized the platter of grits and lifted it from the table.

'What the hell you doin', nigger?' Murphy exclaimed.

'Masta, suh,' Jubal panted. 'Masta, suh. Rafe, he run.'

'Damn his black hide. But what is that to do with busting in like this . . . ?'

Shawn said, 'Poisoned! Rafe did something to the food.'

'Yes, suh,' Jubal said, still breathing heavily. 'Tol' me he goin' to put groun' glass in you grits this mawnin' fo' he runs. I thinks he crazy, but this mawnin' cain't find him. An' when I looks, I sees a paper o' ground glass under his mattress, masta, suh. I comes heah fas' as I kin run.'

Murphy reached over to his wife's plate, picked up a portion of the grits cake she'd served herself with. He crushed it between his thumb and forefinger, rubbed them together. Then he slipped the fingers into a glass of water to remove the grits and grease. He held up his hand. Blood oozed out of the thumb and forefinger.

'I be damned,' he exploded. 'Shawn, get word to every plantation. Send into town with the word. Use one of the houseboys. I'm offering a reward of five hundred dollahs for that black bastard. I want him alive an' kickin'. I want to snake him myself. Go fast – so's he can't get far.'

Shawn rushed out. Murphy regarded his still bleeding fingers. 'This is what would be happening inside all of us, we'd eaten that food.'

Mrs Thibault pushed her plate away. 'Murphy, did it occur to you what we owe this man . . . what's his name? Boy, what is your name?'

'Jubal, mist'iss.'

'Thank you, Jubal. You saved our lives, without question.'

'That Rafe, he sho' crazy. Reckon I whups him so hard he don' know whut he does, masta, suh?'

Jubal was asking a mild question without permission to do so. If Murphy Thibault wasn't going to really recognise the service his slave had rendered, Jubal was going to be reminded that a slave doesn't ask a question without permission.

'You laid it on him good, Jubal,' Murphy said. 'But he's been a troublemaker. You say there's glass under his mattress?'

'Yes, suh, masta, suh. I finds him gone, reckon he run, but he got a few dollahs I knows, hid under the mattress. If that gone, Rafe gone too. Thass when I finds the paper with the glass.'

Murphy scooped up a handful of the small, hot biscuits and began to chew on one as he arose from the table. He spat the dough out in a hurry and then reduced one of the biscuits to a ball as his fingers sought more ground glass. When there seemed to be none, he began eating another of the biscuits.

'Take me to his bunk,' he told Jubal.

'Thank you, Jubal,' Mrs Thibault said again, quietly and earnestly.

Even Pauline smiled. 'Yes, thank you very much, Jubal. I think you should be rewarded.'

'Don't want nothin',' Jubal said. 'Done whut I done 'cause that a bad thing Rafe try. Real bad thing.'

He walked behind Murphy to the barracoon. No doubt he could have walked beside him this morning and gotten away with it, but Jubal was smart enough not to go too far too fast.

Murphy lifted the mattress and took out the paper in which the glass had been kept. He shook his head and swore. Then he faced Jubal.

'Listen to me, Jubal. I means this. You say one word about what Rafe tried to do and I'll see you hang from that tree.'

'Masta, suh, I ain't aimin' to say nothin'.'

'See that you don't. Someone else might get the same idea, and I don't want to go through this again, or expose my family to some crazy man like Rafe.'

'Yes, suh, masta, suh. I keeps my mouth shut.'

'All right, I think you will. I got plans for you, Jubal. Take the rest of the day off. Tomorrow, come to the house.'

'Masta, suh, kin I ask a question?'

'Yes.'

'Masta, suh, I thinkin' Rafe got friends. Crazy way he bin, he tol' 'bout whut he aimin' to do an' he cain't do it, his friends could.'

'Do you know this for a fact?'

'No suh, masta, suh. On'y thinks maybe. An' I don't know who his friends are.'

'What can you do about it then, when you're not sure?'

'Masta, suh, I kin eat 'fore you does.'

'You mean test the food?' Murphy frowned. 'That's a good idea. Are you sure you want to do it?'

'Yes, suh, masta, suh. I kin eat 'fore I goes to wuk in the fields. I kin run heah noontime and eats mo' and goes back to wuk till supper an' I kin taste agin, suh. On'y a taste, suh. My wench, she good cook an' I gits all I craves, suh.'

'Who is your wench?'

'Calinda, suh. She wuk fo' Mist'iss Pauline, suh.'

'Oh, yes. Well, we'll see.' He rummaged in his pocket and handed Jubal three silver dollars. 'You should be rewarded, Jubal. These are yours.'

Jubal's eyes grew moist and his face went slack in gratitude. He bowed his head, kept the coins in the palm of his hand as if they were treasures. He said nothing when Murphy turned away. After he'd left the barracoon, Jubal jammed the money into his pocket and did a fast little dance, shuffling about the floor, humming a tune to keep time. He hadn't felt so good in months. Not since he'd done raping with Malvena on the riverboat.

He had the rest of the day off. The average black would go humping it to the village where he could spend the three dollars. Jubal didn't want them to think he was just average, so he returned to the rear of the plantation house, found a low hummock upon which to sit and he squatted down there.

Mrs Thibault saw him, some three or four hours later, and came out. She opened her parasol and approached. He jumped to his feet, whipped off his cap and bowed his head as she approached.

'Good afternoon, Jubal,' she said. 'What are you doing here?'

'Nothin', Mist'iss. I ain't doin' nothin'.'

'But you've been sitting here all day.'

'Masta say I gits the day off, Mist'iss.'

'Yes, I know, but is this how you spend a day off?'

'Mist'iss, ma'am, I knows Rafe, I do. He a no-good nigger an' he full of hate. Reckon he might come back an' see you is daid. Might try again, mist'iss, an' I don' aim to let him.'

'Well, that's very thoughtful of you, Jubal. I'm obliged.'

'Ain't nothin', mist'iss.'

'I shall tell my husband. I'll also tell the cooks they are to feed you well from now on and call you when the meals are ready.'

'I thanks you, mist'iss, ma'am.'

She walked away, twirling her pale blue parasol. Presently Jubal saw another parasol, one he was much more familiar with. It was Miss Pauline, ambling along the walk to the necessary house. She knew he was watching and the swiveling of her hips was for his benefit alone.

'Reckon you're askin' for it,' he told himself. 'You're an uppity bitch, but a good-looking one, and when I'm ready, you will be too, or I'll make you ready . . . Mist'iss Pauline, you tart, you whore, you great Southern lady with a desire to be screwed by a black man.'

Jubal lowered his head when she was looking. It was still a far cry to the time when he'd dare to address her and perhaps finger her, but the time was coming. He knew it as sure as he knew he'd be back in St Louis, a free man again. The first step toward the journey was completed today.

He would confide none of this to Calinda. He was growing tired of her anyway, though she was far better than any other wench the plantation had to offer, even among the three hundred or so living here. They certainly didn't pick wenches for looks, not even for youth. And he had noticed that whenever a wench, born on the plantation and raised here, got to be fifteen or sixteen, she was promptly sold. It was the one factor in the running of this plantation that the slaves resented deeply.

No handsome wenches, no young girls, there'd be no raping of blacks by whites. A wife who was surely frigid. Jubal began to add these things, and while they didn't make sense yet, he had a feeling that one day they would.

TWELVE

That night Calinda eyed him with a mixture of respect and suspicion. 'Heered you busted in an' tol' masta Rafe try to kill him.'

'That's what Rafe tol' me, he wakes up after I whups him. Say he got glass an' he aimin' to get in the kitchen and put the glass where it do mos' good. Fo' him, not fo' masta an' mist'iss.'

'Jubal, why you wait till this mornin' to tells 'em?'

' 'Cause I thinks Rafe kinda crazy. He got the miseries from the whuppin' an jes' talk. Says he runs too, an' when I finds him gone this mornin', it sho' seem like he mean whut he say 'bout the glass too.'

She put a plate of pork and grits before him. 'You is a sly one, Jubal. I ain't sayin' whut you tol' me ain't right ever-which way, but they fixin' you don' wuk the field no mo'.'

'Seem like they owe me somethin'.'

'Sho' they does. Mist'iss Thibault, she say you earn you keep 'roun' heah.'

'Whut Mist'iss Pauline say?'

'She say you one smart nigger, an' thass the truth, sho' 'nuff. You so smart, Jubal, you goin' to fall oveh you own feet some day.'

'Whut's the matter with you, Calinda? Din' I make you happy las' night? We sho' had us'n a good time.'

She laughed and let the strange feeling about Jubal pass over. 'Sho' did. Got me a feelin' we made us a sucker las' night. Don' know why, just got the feelin'.'

'Wants to have a gal grow up pretty as you, Calinda.'

She shook her head, but happily. 'You knows whut a woman likes to hear. Reckon you knowed lots of gals, eh, Jubal?'

'Well now, you think I learned all them ways 'thout seein' a gal? You wants me to pester you tonight agin?'

'Got nothin' else to do,' she said.

'No sense waitin'.'

He pulled her down on his lap. She squealed and pretended to want to hit him with the cooking spoon she held, but hoisted up her dress, squirmed to get his pants down and he took her sitting in the chair. Presently the cooking spoon made a great clatter as it hit the floor and she used both arms to cling to him. Without separating, he lifted her, carried her to the mattress, knelt and completed the act again. His enormity never failed to satisfy her. She was a vital woman with a sex drive that amazed him, and he gloried in it because it matched his own. But they'd done the same things to each other so many times Jubal knew he was tiring of her.

He remembered the white whore in St Louis, into whose bed he'd been tricked. Even so, she'd been good. Diddling with Calinda was pleasant, but no longer interesting. He knew he needed a change, but it would have to be a secret one. Especially from the white folks, because he now had an image to preserve. He'd have to be careful about Calinda too, because she was a smart wench. A sly one too, quite capable of sliding a knife blade into his back if she ever caught him getting horny around some other wench on the plantation. Not because she loved him. Just a matter of pride. He wondered if she diddled with Miss Pauline. If so, she'd never talk.

In the morning, he refused Calinda's fried grits, headed for the plantation house and walked into the kitchen. Big Harp waddled his way. Little Harp was again wedged between the range and a work bench, so all she could do was turn her head.

Big Harp said, 'You a goddamn nigger, don' stan' back o' you own kin'.'

'Whut you got to say 'bout that, Jubal?' Little Harp asked.

'You know whut you two charmin' ladies are talkin' 'bout?' he said. 'Saves our masta and mist'iss lives, I did, an' you call me a goddamn nigger. Rafe, he crazy. They goin' to hang him they ketches him. They asks me, I'll pull the rope an' be glad to do it.'

'Waffo you talk that way?' Little Harp demanded.

'If I din' git heah in time yestidday, whut we be doin' this mawnin' if they all daid?'

'Singin' and buryin' them,' Big Harp said.

'They all daid. Pretty soon comes the law, a man who sells us. You wants to be sold agin? You thinks this is ha'd wuk here an' these white folks don' treat you good? They puts you on the vendue table and you so damn fat, nobody bids mo'n a dollah and a half, 'cause you eat anybody out till they's busted. Here you eats all you wants 'cause this masta don' care none. Whut good Rafe doin' you, he kills these folks? Think o' that.'

They thought about it. Their massive bodies quivered with their thinking. Big Harp said, 'Reckon so, Jubal. Reckon so.'

'I gets sold,' Little Harp opined, 'mayhap I gits a kitchen don' fit me good. Got 'nuff trouble gittin' 'round heah.'

Jubal sat down. A cracked plate was before him. He pushed

it aside. 'Now you knows better'n that, Big Harp. I tastes the vittles and I tastes the plate too. I gets my own plate.'

She gave him another and she placed samples of the various foods for breakfast on it. He wolfed them down as fast as the twins served them, until he was stuffed.

'Fine eatin',' he said.

'Bes' in the world,' Big Harp added.

'Long's I don' slide offen this heah chair and die on the floor right at you feet. Jes' like this.'

He slid off the chair, landed on his back, reached up under Big Harp's dress, along her tree-trunk style legs and on to the pubic region where his fingers encountered her as she squealed and began to prance with everything on her shaking, along with the kitchen.

She struck at him with a spoon, just as Calinda had done, but when he got to his feet, she threw the spoon aside and embraced him in layers of fat that made him gasp for breath.

Then even this limited amount of air was cut off further and he felt as if he'd suddenly been placed between two riverboats, both pushing at him from front and rear. The panting of Big Harp couldn't be this fast and Jubal realised he'd been attacked from behind by Little Harp, and her fifty-pound advantage over her sister.

He tried to extricate himself, but he was pinned. He managed to bring up one hand, grasp the sack-like right breast of Big Harp and twist it – hard. She gave a screech and backed off. He pulled free of little Harp's grasping, exploring arms and hands and sat down promptly.

'Whut you tryin' to do, kill me?' he gasped. 'If they's rapin' to be done, I does it, and one at a time. Don' see how you could be raped anyways. Even by somebody as big as me. How's anybody gonna get past you legs an' find your juicy spot?'

'It ain't how big you is,' Little Harp squealed. 'It's how long you is, Jubal. You sho' welcome to try any time you wants.'

Jubal nodded. 'Might try tonight. Cain't tell.'

There was movement outside the kitchen. Big Harp pulled the pan of biscuits from the oven just in time. Little Harp began frying more grits. The houseboy in his green coat shuffled into the kitchen and demanded food. Big Harp fed him.

'You is goin' to git bigger'n me or Little Harp, you keeps eatin' this way, Kip. Little Harp, pass him some grits.'

Kip showed rows of large, very white teeth as he glanced at Jubal. 'You gits to go to N'Awleans, Jubal. Masta takin' you, he is.'

Jubal could hardly conceal his excitement, but when he answered, it was like a shrug.

'Been to N'Awleans.'

'Mayhap Masta shows you a nice place whar you kin

pleasure yourse'f while he pleasures hisse'f. Likes to go to N'Awleans, I does. Gettin' horny, I gettin' older.'

'Shush that kinda talk,' Big Harp said good-naturedly.

'Reckon I knocked up two-three wenches already,' the boy said. He was no more than twelve. 'Hopes I grows to be as big as you, Jubal. Likes it, I do.'

'When we leavin'?' Jubal asked.

'Masta say you come runnin' soon's he through eatin'.'

'You tell me when,' Jubal said.

'Might. You fetches me a present from N'Awleans.'

'Fetch you a present right agin' your ass, you keeps pesterin' me like this. You come back and tell me, hear?'

Calinda hurried in and promptly provided herself with a tray on which she put a small, thin vase with a late autumn rose in it, a creamer, sugar bowl a small jar of jelly and a plate of hot rolls with butter in a side dish. Big Harp placed strips of bacon, a small slice of ham on a large plate. Little Harp added two eggs and a generous square of the fried grits.

Calinda said. 'Hears you goin' to N'Awleans, Jubal.'

He shrugged. 'Seems like I the onliest one who ain't heered 'bout it.'

'Masta buyin' a new coffle 'cause he says he needs mo' help in the fields when the cane's ready fo' cuttin'.'

'Reckon I asks him to bring me back a nice wench,' Jubal said with a grin.

'You do, an' I slices you like you is a side o' bacon. I'se 'nuff woman fo' you.'

'Big Harp an' Little Harp don't think so,' Jubal teased her.

Calinda eyed the two massive, grinning cooks. 'You get lost sho',' she said. 'You dive, in, an' no mo' Jubal.'

The two Harps quivered with laughter and Jubal had to join in along with the houseboy and finally Calinda giggled as she picked up the tray to be carried upstairs to Miss Pauline's room.

'Wants I should take the tray up?' Jubal continued the teasing.

Calinda wasn't amused this time. 'You stays 'way from Miz Pauline you knows whut's good fo' you.'

She stalked out, laden with the heavy tray. The two Harps laughed uproariously and Big Harp slipped a thick piece of ham on to the plate Jubal had used. He ate it, but began to worry about getting as fat as they were.

Kip scurried back to the dining room and returned almost at once, breathless with the importance of his message.

'Masta Murphy, he say you gets dressed and meets Drill at the stable. You runs, Jubal, 'cause Masta 'bout ready now.'

Jubal darted out the back door, raced down to his cabin where he changed into the only other clothes he owned, a good white shirt, a pair of cotton trousers and heavy shoes. He rubbed his thatch of wool with water, washed the back of his neck and under his arms. He reached the carriage as Drill was mounting it. Jubal swung aboard and sat down beside him.

'You comin' too?' Drill asked.

'Masta say so.'

Drill eyed him in disapproval. 'In them trogs?'

'They's all I got,' Jubal said. He noted that Drill now wore tan pants, highly polished boots, a yellow weskit and a frock coat the color of coffee. On his head was a tall beaver hat.

'You any otheh nigger, I makes you run behin' the carriage. Whut he takin' you 'long fo'?'

'Don' know, Drill. Reckon he fo'got to tell me.'

Drill gave him a baleful look, slapped the reins and got the carriage moving. He pulled up before the plantation house and quickly climbed down. So did Jubal.

Murphy and his wife came out at once. Murphy indicated the bag on the porch. Jubal sprang forward to carry it while Drill dusted the carriage step ceremoniously. Drill clambered into the seat and the journey began. Murphy's wife didn't wait to wave goodbye, Jubal noted.

Ten minutes along the road, Murphy took a flask from his pocket and enjoyed a long pull at it. Then he tilted his wide-brimmed hat forward, covered his face, and fell asleep.

It was a long journey, broken only by the overnight stay in the little town they'd come through before. Jubal wondered if he and Drill were going to be locked up in the Negro jail. He didn't look forward to it.

When Drill pulled up before the inn, Jubal jumped out of the carriage, procured the suitcase and stood waiting for Murphy, who was verging toward a state of drunkenness, but not so that he couldn't handle himself.

He gave Drill and Jubal each a dollar. 'Get yourself some food,' he instructed. 'Do what you wish tonight and sleep in the carriage. Be ready at sunup.'

'Yes, suh, masta, suh.' Drill tipped his beaver hat. Murphy glanced at Jubal. 'You look like hell. When we get to New Orleans remind me to buy you some trogs.'

'Yes, suh,' Jubal said with emphasis.

'Bring my bag up to my room. The innkeeper will tell you which one. That's all.'

Jubal walked behind Murphy and saw him veer off to a small cafe adjacent to the inn dining room. Jubal inquired at the desk and was told where to deliver the suitcase. He ran lightly up the stairs to the second floor where he found the room without any trouble. He placed the bag inside, inspected the room to make certain it was absolutely clean and tidy. Then he left it, closing the door behind him. His eyes fell upon the metal numbers tacked to the panel. The innkeeper had designated the room by number, and Jubal had simply gone to it. Not many slaves could read numbers. He'd have to watch out for that. One error of this kind could ruin everything, for Jubal realised very well now, that if he was known to be educated, something drastic would happen to him.

He left the inn by the rear door, as he was supposed to do when not in the company of his master. Scattered around a pile of rubbish at the rear of the inn were pages of a New Orleans newspaper. He looked about, saw no one, swiftly seized one double page, crumpled it and thrust it under his shirt. He hadn't read anything in so long he had a hunger for it.

He found Drill unharnessing the horses so Jubal didn't enter the stable, but went around to the side of it where there was some degree of privacy. There he flattened out the newspaper and once again felt the thrill of being able to read – and understand what the words meant.

The only item of interest he saw was an article scathingly referring to the Liberty Party, a northern group of anti-slavery advocates. Jubal found little information in the highly biased article, but it was the first time in his life he'd even known a movement against slavery existed. Certainly no one had talked about it in St Louis.

He wondered if such a movement could possibly gather enough momentum to have a meaning for the Negroes. It was, at least, some faint hope. He longed to spread this news, but decided against it. If it was traced to him, he'd have to explain where he heard it – or confess that he could read. That crime, compounded with the spreading of such information, could very likely get him whipped to the point of death. This ever-present threat kept his lips sealed and made him continually cautious.

He and Drill ate for two bits each at the home of a Negro couple. They were both tired, slept well in the carriage after washing down the horses with warm water and drying them thoroughly. The stableman baited them and Jubal had nothing further to do.

In the morning, Jubal sat on the porch steps of the inn, waiting for Murphy to come out. Drill stood beside the carriage, occasionally flicking specks of dust from the seat and the step.

Murphy stumbled out, in a vile mood, still half drunk. He said nothing in response to their greetings, but fell asleep in the back seat at once.

Jubal and Drill were silent, out of respect to his being asleep, but when the carriage rolled into the outskirts of New Orleans, Jubal emitted a long, grateful sigh. This was what he wanted. People about, wagons, drays, buggies, carriages, barouches cramming the streets. Store windows that were the most fascinating scenery in the world to him.

Drill, accustomed to the traffic, maneuvered the carriage expertly. He knew where he was going and he pulled up, finally, before the enormous St Charles Hotel on St Charles Street. Jubal stared in wonder at this marvel of the 1840's. Beyond the great doors he could see part of the rotunda for which the hotel was justly famous. Two Negroes, at least six feet seven or eight inches tall, promptly appeared. They were dressed in red trousers, black boots, shinier than any Jubal had ever seen before, long red frock coats and black fezzes.

They took possession of the bag, helped Murphy down and greeted him respectfully. Murphy walked to where Jubal and Drill stood, awaiting orders.

'Drill, see to the horses. We'll be here until day after tomorrow. I'll be getting more niggers to help with the crop. Jubal, help Drill and then go down to Nate's Clothing Store. Drill knows where it is. I'll send word you're coming. Get yourself togged out. Everything you need. Two outfits, understand? Two of everything. I leave the colors up to you. Remember, I want to show you off, so don't come back looking like a clown.'

'No, suh, masta, suh,' Jubal said happily.

Murphy gave them each five dollars. 'That's to spend as you wish. Eat with it, find a wench, get drunk – but stay in the stable if you do. That's all. And, Jubal – meet me here at seven.'

'Yes, suh, masta, suh.'

They boarded the carriage and Drill drove it quickly to the stable Murphy always used. He and Jubal groomed the horses, baited them well and left them to rest. They walked several blocks to a less magnificent section of the city and they were greeted by two tailors as they entered Nate's Place.

Jubal would have liked cream-colored pants, tight at the thighs, held beneath the boots with a strap, a white shirt and wide black tie. A black frock coat and a black hat with a medium brim. That was what he craved, but he knew what Murphy expected him to buy. So he procured trousers so tight in the crotch he was going to have difficulty sitting down. For some reason, white men admired the crotch bulge and women regarded it with considerable interest. He selected them in dark purple, both pair the same color. He picked out a pale lavender shirt, ruffled in white, and frock coats of a medium lavender shade.

He crammed his feet into shiny boots and regarded himself in the mirror. He liked what he saw. His skin, a pale brown, contrasted softly with the lavender. The coat made him look even more broad-shouldered and narrow-hipped.

Drill clucked his tongue in delight. 'Man, you sho' goin' to get youse'f screwed tonight. Wisht I could. I too old any mo'. All played out. No juice lef'. I gits drunk, reckon.'

'Don' know whut I kin do,' Jubal said. 'Masta wants me fo'

somethin'. Show me off, he said. Whut he mean by that?'

Drill thought he knew, but he decided to refrain from telling Jubal the bad news. A fighting man meant a dead man sooner or later. If Masta Thibault meant to match Jubal with the Devol fighter, it would be sooner.

'White folks like to show off they bes' niggers. Make 'em feel impohtant you tags 'long an' folks admires you. You knows whut to do in a big city like this? You waits at the hotel fo' masta. You finds a bench near the do'. That's whur you waits. You goes inside you gets you ass kicked real good. See you in the mawnin', Jubal.'

Jubal, feeling resplendent in his trogs, returned to the stable, where he put his plantation clothes and his duplicate wardrobe in the carriage. Now he was free to roam the streets until seven. He had about an hour and a half.

He unerringly made for the Negro section and paraded himself up and down the street, answering interested calls from girls, and often lewd ones from bucks, with good-natured repartee. He hadn't felt this good before in his life.

At half-past six he was at the hotel where he located the bench and sat down to wait. The town was lighting up now. The gas lamps cast a soft glow over the street, windows were illuminated, the business activity slowed down, and where wagons and drays had predominated the traffic, it was now composed mainly of barouches and fancy carriages.

Jubal had no idea what Murphy Thibault had in mind for the evening, but he expected it to be an interesting one. He was not to be disappointed.

THIRTEEN

Murphy, after a bath and a change of clothes, went down to the lobby for a drink. He wasn't hungry, so he satisfied what appetite he had with small portions of the free lunch on the bar. He consumed half a dozen oysters, followed by a slab of beef between two slices of bread, well-buttered.

'Well, Mr Thibault,' a voice breathed softly in his ear. He didn't turn his head.

'Hello, Devol.'

'Just came in,' Devol said. 'I saw your boy sitting out there. Are those your colors he's wearing?'

'Don't know what he's wearing,' Murphy said. 'Told him to pick 'em out himself.'

'How about talking a little business? You brought him with

you to show him off, didn't you? That means you plan to fight him.'

'It don't mean a goddamn thing.' Murphy said. 'I ain't aiming to fight him.'

'You know, we could rent the slave market on Royal Street. Big enough to get six-seven hundred in there. Maybe more. They'd pay well if a boy big as yours fought my boy. I could afford a very good-sized bet. Say . . . twenty-five thousand.'

'Not interested,' Murphy said.

'That is only half of it, Mr Thibault. We charge twenty dollars for each and every man who wants to see the fight. That runs into a lot of money. I might bet you this way – your boy wins, you take the whole business. Come to fifteen thousand and more. Maybe lots more, if you give me time to promote this right.'

Murphy shook his head. 'I don't need money. I don't like this kind of fighting, and I don't like you. Do me the great honor of staying away from me, Devol, or, by God, I'll give them a chance at the hospital to bet on whether you live or die.'

Devol's face flamed. 'Suh, I've sent my seconds 'round for less than that.'

Murphy grinned at him. 'I can outshoot you; I'm a better swordsman than you are; I can outbox you; but damn it, I can't outtalk you. Go 'way! Git!'

Devol chewed his lower lip for a moment, contemplating his chances in a duel, and decided they were not very good. He knew Murphy had fought two or three, and if he hadn't won, he wouldn't be here now. Devol had talked many a duel, but never actually fought one. He was too cagey for that. He walked away without another word. Murphy finished his drink. It tasted bitter.

He saw what Devol had meant when he left the hotel lobby and Jubal jumped to his feet. He was certainly resplendent. Leave it to a nigger to choose clothes like these, but he had to admit that Jubal looked good in them. Suddenly he felt sorry for Jubal, for his place in the world, his lot in life. Ann always felt sorry for them. That was one of the sore points between them, though not the biggest. He felt sorry for himself too. He was a man with a wife, but without his wife. He hadn't slept beside her now in almost twenty years.

He wondered: If he ever did again, would he respond to her as he used to? A succession of whores, many of them extremely clever, hadn't been able to cause an erection. His only satisfaction came from the endurance of sharp, stinging pain. When the pain grew great enough, he experienced something akin to an orgasm. He wasn't certain what it was, but it served.

He felt a desire for that feeling tonight, forgetting it for a moment while he admired Jubal.

'You sure are something,' he approved. 'Wonder to me the gals let you get this far.'

'Thank yo', suh, masta, suh.'

Jubal grinned from ear to ear.

'I'm going to visit a friend of mine. When we get there, you can sit in the bar off the parlor. If you touch any liquor, I'll have you hided. Niggers and whiskey don't go together. Mean nothing but trouble.'

'Yes, suh, masta, suh, I don' drink nothin'.'

'All right. Anyboy asks you who you are, tell them you're my nigger. If they gets too nosey, lose your voice. Come along.'

Jubal trailed behind him. It was a distance to Basin Street, the part of it where Murphy wanted to go. When he stepped on to the porch, Jubal scampered ahead of him to open the door, but it opened before he could touch it. A light-skinned girl in a maid's uniform greeted Murphy very politely and after he passed, she eyed Jubal with considerable interest, but she didn't say anything.

'My nigger can sit in the bar,' Murphy said. 'Your mistress about?'

'Waitin' for you, suh,' she replied. She crooked her finger at Jubal and he trailed behind her through the reception hall, then the big room where the bloody fight had been held, and finally into a smaller room off which was a service bar. Behind it were a couple of stools. Jubal seated himself, stretched his legs, put his hands behind his head and arched his hips slightly. The maid watched him with undisguised interest.

'You stays heah, nigger,' she said.

'Alone?' he asked innocently.

'You think I stays with you? Whut you think I am?'

'Don' know what you is, but I knows whut you wants an' I got it.'

She nodded. 'You sure have. My name's Pet. What's yours?'

'Jubal.'

'You Mist' Thibault's nigger?'

'Thass what he said.'

'I'll come back,' she promised.

Jubal nodded. He didn't mind the wait. From where he sat, he could see Murphy Thibault going up the wide staircase with a dark-haired girl beside him. Presently he saw two other men select girls and take them up the same stairs. More men came in. Now and then, one would stop and stare at him and Jubal would promptly lower his head until the inquisitive ones went away. One man didn't. Jubal jumped to his feet.

'You – nigger – who you belong to?'

'I's Mister Murphy Thibault's boy, suh.'

'Oh, yes. Heard about you. Fighting nigger?'

'Me, suh?'

'Who else am I talking to?'
'No, suh, I ain't no fightin' man, suh.'
'You look like you could be.'
'Yes, suh, reckon I kin fight, has to, suh.'
'You're the first buck I'd ever bet on against Devol's boy. But I reckon Thibault, he don't want to fight you so don't make any difference.'
The man wandered away and Jubal frowned. A fighting man? Devol's fighter? This was something new. He wasn't quite sure what it meant except that he was regarded as someone special enough to take on Devol's boy, whoever he was.
Jubal promptly forgot about fighting. The maid returned and eyed him hungrily. 'Your masta mighty busy for two-three hours. You wants to sit heah by yourself, or would you like to come to my room?
'Craves your room, I does,' Jubal said quickly.
'Got any money?'
'Got five dollahs,' he said, not mentioning the three he'd saved before.
'Maybe you'd be worth it at five dollars. What's that pushing out between your legs?'
'What sticks in you,' he said casually.
She sneered at him. 'Pretty sure of yourself, ain't you?'
'No, ma'am, but I pretty sure o' you. Kin smell a gal she gits horny. Kin smell you.'
'Follow me,' she commanded imperiously, taken aback by this outspoken man.
He trailed behind her. He realised he'd been sitting there for quite some time, and it must be late. There were no more visitors for the maid to greet; the music he'd enjoyed had stopped. He looked up the staircase as he passed it by and smiled to himself. He wondered if Murphy Thibault thought him so stupid he didn't know what went on up there.
The maid led him down a flight of stairs to a basement where there were three small rooms. She entered one and lit a candle. It was a nice room, plainly furnished. The bed was big and looked comfortable. It smelled good too, of white woman's perfume. No doubt the maid stole some of it from time to time.
She sat down on the bed. 'Put the five dollars on the bureau,' she said.
Jubal took the five coins from his pocket, made a little stack of them and then walked up to her, sat down beside her. He intended to remove her clothes gradually, work her to a pitch he'd enjoy, but before he could act, she had a hand down his pants and her fingers closed around his penis. At the same time she lay back and pulled him over top of her.
'Can't wait this time,' she said in a hissing whisper. 'Shuck your pants . . . hurry!'

He got up long enough to step out of them, remove his coat and get his shirt partially unbuttoned before she dragged him down on top of her. She moved her legs, grasped his penis again, pressed it against a thigh, moaned softly, maneuvered it inside her and Jubal lost control. It was over so fast he barely knew it had happened. He withdrew, turned toward her. She lay on her back, eyes closed. She had small lips. He kissed them and caressed her breasts. They were small and hard. He didn't mind that. The rest of her was lush and soft.

He brushed her hair back. It wasn't wiry as Calinda's was inclined to be. His fingers fumbled with hooks and eyes. She opened them for him. He removed her dress. Beneath it, she was nude. She cupped her round breasts and shook them for Jubal's benefit. His smile was pleased as he removed his shirt, hanging it up carefully. He got back into bed.

'You wants diddlin' or you wants more whut you jes' had?'

'Diddle,' she whispered.

He began to stroke her breasts to firm the nipples. He laid his cheek against them and let one hand pass down over her flat belly. Her hips began to move. He skipped her genitals and caressed the inner part of her thighs, slowly working upwards until his hand rested lightly on her pubic hair.

She gave one shriek, raised her legs, scissored them around his body and loosened her hold only enough for him to enter her. This time took much longer because he made it so, for, at intervals, he'd extricate his penis, making her cry out in frustration. It excited him to have her move frantically against him as her organ sought his

'Stop takin' it away fum me like that. Drives me crazy.'

'I drives all black wenches crazy,' he said, easing his penis back inside her.

'You one smart nigger,' she cried half in anger. 'Too smart.'

'I one good screwin' nigger,' he replied.

'Then screw and stop the damn talkin' an' teasin'.'

He was ready and they both worked off their passion in a frenzy of movement that left them limp and satisfied.

'When your masta comin' again?' she asked, after they'd rested a while.

'Reckon he don't tell me that. Sees him take a gal upstairs.'

'You know what this place is, Jubal?'

'So'. It's a whorehose.'

'Cathouse,' she corrected him. 'A palace of pleasure, but your masta sure don't get pleasured.'

Jubal was interested. 'Whut that mean?'

'He been comin' here now for maybe fifteen-sixteen years. What his wife like?'

'Don't seem like she do much diddlin'.'

'He a sick man or something? I hear what goes on here. I

heard them say he ain't stuck it into no woman here all the time he been comin'.'

Jubal was astonished. 'Well, whut in hell he comin' here fo'?'

'They tries everythin', Jubal. Sometimes two, three gals work on him. They frenches him, lets him bugger 'em . . . anything, but it's no use. He just small and no good.'

'Glad I ain't like that.'

She giggled. 'I had big men before, but you the best.'

'Had any white men?'

'Sure . . . lots. They changes their luck. Don't mind none. They pays me good.'

'They fix you up like I do?'

'You know ain't a white man livin' could do that, Jubal. How come you so gentle and so big?'

'Hurts a gal they ain't no mo' good, thass why.'

'Kinda hurt me some, Jubal. I gots to go upstairs pretty soon. The gentlemen start leavin' and they gives me nice tips.'

'Whut my masta do up there, he don't pester the gals?'

'Jubal, I tells, you tells nobody else.'

'I tells nobody.'

'The gals take off his clothes. They see if they can get it up an' when they can't, they turns him over on his belly and they whups him.'

'You plain crazy, gal. White men don't get whupped.'

'He do – and he pleasures hisself that way. Don't blame you for not believin' me, but he sure goin' to be sore tonight where they whup him.'

'Reckon I whups you 'bout now.' Jubal slapped her bare behind gently. She twisted around, drew him to her. She slid down the bed and pressed his face against her breasts while the rest of her moved violently. He slid down. They were off the bed and on their knees. He forced her legs apart. He went back and plunged his organ into her. His hands supported her buttocks, leaving her free to writhe and keep her body in motion till they reached their climax.

After they rested a few moments, she kissed him and put on her uniform. Jubal buttoned his shirt. He pulled up his trousers and then calmly picked the five silver dollars off the bureau and dropped them into his pocket.

She nodded, kissed him, felt him again and then fled. He made his own way upstairs. When he resumed the stool behind the idle bar, he watched her usher the men to the door, help them with their coats, brush against them quite accidentally so they had an encounter with breasts and sometimes thighs. She knew her business. Her eyes were alternately coy and teasing, meek and willing. Jubal saw silver dollars fall into her hands. Twice the men insisted on dropping them down her low-necked uniform. She bent forward obligingly, pushed up her breasts with her hands until the nipples popped free of their confinement. The men paused long enough to nuzzle a nipple. She moved it along their lips in a slow, teasing manner. One of them bit and she cried in delight. The other slipped his hand between her legs and forced his finger up inside her, through the material. The hand moved up and down and she responded skillfully, causing him to laugh heartily. He extracted his finger and went out. The other man followed.

One of the last to appear was Murphy Thibault. He walked, unaccompanied, slowly down the stairs. Jubal arose instantly. He moved out and fell in behind Thibault. Pet had had his hat and cane ready. Thibault handed her a piece of silver. She curtsied politely. Thibault glanced behind him, crooked a finger and Jubal followed him on out.

On the street, Thibault came to a halt. 'Won't need you again tonight. Wants you first thing tomorrow. Get yourself dudded up like tonight.'

'Yes, suh, masta, suh, I get dudded up good.'

'That's fine. Good night, Jubal.'

Jubal said good night and stood there while Thibault walked slowly away, heading in a direction opposite the one he'd take if he were returning to the hotel. Jubal knew Thibault would glance behind him soon to see that he was obeying the order to go to the stable and sleep. Jubal had no such intention.

He'd never before heard of what Thibault did in that whorehouse. Letting the girls try to pleasure him and when they could not, allowing them to whip him. It didn't make any sense to Jubal. A whipping was punishment. How could a man get any enjoyment out of that? Yet, according to Pet, he came here time after time, year after year, and it was always the same.

Gradually Jubal began to see a few things in their proper light. Thibault's wife had acted especially cool when he left for New Orleans. It was likely she knew why he was going there, and she resented it. But how could she, when it was her fault? If Thibault was properly taken care of, if his needs were satisfied, he certainly wouldn't do such a crazy thing.

Jubal guessed that she probably hated her husband. That was why she never went to bed with him. Yet she had birthed a son, and there was no question but that Shawn was sired by Thibault. They were so much alike, it was impossible to think otherwise.

So Jubal thrust the mystery from his mind because there was no answer that he could find now. He looked back. Thibault was just turning a corner to the left. Jubal walked with long, fast strides over a side street, came out to an avenue in time to see Thibault cross it. At the next block Thibault crossed the street and seemed to be heading for a pleasant-looking dwelling with an outside stairway and a grill-railed veranda overlooking the street.

Jubal's long legs took him down the deserted street quickly. He was in time to watch Thibault climb those stairs, walk along the veranda, knock on a door.

When it opened, there was plenty of light behind it to illuminate the girl who went quietly and lovingly into Thibault's arms. Jubal's eyes widened in amazement and he felt his senses reel. He felt weak and trembly all over. She was the loveliest girl he'd ever seen in his life. There he stood, a good distance away, and fell in love with a girl he'd never seen before. A girl he didn't desire sexually half as much as he wanted her to belong to him. He wanted to protect her, to love her, to be her man and have her for his woman – for always. She was Negro, she accepted Thibault happily – the man who had to be whipped to be pleasured. If Thibault couldn't satisfy himself with the clever whores at the cathouse, how could she pleasure him?

Jubal suddenly hated Thibault. He visualised him taking the girl's clothes off, laying her down, mounting her, doing whatever a man of his kind could do – which certainly couldn't be much. Jubal wondered how she could stand him. This old man with a useless thing between his legs who dared to leave a whore and come directly here to a girl like this!

Jubal turned away reluctantly. What he really wanted to do was go up there, strangle Thibault and take the girl away with him. He cursed himself. He was as unable to help her or himself, any more than Thibault could pleasure a woman.

Jubal knew he'd be back. He wouldn't be able to remain away from this girl, whom he had seen only from a distance, whose voice he'd never heard, whose body he'd never touched. Whose golden skin enticed him as no other woman had ever done.

He'd be back. He didn't know how or when, but he knew he'd return and somehow meet this girl. He felt that it was his destiny to do so, and meanwhile he could dream about her. His life would be filled with thoughts of her. Now he had an overwhelming ambition. One he couldn't possibly satisfy, but it was there. He could think. He was educated. There'd be certain things he could do and he'd think of them eventually.

The galling thing now was his vision of Thibault diddling with that girl. Jubal felt like throwing back his head and baying his frustrations to the stars.

FOURTEEN

The journey back to Briarfield was a duplicate of the one which brought Jubal to the plantation. Two carts, to be used in the fields, were piled with supplies and each carried four wenches, while behind the procession walked the new coffle of eighteen slaves whom Murphy had bought. The only difference in the procession was that no runaways were chained in the carts, and Jubal rode in the carriage beside Drill.

Jubal was silent most of the time, not even talking to Drill. He could think only of that girl. Of her trim figure, the neatness about her, the straight hair which she let cascade down over her shoulders. She'd have brown eyes, of course. That she was a mixture of bloods was apparent – she was a mustee.

He spent most of the journey trying to figure out some way he could return to New Orleans and meet her. He felt he couldn't go on unless he did this. He deeply resented the fact that Murphy had stayed the night with her which meant he'd bedded down, of course. Until now, Jubal hadn't cared how many men had possessed any woman he took to his bed. This time it was different.

When they hailed the plantation house, Shawn came running out to greet his father. Miss Ann was not as enthusiastic. Miss Pauline, clutching her ever-present parasol, joined the group. She did cast one steady look at Jubal, attracted by his clothing and new appearance. She even smiled just a little as he bobbed his head and lowered his eyes respectfully.

Ann Thibault kissed Murphy this time, but a perfunctory kiss that seemed one more of duty than love.

'Did you make all the arrangements?' she asked her husband.

'Yes. Reckon there be eighty people here.'

'Then we'll have to get busy,' she said. 'There isn't much time.'

As if she expected to begin preparations at this very moment, she hurried back into the house. Murphy didn't seem annoyed at her abrupt departure. Mason appeared to take charge of the coffle and the wenches. Jubal, after turning the luggage and the purchases over to Kip, was allowed to go. He returned to his cabin. Calinda was, of course, busy caring for Miss Pauline and she'd not be back until later. Jubal didn't take off his new clothes, but he did hang up his second suit and then his old trogs. He wanted Calinda to see him dressed well for once.

He stirred up the fire some because it was getting cool these evenings. Soon now it would be time for the harvest to begin, and from all accounts it would be a madhouse of activity for a few weeks, with everyone on the plantation straining to the utmost to get the crop in before the black frost could reach the fields.

The cane was higher than Jubal's head now, and a stalk broken off contained plenty of sweetening to be sucked out of it. The pickaninnies were forever getting spanked because they stole so much cane.

Jubal again brought out the newspaper, reading the short article about the Liberty League, wondering who these people were and why they bothered to take the side of a southern Negro. He crumpled the page finally and dropped it into the middle of the fire, watched it turn to ashes and he felt safer. If he'd been caught with that newspaper, he'd have been surely whipped.

When Calinda returned, Jubal was dozing by the fire. She slammed the door to wake him up. He got to his feet and grinned at her as he put on his lavender coat.

'Ummm . . . ummm. . . . ' she exclaimed. 'Looks like one o' them riverboat gamblers, you does. You see any gals in N'Awleans?'

'Lot's o' gals in N'Awleans,' he teased her. 'Bedded down with two or three. They wasn't as good as you.'

'Wouldn't s'prise me none you did. Got somethin' to tell you. Two things.'

'It kin wait,' Jubal said.

He went to the mattress on the floor, rolled it back and took out a flat, gaily wrapped package. Calinda gave a squeal of delight, snatched it from him and ripped the paper away. She took out the silken scarf of pale green with yellow borders. She gasped, ran it through her fingers, pressed it against her cheeks. She tied it around her head and wished she had a mirror. She would take it to the big house in the morning, hidden under her dress, and when she got the chance, she'd put it on and preen before Miss Pauline's mirror.

'Jubal, I nevah had anythin' like this befo' in all my life. Pleasures me mo' than anythin' 'cause I got good news for you.' She stepped close to him and touched his face. Then she stepped back with a tremendous scowl. 'Whur you gits the money to buy this?'

'Masta Murphy give me an' Drill five dollahs each to spend. Nothin' I wanted so I bought you this. Din' steal the money.'

She embraced him then. 'Jubal, I's knocked up.'

He lifted her off the floor before he held her to him and hugged her until she yelled. After that, she had his supper to make. She'd brought leavings from the plantation house and they made a fine meal on them. Her chatter was sometimes annoying, but Jubal was glad to be back.

'Jubal,' she said, 'I done fo'get to tell you we's havin' a big dinnah an' a ball. Next week. Masta Murphy called on friends in N'Awleans and sent word to white folks hereabouts. Maybe a hundred'll come.'

'Wondered why Masta Murphy made Drill drive him all over N'Awleans. Masta done went to a cathouse an' he got a wench he sees to. Whut the matter with him? He got hisse'f a nice wife.'

'She don't have no truck with him no mo',' Calinda said. 'Hear tell been like that fo' mos' twenty years now. Cain't find out whut happened. Nobody knows, it was so long ago.'

Jubal decided not to reveal that their master also paid whores to whip him, and that he derived some sort of queer satisfaction from the pain. He doubted Calinda would believe him anyway, but more than that, Jubal felt a slowly widening gap between himself and Murphy Thibault. When he searched his mind, the only reason for his hating Thibault was because of the mustee back in New Orleans.

'Cane gettin' mos' ready,' Calinda remarked as she bustled about the cabin, the long ends of the scarf trailing behind her.

'Whut?' Jubal asked, rousing himself from a mind fogged with memories of a girl whose name he didn't even know. Who served a man far too old for her, let him stay all night, after he was fresh from a whorehouse where he'd been diddled with by prostitutes and whipped at his own request. He wondered what sort of girl she could be, and he knew he didn't care what she was.

'You dreamin',' Calinda said.

'I'm tired. Right tired. You reckon I goes to the kitchen tomorrow to test the food?'

'Ain't said you wasn't to. Might send you to the fields. They's not enough niggers.'

'Brought back eighteen new ones.'

'Won't be 'nuff anyways. Got us a mighty good crop this year. It good 'nuff we gets a week off 'fore Christmas.'

Jubal nodded. A week off at Christmas. If only he could think of some excuse for him to go to New Orleans. Some way to get there. He realised how imposible it was, so he forced the girl out of his mind and turned his attention to Calinda.

They ate, while he told her about the city, and she chattered about the small details happening in the plantation house. There was great excitement about the coming social affair. Calinda was going to enjoy it even if it meant much more work for her. She also felt a quiet satisfaction that Miss Pauline hadn't been angry at the news she was going to have a sucker by Jubal.

They took off their clothes finally, blew out the candle and lay down on the mattress. They pulled up the blanket because the nights were gradually getting chillier. Jubal wondered how he was ever going to make love to her tonight. He was tired, and even more than that, he couldn't shut the memory of that lovely mustee out of his mind. He even felt shame when his penis rose and hardened.

Calinda's hand slipped down, enclosed it and she sighed pleasurably, believing she had caused it. She moved the skin up and down slowly, gently, felt his juices start to trickle over her hand. She slid to a point where she could kiss and fondle him at the same time. Jubal knew he had to go through with it and decided to get it over with fast. He whipped her on her back, entered her almost cruelly, brought his body down hard. She cried out, but if it was pain, that didn't last long. She set her hips in motion, matching each thrust he made, building him up and up until their passion crested and she felt him grow limp.

'Jubal, you acted like you ain't had it in a month. Reckon you ought to go to N'Awleans ev'y day you kin. Comes back to me primed like that an' we make suckers ev'y year. Jubal . . . you all right?'

He began to snore softly. She smiled and covered him before she curled her body against his.

Jubal's eyes were soon wide open. He'd only pretended sleep, for Calinda was smart. He was pleased she was going to birth his first child, but when he'd rammed himself into her a few moments ago, it was not Calinda he lay upon, but that girl. Some day, he told himself, he'd do the same thing to her. It would be no dream, there'd be no substitute beneath his loins. She'd be there, every golden inch of her.

Calinda shook him awake at dawn. He washed in icy water in the basin outside the cabin. He dressed in his plantation clothes and hurried up to the main house.

He was greeted by Big Harp's thick arms and massive body. Little Harp couldn't extricate herself from the stove and the table in time. They served him huge quantities of food, and he ate it all. He realised that he wouldn't be allowed to spend all his time in the kitchen, and he wondered what they had in mind for him. Perhaps the fields, because when the cane was ready, there were no shirkers on this plantation. Manpower was used down to a pickaninny who could do nothing more than tote drinking water.

Kip, in his green coat, brought the word to Jubal 'Masta Shawn he say you goes down to whuppin' shed.'

'I ain't done nothin',' Jubal declared in sudden alarm. 'Sweahs I ain't done nothin'.'

'Ain't goin' to whup you,' Kip said. 'You don't git theah soon, mayhap he will.'

Jubal loped over the distance to the whipping shed. He found Shawn inside, seated on a bench waiting for him.

Jubal whipped off his cap. 'Yes, suh, masta, suh, I'se here.'
'Jubal, did you see that big buck my daddy brought back?'
'Yes, suh, sees him.'
'Think you can fight him?'
Jubal was dismayed. This was something he wanted no part of.
'Ain't a fightin' man, suh.'
'We think you are. I do, especially. Now, you know we're having a big affair here next Saturday and Sunday. Might be a hundred people coming. I want you and the new buck to put on a fight for us.'
'Masta, suh, tells you the truth, I ain't a fightin' man.'
'You're big and strong. You move well.'
'Masta, suh, we niggers fight, one of us gets to die. I'm too scared to be a fightin' man.'
'I promise you there'll be no killing.'
'Wishes you get somebody else, masta, suh.'
'Jubal – I'm telling you to fight the buck. Is that clear?'
'Yes, suh,' Jubal said unhappily.
'Tell you what. Next week I'm taking twenty men and every cart and wagon we got to New Orleans. We have to get more hogheads for the sugar. If you whip that buck good, I'll take you along and put you in charge.'
'So' 'nuff?' Jubal asked in sheer delight at the prospect.
'And I'll give you five dollars to spend.'
'I fights him,' Jubal said quickly. 'I whups him good.'
'I warn you, if either of you quits or fakes, you'll get hided.'
'I whups him good,' Jubal repeated emphatically.
'I think you'd be one of the best fighting men in the state if you were trained.'
'Yes, suh.' Jubal showed no enthusiasm beyond this fight which would get him to New Orleans.
'I'll tell you why. You're the smartest nigger I ever met.'
'Me?' Jubal asked, partly in alarm.
'I've watched things you do, and you do them well. You don't have to be told everything, shown everything. You've got a brain under that wool of yours. You're doing very well on this plantation.'
'Me and Calinda, we made us'n a sucker, masta, suh.'
'Good. I hope it's a boy and he's built like you. Well, are you going to be ready Sunday?'
'Yes, suh, masta, suh. I'se ready now.'
'Eat all you wish. More than just testing the food for my daddy. I want you good and strong.'
'Yes, suh, I eats.'
'Jubal, did you come down from Major Sedgewick's farm?'
'Yes, suh, I gets sold Major dies.'
'Funny, I used to go there to see a girl. His niece. I never

remember seeing you and I think I would, you're so damned big.'

'Seen you, suh.'

'At the Sedgewick plantation?'

'Yes, suh. Seen you there.'

Shawn nodded. 'All right, Jubal. You can go, but remember I want you in shape for Sunday.'

'I be ready, suh. Sweah's I will.'

Jubal left the shed, but Shawn continued to sit on the bench, thinking quite deeply about this unusual Negro he'd just dismissed. He was an interesting slave. So far as Shawn knew, Major Sedgewick didn't have a niece and, what he knew for an absolute fact, he had never set foot on the Sedgewick Plantation. Jubal had walked into the trap Shawn set for him. This surprised Shawn too, because he meant what he'd told Jubal, that he was smart. There was that look of intelligence in his soft brown eyes, and he was quick to respond no matter what the order was. He worked with a precision that showed he was capable of thinking of what he was doing, often improving on it.

Jubal was a mystery to Shawn, but he wasn't anxious to solve it now. He was far more eager to find out what kind of a fighting man he was.

Jubal was worried. He felt that suspicion of Shawn's. He'd have to be very careful. Then he recalled the promise he'd be taken to New Orleans next week. He would find a way to see that girl. Nobody could stop him. If he had to kill this new buck to get there, he'd cheerfully do so.

But it might be well to see just what kind of a buck he was going to fight, so Jubal made his way to the barracoon where the new men would be resting for this one day, after the long trek. Jubal strode into the building.

The new men sprang to their feet as he entered, but when they saw he was just another slave, they resumed their slothful positions again. Jubal walked slowly the length of the room until he came to the buck.

'Wants to talk to you,' he said.

'What fo'?' The new man wasn't moving if he could avoid it. His legs felt as if they wouldn't hold him up and he could still taste the dust from the trek.

'Get up!' Jubal ordered sharply.

The slave gave him a flash of white teeth. 'Who you, man? Jes' 'nother nigger. You ain't white, is you?'

The slaves laughed gleefully. They were all members of the new group. They would stick together and favor their own against any other slave, especially one inclined to be bossy.

'You gits on you feet in one minute,' Jubal said, 'or I whups you one.'

The slave sprang to his feet. Jubal saw how big he really was. He looked to be strong too. Jubal slapped him across the mouth. The buck gave a roar and made a drive for Jubal. His fist was well aimed, but Jubal ducked in time and he only got his jaw skinned a bit. Jubal hit him on the chest, drove him back, but it seemed to have no effect on this man. Jubal took two hard punches, the second of which could have broken his shoulder if he'd been in the wrong position.

He lashed at the slave's face. He could take that too, Jubal was getting winded, but this buck seemed fresher than when he began. It was all that food, Jubal's brain told him.

The buck whizzed a fist half an inch from Jubal's face. For a second, he was vulnerable and Jubal aimed two fast, hard punches to the stomach. The slave howled in pain, doubled up, clutching at his belly.

Jubal backed away, still ready to fight, but there was no argument left in this buck. Jubal now knew the buck could absorb punishment anywhere except his stomach. It might be the buck's one weakness and Jubal would have to capitalise on it. If the buck's fist ever connected with Jubal's jaw, there would be a quick end to the fight and Jubal wouldn't get to New Orleans. He intended to go.

'What fo' you do that?' the buck asked. 'Don' even know who you is.'

'I'se the peacock 'round heah, boy. I'se Masta Murphy's boy and I Masta Shawn's boy. I tell you to hump, you humps. I does the whuppin' on this heah fa'm too, an' I kin skin a man good I don't like him.'

'Ain't done nothin' to rile you,' the slave persisted. 'Don't aim to make any trouble.'

'Whut you name?'

'Cully. I'se Cully.'

Jubal turned around and walked out. He was well satisfied. He was going to New Orleans. He'd see that girl. He didn't know what he'd say to her, or what excuse he'd give for calling on her, but he'd find one. Jubal felt as if he'd had half a bottle of tafia.

FIFTEEN

The workers were getting ready for the harvest. The men were in full charge now, for there was no longer any field work for the women. The hoeing was dispensed with and the stalks were ready to be cut.

The seed stalks were being laid by. Bucks, stripped to the waist, sweated profusely in the hot sun. The nights were getting definitely cool and there could be frost before too long, but the sun was still hot.

Armed with the big knives, the bucks started down a row of cane. The knives slashed away the leaves on the right side of the stalk, another blow trimmed the left side. The third slashed through the base and the stalk was picked up, held at an angle and the top lopped off. It was then loaded on the carts which followed the workers.

This was the seed for the next crop. It was stored in huge 'mats' or beds, to be planted the following February. The seed stalks looked very good to Murphy and Shawn. Next year's crop would be even better, though this one should be a bumper. When the refined sugar reached the sugar wharves in New Orleans, it would be sent to many parts of the country and the world. Murphy was sure the proceeds would pay off the plantation and leave a generous profit. He had much to be thankful for.

Jubal took no part in any of this, beyond jogging down to the fields for the exercise. Shawn had ordered him to run wherever he went, never walk. To lift heavy barrels and hogsheads, slung from tree limbs, anything that used the muscles. Jubal was enjoying it, especially when he rested and spent that time watching the slaves breaking their backs in the very work of cutting cane.

Jubal visited the sugar house and watched them getting everything ready for the harvest. The cane would be brought in carts, fed on to a belt which brought it between three massive rollers. There the cane was pressed, crushed and squeezed. Then the cane juice passed into great vats from which it was sieved and cleansed of debris. Now it passed through tubes into huge kettles where slaked lime was added, the boiling process began and the syrup transferred through four different kettle boilings before it was ready to be paseed into the large reservoirs where it would be left to cool and granulate.

In the plantation house, slaves were busy washing, polishing, mending. In the kitchen, Big Harp and Little Harp strained the capacity of the large room with their own enormous bulks and those of the half-dozen slaves they'd been assigned to help. Baking was being done in relays, and four slaves were kept occupied all day cutting and toting firewood for the big ranges.

Calinda followed Miss Pauline about, applying herself to whatever tasks her mistress found for her. She did very little cooking in the cabin, for she ate in the kitchen or with Miss Pauline, and Jubal was well taken care of by the Harp sisters and the orders of Shawn and Murphy. She was glad, for from time to time Miss Pauline would nod to her and they would retire to the room upstairs. The moment they entered, Calinda locked the door, drew off her dress and attended to the sex needs and desires of her mistress. In doing so, she satisfied her own. She was glad she was carrying around a sucker. Even Miss Pauline was excited by it. She told Calinda she couldn't wait to suck on her titty and taste her milk.

The thought delighted Calinda. Miss Pauline could think of more ways of satisfying herself. Even this morning when they were in the parlor, she forced Calinda to bend back, pull up her dress, spread her legs and expose herself. Miss Pauline thrust a finger up inside Calinda, probing, feeling, exploring. She told Calinda she wanted to see if she felt different in there now that Jubal had planted a sucker in her. When Calinda had looked nervously toward the open door, fearful of their being seen, Miss Pauline smiled recklesly, pulled up her own skirts, revealing her nakedness and pushed her genitals against Calinda's.

'Be Jubal, Calinda,' she urged. 'Be Jubal.'

Calinda did as she was bade. She suspected Miss Pauline wouldn't mind one bit if Jubal planted a sucker in her. She wanted more than rape by Jubal, she wanted a sucker by him. But by now Calinda didn't mind, because she was tired of Jubal and she knew no matter how many Jubals Miss Pauline wanted, she liked Calinda best. Calinda never talked and she loved pleasuring her mistress, who was happiest behind the locked door of her bedroom with her clothes off and being ministered to by Calinda's hands, mouth and body. However, she made Calinda tell her everything Jubal did to her on the mattress they shared. Calinda did, even elaborating on it, liking to see her mistress's eyes narrow, her breath quicken, her nipples harden and her body start pumping as she imagined Jubal on top of her.

As for Jubal, he was finding out that all that food distressed him. He decided he'd fight better with less of it so he ate only the samples he was supposed to test before Murphy would eat of the same food. From time to time Rafe's name came up in the household, with the comment that no trace of him was ever found.

Each time, Jubal would worry about the grave in which he'd interred Rafe and he trotted down there to rid himself of these cares. The rapidly growing turf and shrubs had already erased any signs of the grave. If it was found now, it would be by pure chance, so Jubal ceased to worry.

The dinner was to be held Saturday afternoon and the festivities continue on into Sunday. By that morning the house was crammed with guests who came from distances beyond a day's travel. Those who lived closer would be coming later in the day. Sunday there'd be another dinner – and the fight between Jubal and Cully.

Several times Jubal saw Cully at work in the fields. He watched him march back to the barracoon in the evening and noted how slow his steps were, how his back was bent under all that hard work. Cully wasn't going to be easy to whip, but it could be done. Better, anyway, to make it look like a good fight with no advantage on his side.

Cully still resented the way Jubal had treated him the day of his arrival and he showed it. Whenever they met, Cully's greeting was sullen. Cully hadn't the slightest idea that he was going to fight Jubal.

'I do declare,' Calinda said the night before the party, 'this heah the bigges' an' best dinner I evah heered 'bout. Got 'nuff vittles to feed three times whut's comin'. Don' mind that none. They be 'nuff leftovers fo' everybody on this here plantation to get some.'

'You hears them talk 'bout me and Cully fightin'?' Jubal asked.

'So' have. All the men talks about. Miz Pauline too, reckon. She 'bout as excited as the men. Miz Ann, she agin' it. She say fightin' a sin.'

'Sho' is,' Jubal commented wryly, 'for them that does the fightin'.'

'You thinks you kin lick that big man, Jubal?'

'I lick him good 'cause if I do, I get to go to N'Awleans with Masta Shawn.'

Calinda eyed him suspiciously. 'Why you so set on that? Been to N'Awleans, ain't you?'

Jubal smiled at her. 'I gets five dollahs too, and I wants to buy you a dress to go with the scarf. That's why I wants to go.'

She smiled. 'Wish I wasn't so tired. I'd take you to baid an' stay 'wake all night pleasurin' you. Wants a dress real bad, I does.'

'You'll get it,' Jubal promised.

'You gets to kill that buck, you wins?'

'Masta Shawn, he say no killin'. Don' want to kill nobody.' Jubal recalled Rafe and the way he died and shuddered slightly at the memory.

'Way they talkin' they aims to make you a fightin' man.'

'Not me.' He shook his head. 'Fightin' man is a killin' man an' I got no want to kill or be killed. I whups Cully good 'cause I got to go to N'Awleans, but they make me a fightin' man, goin' to be a mighty poor one. Cain't make me fight I don't want to.'

'Don't want you no fightin' man,' Calinda declared.

'Runs with you fo' I let's 'em do that to you.'

Jubal seemed mildly interested. 'You'd run with me, Calinda, I asks you to?'

She walked over to where he was sitting, bent and put her face against his. 'Whut you wants me to do, I does. Runnin', stayin' or pleasurin'. Your sucker growin' in me. Goin' to be a boy, jes' like you, Jubal. Jes' like you.'

Calinda was as surprised at her burst of affection for Jubal as he was. Lately, they'd been taking one another for granted. Calinda let her hand rest on her abdomen. Her lips parted in a tender smile. Must be the sucker inside makin' me go soft, she thought. Didn't think I could ever leave Miss Pauline, but guess I could. This sucker really doin' somethin' to me.

Jubal drew her close, let his head rest against her stomach, his thoughts similar. He wanted to love Calinda like he loved that beautiful girl in New Orleans. Wanted to real bad, 'specially since she was carryin' his sucker. He made up his mind he'd try. Their love-making that night was tender, all-satisfying and they both believed that from then on it would be different. Better.

Saturday morning Kip came running to the cabin. 'Jubal,' he said, 'Masta Shawn he say you gits in you new togs an' you stands at the do' to open it fo' the white folks.'

It was the beginning of a good day, Jubal thought. He dressed in his extra suit and paraded along the slave quarter street for the admiration of all the wenches and the children. He reported to Shawn later and was told what to do. It was a task that was quite unnecessary and Jubal knew very well all Shawn wanted to do was show him off as the new fighting man.

Kip looked at him in awe. 'You sho' splendiferous, Jubal. You the mos' splendiferous nigger I evah seed. Jubal, when I grows up, do I gits to look like that, please?'

'Reckon you does, you keeps growin',' Jubal said. Kip's chances of the luck he'd encountered was going to be slim indeed. Once Kip reached the proper age, he'd be promptly shipped to the fields and some new boy picked as a house servant.

Ann Thibault, in her afternoon party finery, was making a final inspection of the premises and she stopped to talk to Jubal on the porch.

'Jubal, you are not to hurt the boy whom you fight tomorrow. I don't want you – or him – injured. I don't mind a fair fight according to the rules, but we will not indulge in the sort of thing that's popular in New Orleans.'

'Yes, mist'iss,' Jubal said fervently. 'I ain't cravin' to kill nobody and I sho' don't crave gettin' killed. Makes it a fair fight, I kin help it.'

'Good. You're a very intelligent boy, Jubal. And you look . . . ' She fanned herself industriously while she tried to think of the right word. 'You look gorgeous.'

Thank you, mist'iss.' He bobbed his head.

Pauline sauntered by him several times. When there was no

one about, she stared quite openly at the bulge in his trousers and once she gave him a quick smile. He thought she came by more often than was necessary. He wondered, idly, what she'd do if he told Masta Murphy what Pauline had done on the riverboat. Quite likely she'd deny it in the high anger and he'd get himself whipped . . . or hanged. He had no intention of risking that, so Pauline was quite safe. The way she acted, she knew it.

When the carriages began to arrive, Kip and two other boys, also in green coats, opened the carriage doors. Other boys toted luggage. Jubal, in his finery, instantly attracted attention. He would bow low and open the front door for the guests. That was all he had to do. Shawn was taking no chances on tiring him before tomorrow's fight.

In the evening, kegs of tafia were sent to the slave quarters, along with a large quantity of food. The slaves gathered around several big fires where they roasted meat and drank tafia; couples went off into the forests; others danced and everyone sang. There'd be no work done the next day. The following week would see to the final preparations for beginning the harvest and then they'd make up, in hard work, for this pleasuring.

That night Calinda stumbled into bed without undressing. Jubal, with a good portion of tafia in his stomach, was in a mood to be doing some pestering, but when she didn't respond. he fell to dreaming about the golden-skinned girl and what he'd do to her in the lucky event they met. He felt his penis rise and harden and he had to clench his fists to keep his hands from going down there. He wasn't so hard up he would revert to that. He could take Calinda, but he didn't want her to be a part of his imaginings, so he turned on his side. Her back was to him, but he pushed his penis between her legs, moved slowly until his juices had moistened her, after which his thrusts quickened as his passion rose, reached its peak and subsided. Calinda didn't even stir. Jubal turned his back to her and promptly fell asleep.

Guests were up and about early the next day, inspecting the crop and the sugar house. The men made frequent visits to the spring house where cold water was available to mix with their corn whiskey. Miss Pauline, with her parasol, flirted with the men quite openly, making a little game of it. Ann Thibault seemed to be everywhere, tending the wants of her guests and glowing with excitement and happiness. Shawn was usually in the midst of a group of unattached, giggling girls, voicing compliments and evincing charm. Murphy stayed close to the spring house and by early afternoon he was happily drunk, as were half the men.

Jubal saw that Shawn had caused a roped-off space to be

created on the lawn in front of the house. It was large, providing plenty of room for the rough kind of a fight they'd expect.

Jubal no longer thought about the fight. That was something to be gotten over with. He couldn't get that girl out of his mind. Upon his success as a fighting man this afternoon depended his chance of meeting her, of seeing her again. He would give the white folks a good show, but he didn't intend to get marked up by Cully. Some of the bruises inflicted in these fights didn't heal for weeks and he wanted to look his best when he presented himself to the girl in New Orleans.

After a Sunday two o'clock dinner, Jubal removed his splendiferous clothing and donned pants torn off at the knee, and an old shirt. In his bare feet, he trudged toward the fighting ring where the men were already beginning to gather. Jubal moved reluctantly. This was not something he wanted or would enjoy. There was always the chance he might get hurt or, by some unlucky accident, be rendered unable to fight, so that Cully could tear him apart for the pleasure of the audience.

Cully, who had been finally notified of his part in the fight, was being half pushed to the ring by Mason. Cully had looked forward to another night of tafia drinking and frequent little trips into the bush with one wench after another.

When he saw whom he was going to fight, Cully lost his reluctance. He ducked under the rope, grinningly raised his hands above his head and grasped his fingers together in a steeple, indicating victory. Jubal, watching him, realised that Cully had been a fighting slave before. Little wonder he'd been a tough man in their first encounter. Jubal began to worry. If he could get at Cully's midsection early, he could stop him with little trouble, but if he didn't, if Cully knew his weakness and guarded against it, Jubal was going to have a time.

Jubal entered the ring and looked about uncertainly. It seemed to him that this sea of faces represented half of New Orleans. There was a great deal of talk about his muscles, his size, and a number of bets were being made.

Cully pranced about, pausing to glower at Jubal from time to time. Once, as he passed by, he managed a whisper. 'Goin' to pull your balls clean off, nigger. Pull 'em off an' make you eat 'em.'

Jubal's ire began to rise. Here was a stupid, thick-headed nigger with nothing but strength to depend on. Jubal was educated. He could think, and if he couldn't outthink this man, he deserved to get himself killed, even by that fantastic method Cully described.

Shawn stepped into the ring. 'You two fighters – take off your shirts, but don't shuck down. You fight until one gives up or is knocked cold. I'll give the word when to begin.'

'Masta, suh,' Cully complained, 'we don't git to shuck down, I don't get to grab he balls.'

Shawn choked back the laugh, but nobody else seemed to, except Ann Thibault, who turned away. It was she who'd probably given the command for no shuck-down. Jubal was satisfied with it, but Cully still grumbled that it wouldn't be a fair fight.

Jubal waited for the signal to begin. Cully was half crouched. Jubal guessed that he would use this position to spring from, to charge and try to get the fight over with quickly. Jubal let himself present a fine target.

'Start fightin',' Shawn yelled.

Cully came out of the crouch in a savage rush. Jubal swung to one side, stuck out his foot and Cully tripped over it, hit the ground, slid about six feet and sat up, dazed. Jubal could have kicked him into unconsciousness, but he still had no heart for this.

Cully mistook Jubal's reluctance to take advantage of a situation for cowardice. He jumped to his feet, laughed aloud and came in again. Jubal ducked a swinging right and ran into a left jab. It was short, but had power behind it and the wind was knocked out of him for a few seconds. Cully had no intentions of showing any mercy. Before Jubal could regain his wind, he was at him with a two-handed grip on Jubal's right arm. Cully began to yank. If he had his way, he'd pull the arm clear out of its socket. Cully had seen it done. He knew how. Jubal, who'd never even heard of this form of mayhem, brought up the fist of his free arm and hit Cully squarely under the chin. Pain ran down Jubal's arm to the shoulder blades. Cully's grip weakened. Jubal hit him again, this time on the nose. He broke it, as he intended to do, because he suddenly realised that Cully was going to kill him if he could, despite the orders against it.

Cully shook that blow off, but it did serve to weaken him a little more. Jubal backhanded him across the face, inflicting more pain on the now-throbbing broken nose. Cully let go, howled in agony and rage. The nose might interfere with his breathing, but it didn't slow him down much. He lowered his head and rammed Jubal in the stomach, sending him careening backwards until he was actually against the single rope and the men who lined it. Two or three of them put their hands against his back and pushed him violently back into the ring while they shouted encouragement and a demand for more blood.

Some of the women had turned away. Ann Thibault was already on the porch, refusing to witness any more of this. Slaves, not permitted near the ring, had gathered well off where they could see little, but they could hear the shouts of the crowd. That told them, vaguely, which way the fight was going.

Jubal thanked his foresightedness in preparing himself for the battle, Cully was getting winded and he was no doubt breathing blood from his nose because he coughed every few seconds and spat blood on the ground.

He was still powerful, still a dangerous menace. Jubal decided he could no longer risk any more of Cully's attacks. One punch just might hit him in a vulnerable place and send him crashing to the ground. If that happened, he was going to be killed. He knew that now. He also knew that the crowd not only expected it, but wanted it. They didn't care if a man died, so long as it was to the accompaniment of screams and pleadings, which the winning fighter would ignore.

Jubal crashed home a straight right to Cully's stomach. Cully cried out in pain and doubled up, exactly as he'd done in the first fight Jubal had with him. Jubal hit him twice more in the belly, then backed off. Cully, still doubled up, seemed to be in the direst agony. Jubal lowered his hands and Cully came at him out of the doubled up stance. Jubal went down under the savage, unexpected onslaught. He tried to roll over. Cully kicked him alongside the head, but a kick with a bare foot isn't too bad. Cully, however, next used a heel as hard as steel on Jubal's face, bringing it down in a smashing blow. Jubal felt teeth loosen, tasted blood and his wits began to reel. The heel came up for another blow. Jubal reached out, grabbed Cully's ankle, twisted it as hard as he could. Cully, off balance with the foot already raised, tilted over like a tree sawed through. As he went down. Jubal got up. He used his arm to wipe blood from his face and then he went into a flying leap that put him on top of the now squirming, kicking and elbowing Cully.

Jubal could take these blows, for they were too short to be effective. He drove a knee into Cully's stomach, bounded up and down twice. with the knee going in deeper each time.

Culley was clawing at Jubal's crotch. If he got a grip on him there, even with trousers on, he could inflict a horrible punishment that would likely end the fight with Cully kicking him to death.

Jubal pulled himself up, bent his leg hard, aimed the knee at the stomach again and threw himself down with all his weight behind him.

Cully screeched and his face became contorted in agony. He was bleeding so hard from his broken nose that Jubal was painted with the blood. The crowd cheered and yelled itself hoarse, crying for more blood. Bets were changing as the odds alerted. Jubal had not time to find out who was the more popular at this moment.

Cully, bent double, and this time unable to straighten up, did claw again in the direction of Jubal's crotch. He almost got a grip on it, for Jubal had to come in very close for his next attack. Using the knee again, he brought it up sharply under Cully's chin. There was a loud cracking noise. Cully's jaw hung lopsided. He began to scream and hold his face with both hands while he ran around the ring to escape Jubal.

'Kill him,' the crowd yelled. 'Kill the sonabitch coward, runnin' like that.'

Jubal debated briefly whether or not to finish Cully off. It would be easy now, but he didn't want to kill him, and he remembered that Shawn had said there should be no killing. Jubal merely walked up to the thoroughly disabled buck. He grasped his wool, yanked his head up, hit him in the face again, completing the job of thoroughly wrecking his features. Then he hit him in the stomach to double him up, and when he bent over, Jubal used both hands, clasped together, to bring down a posible neck-breaking blow to the back of Cully's head. He fell down on his face and stayed there.

Jubal wasn't sure but that the man was dead, until Cully groaned a few times and turned over on his back. The crowd jeered at him, but Cully could take no more. He made no effort to get up.

One of the men dived under the rope, stepped up to Cully and kicked him in the face, bloodying his highly-polished boots. He wiped the blood off on Cully's pants. Apparently he was a poor loser.

Jubal staggered up to the ropes. Someone pushed him back. 'Finish him off,' he was encouraged. 'Let's see you twist his leg off. Bust his goddamn neck! Kill him!'

Jubal, with wave after wave of pain running through him, stood there unable to move. Shawn raised the rope and stepped up to him. He waved his arms at the crowd.

'I told this buck – no killing. I told him he could go almost as far as that, but not to finish him off. We don't want a killer fight on this plantation, my friends. That's for city fighting.'

There were some grumbles, but most of the men were satisfied, some even sated. The group began to break up. Kip and his two assistants were approaching with trays. The men advanced on the three boys and the glasses vanished from the trays.

Shawn looked keenly at Jubal. 'You all right?' he asked.

'Hurt some, masta, suh, but I all right. He sho's a tough man. Reckon I killed him?'

'No. He's groaning over there and beginning to move. I'll have them carry him to the slave sheds.'

'I takes him,' Jubal said. 'He hurt bad.'

'You did a fine job.'

'I gets to go to N'Awleans, masta, suh?'

'I won three hundred dollars betting on you today. I'll give you ten dollars to spend. And you'll be in charge of all the men I'll bring.'

Jubal murmured his gratitude and wished his face didn't hurt so much. He managed to lift Cully's head and shoulders as Shawn made his way out of the ring and returned to his guests. Murphy, teeth clamped on a dead cigar, was still watching Jubal, wondering if he should risk him in a fight with Devol's boy. Murphy didn't need the money, the crop was going to make him comparatively wealthy, but a challenge was something he'd always met, and he'd never been known as a man who ran away from any sort of fight. Either a personal affray or using a slave. Finally he turned way, still undecided.

Jubal got Cully to his feet, supported him, though he was having trouble moving about himself. The two men staggered toward the barracoon.

SIXTEEN

Once again Jubal made the long journey to New Orleans, under the same circumstances as before. The only change was that Shawn headed the much larger party. Six wagons and horses and twenty slaves followed the carriage in which Jubal rode beside Drill.

Jubal had recovered from the effects of his fight promptly, but Cully was still not able to work and his fractured jaw was being held in place by rags tightly binding it. There's been no more talk about other fights and Jubal still dreaded the thought of one.

In New Orleans, the slaves were turned loose with a dollar each. Drill preferred to stay with the carriage and Jubal promised to return and share it as sleeping quarters. As Murphy had wanted it, Shawn also had Jubal dress in his finery and accompany him wherever he went. Jubal walked a dozen steps behind his master and when Shawn entered a building, Jubal would seek out the slave bench, sit down and wait. This gave him time to think. More and more, he considered running. If he could reach St Louis, there might be some way there of proving that he was a free man. In Louisiana he might as well have been brought in on the last slave ship.

Shawn visited no cathouses, at least while Jubal was with him, and he kept very busy going about buying hogsheads and other supplies for the plantation. He talked at length with ship captains down at the docks so that there'd be room for the sugar to be carried north or to Europe.

Jubal thought, too, of the golden girl and how he was going to meet her. He needed a reasonable excuse, but he couldn't think of one. Murphy's visit had been so long ago that he couldn't use that. Nor could he use Murphy's name, for she'd be bound to tell him of it when he came again. Murphy would have cause to be angry then, and Jubal knew he'd be whipped until the flesh left his bones. Yet he had to see her, even if it meant taking great chances.

On Saturday night, Shawn left Jubal at the door and entered the Royal Palace Cafe where he was boisterously greeted by old friends. The corn liquor here was good, served in generous quantities, and there was a substantial free lunch so that Shawn settled down here for part of the evening.

He discussed horses, whores, wenches and sugar, in that order. The horse racing was extremely popular, the whores were an everyday matter, but interesting nonetheless, the mulattoes were a source of gossip and sugar had become one of the staple industries of New Orleans, so the talk concerning it involved everyone there.

After a while, and several potently large glasses of whiskey, someone mentioned the fight held at Briarfield Plantation.

'Mighty good fight,' one of those who had witnessed it remarked, 'but whyn't that big buck kill the other'n? Had him down real good. Craved to see him twist his head and bust his damn neck, or bite off his nose. Saw a buck fighting-man eat the ear off one man last year. Just got it 'tween his teeth and *snap* – the ear was off. Told me later he swallowed the dang thing, but I don't believe it. They were just trying to build up his reputation.'

'Too many ladies present,' Shawn explained. 'Wasn't like a regular city fight where you pay to see it. My daddy told them two bucks not to kill one another, but to fight until one couldn't fight anymore.'

'That's sure what they did, Shawn,' one man said. 'Like that buck. Looks smarter'n most of 'em and the way he fights makes me think he ain't no ordinary nigger.'

'That's what he is,' Shawn said. 'Just an ordinary nigger.'

'Then why don't you fight him against my boy?' another voice asked.

Shawn looked around lazily. Devol had been seated at a table close by all the while. He'd been drinking too; his face was flushed and his manner aggressive.

Shawn sipped his drink slowly, looking at Devol over the top of the glass. 'I haven't had the honor of making your acquaintance,' he said, though he knew very well who Devol was.

'I'm Devol, and I own the best fighting nigger in Louisiana, bar none.'

'You own the second best,' Shawn taunted him.

'I'd be willing to bet the whole purse on my boy, Mr Thibault.'

'And if it was my place to take you up on that, Mr Devol, I'd do so right now. But the slave belongs to my father and if he does not wish to fight him, that's his business. If you know my father, you know no one makes any arrangements for him.'

'I don't reckon he'd make a big fuss, you let your nigger fight my boy.'

Shawn exploded a large laugh. 'You don't know my daddy.'

'Seems like I do. Seems like I challenged him and he backed off right fast, suh. Got him wrote down he's a coward, comes to risking his boy.'

Shawn said, 'Say that again, Mr Devol, and I'll put on a little fight right here for the benefit of my friends and yours. Only it won't be our niggers doing the fighting, but you and me, suh.'

Devol was pink with anger and the embarrassment of knowing he'd never have the nerve to fight this man, and also knowing that all his friends were quite aware of it.

'I didn't call your daddy a coward all ways, Mr Thibault.' He was temporising now. 'Only where it comes to risking his nigger 'gainst mine. Don't mean to be disrespectful 'cept in a sporting sort of way.'

'You just saved yourself some busted bones,' Shawn said with a grin.

'I'm a sporting man myself,' Devol went on. 'That's why I want to find the best opposition there is for my boy. But I can't make anybody fight their slave against mine. I'll be honored to buy a gentleman like you a drink, suh.'

'No, thanks,' Shawn said. 'I'm not drinking your whiskey, Mr Devol.'

Shawn turned his back on the man, quietly seething with rage. Had Devol persisted, he might have gotten his boy a fight tonight. Shawn was sure Jubal would win. He thought better of this mad compulsion and settled down to his drinking.

By eleven o'clock, he was unsteady on his feet. Devol had wisely departed before Shawn became too drunk and, perhaps, belligerent. Devol thought he'd taunted him enough anyway. If Shawn could persuade his father to let Jubal fight, there would probably be the largest audience ever assembled in New Orleans.

Jubal jumped to his feet when Shawn swayed and reeled out of the cafe. He moved up to him, but Shawn waved him back with a muttered imprecation. Jubal fell in behind, ever watchful that Shawn didn't trip and fall. They were proceeding toward Basin Street and Jubal wondered if Shawn was going to follow in the steps of his father and head for one of the bawdy houses.

They had almost reached the area when Shawn pulled himself up and ceased staggering. He summoned Jubal with a crook of his finger.

'Don't need you no more tonight, Jubal. Tomorrow I'm going to sleep late so you don't have to come for me until evening. Gave you ten dollars, now go and enjoy it.'

'Yes, suh, masta, suh,' Jubal said. He should feel elated, but he wasn't.

Shawn made waving motions. 'All right, go away. I said I didn't need you anymore tonight. Go on. Find some of your own kind. Must be a wench you can get for less than ten dollars.'

'Yes, suh,' Jubal managed to grin broadly. 'Reckon that's whut I does, suh.'

'Be at the hotel about six tomorrow night.'

'I be there, suh.'

Shawn left him and began walking rapidly away. Jubal watched him for a moment and then frowned. He was heading in the same direction Jubal had intended to take. He meant to haunt the neighborhood where that golden-skinned girl lived, on the bare chance that he might see her. If Shawn ever spotted him there, and told his father, there'd be something to explain which Jubal wouldn't be capable of. He decided to take a roundabout route.

Moving fast, in a half-run at times, Jubal darted down one of the side streets and finally emerged to a point opposite where the girl lived. He was in time to see, with a sinking heart, a man standing before her door. Just as Murphy Thibault had done there on the railed balcony.

The door opened. Jubal saw her again and marveled at the perfection of her. She was lighter of skin than he thought. He wasn't paying any attention to the man – except for a momentary urge to kill him – because the girl attracted him so.

She opened her arms to the man and he enveloped her in a great hug before he kissed her. As he entered the room, the light shone well on his face and Jubal recognised Shawn. This was where he'd come. To the same girl his father favored. Jubal wondered if either one of them was aware of this.

Jubal felt as if he'd just been lashed. His soaring spirits shrank to nothing. What chance would he have with a girl who favored his master and his master's son? She'd certainly not be attracted to a buck like him. And maybe it was just as well. If she spent the night with father and son, she was nothing more than a common whore. Not that Jubal minded it so much, except that she was sleeping with two men he not only served, but actually liked. He turned away and New Orleans became a dreary, unwelcome place.

He made his way slowly back to the stables. Drill was already curled up in the front seat, snoring lustily in a drunken sleep. An empty bottle lay beside him.

Jubal removed his fancy clothes, folded them neatly, settled himself in the back seat with a blanket for cover and tried to go to sleep. All he could think about was that girl – nude, every inch of her lovely body under Shawn's caresses, under his body, filled with his tumescence. Responding to him, returning his kisses, spreading her legs to accommodate him, and returning his passion with a fervor to be expected of her.

That night Jubal really considered running. He still had the ten dollars. He could sell his clothes for two or three dollars more. He might be able to slip aboard a river boat or, better yet, a schooner on her way to the open sea.

Of course if he was discovered on the schooner, they'd simply throw him overboard. If they caught him on a riverboat, they'd turn him in for the usual cash reward. If he merely ran for the bayou country, the dog packs could be sniffing his trail tomorrow and they'd find him. Very few slaves ever escaped, though many were never seen again, for they died somewhere along the route to safety.

In the morning, quite late, Jubal awoke. Drill was already gone – to where he had no idea. Jubal kept the blanket wrapped around him, went to the stable through where the blacksmith dipped his red-hot irons, and washed himself thoroughly. He took time to shave because he must look neat when he met Shawn. He hoped he wouldn't show any of the resentment he felt toward his younger master.

There was the whole day to spend, however, and he had money. Of course he'd buy Calinda her new dress, but that shouldn't cost more than three dollars, so he had plenty left. The thing to do, he made up his mind, was to find a wench and take her to bed. At least the day wouldn't be wasted.

He wandered out of the stable and was instantly attracted by the sound of what must be strange drums. He followed the noise and noticed that the streets were full of slaves, all dressed in their finest, all heading in the same direction, toward the sound of the drums.

There were fancy carriages too, some bearing white folks, others beautiful mustees in silks, big hats and parasols, with black coachmen. Soon Jubal was part of the parade, but until he reached the spot where the drums originated, he had no idea what was going on.

Then he remembered someone had mentioned Congo Square and this was it. Each Sunday the slaves were allowed to congregate here and sing and dance. Jubal became interested. The bucks were dressed in their masters' cast-off clothing, mended and pressed, and the slaves could be proud of the way they looked. The wenches wore dotted calicoes with Madras kerchiefs in riotous colors tied about their heads to form a popular slash of fashion known as the tignon.

Children, just as colorfully dressed, scampered about everywhere. In the center of the large cleared area were the drummers. Their instruments consisted of vats and kegs, upended. Their drumsticks were enormous beef bones. Along the sidewalk, tables had been set up, screened from the sunlight by awnings. They were laden with pies, cakes, ginger beer and lemonade, offered for pennies.

The dancing began promptly and Jubal found himself a favorable spot where he could stand and watch. The men pranced. Little bells attached to their wrists and ankles tinkled merrily. The women chanted with a frenzied zeal and the wenches, engaged in the dancing, swayed and moved without lifting their feet from the ground.

The drums grew louder. Soon the square was a mass of dancing, stamping, squirming black bodies. Some of the men shouted, '*Dansez Bamboula! Dansez Bamboula!*'

'They are saying that they dance the Bamboula,' a gentle voice breathed in Jubal's ear. He turned his head and a dizziness took possession of him so that he was tongue-tied, his stomach churning into a knot.

The golden girl was beside him, smiling at him. She barely came to his shoulder and while he knew she was lovely, he didn't expect her to be this outrageously beautiful.

'The dance is from the Congo Plains in Africa,' she said. 'The Creoles call it the Bamboula.'

'Missy . . . I thanks you. Was wonderin' whut . . . whut. . . .'

'Go on, Jubal,' she urged. 'What were you going to say?'

He was more dumbfounded than ever. 'You knows me, missy? Knows my name, you does?'

'Of course I do. You are the slave of . . . of . . . some friends of mine.'

'How did you know me?' Jubal asked.

'Mr Murphy Thibault saw you from my window. You'd followed him, and he was very proud of the fact that you did because he was . . . shall we say . . . somewhat inebriated? And you were protecting him, even though he had ordered you to go to the stables and get some sleep.'

'Din' know he saw me, Missy. Don' rightly know whut to say.'

'Let me explain about Congo Square,' she said. She spoke perfect English and in a warm, mellow little voice. 'It was decided some years ago that the New Orleans slaves were being treated too harshly. In those days the ships brought them here from Africa and they were sold right after they got off the boat. They were chained in long rows, with iron collars around their necks and their ankles fastened by more chains. That's how they were put to work. But many of them died under this treatment and gradually the owners realised that when a slave died from neglect or overwork, they lost a great deal of money. So they decided not to be so harsh.'

'You knows all this?' Jubal marveled.

'I've attended the Catholic schools and the nuns have taught me well, Jubal. Nowadays, Sunday is the day of leisure and the slaves have nothing to do so they often got into trouble. That's how Congo Square began. The police allowed them to congregate here, to dance and sing, and find whatever entertainment they could. At sundown, it all stops for another week, but these people do love it so.'

'Yes, missy,' Jubal said.

'My name is Marcy Fournet. You do not have to call me "Missy". I'm a Negro too.'

'But you ain't a slave?'

'No. I'm free. I'm called a person of color, because I'm not black. But you aren't either.'

'I'se a nigger,' Jubal said cheerfully. 'That's whut I is and it don' rile me none.'

'Good. I'm glad to hear you say that. Jubal, would you like to come to my little home? I'd be glad to serve you tea and I have made some very nice little cakes.'

'Missy . . . Miss Fournet,' Jubal said. 'Wouldn't be right.'

'Of course it would. You work for my friends. I like the way you serve them, so you're my friend too. If I was white, I couldn't say that, but I can to you. And I'm not so dark I can't say friend to some white people too. I have it rather pleasant – compared to you.'

'Likes to call on you, Miss Fournet,' Jubal said, holding down his eagerness.

'Then you may meet me there. I'm sorry I can't allow you to ride with me. That's against the rules. But I'll be very glad to see you.'

He could only nod. She twirled her little pink parasol and moved away from him. He trailed behind her at some distance until he saw her summon a barouche driven by a mulatto, who jumped down to help her into the seat, and treated her with the greatest respect. Apparently Murphy Thibault had given her the barouche and paid the driver.

Jubal made his way into what was now a fairly familiar area. When he reached the house, the barouche was pulling away, so the girl must already be in her apartment. Jubal walked slowly toward the stairs. He'd seen Murphy Thibault go up them, then Shawn. Now it was his turn, but while he didn't question but that their maleness grew in them with each step as they drew nearer and nearer to this unusually and extraordinarily beautiful girl, his desire remained sexually dormant.

He judged her age as about eighteen or nineteen. She had soft brown eyes, as he knew she would. Her lips were straight and without the fullness of at least part of her ancestors. Her nose wasn't flat nor flared out. She had straight hair, a medium shade of brown with no kinkiness. Except for the golden hue of her skin, she could have easily passed as white.

When he knocked, she let him in and he found himself in a small but very colorful and pleasant parlor. He hadn't been in a room like this since he lived up north.

The furniture was fragile-looking, with curved backs and legs, and covered with pale material into which designs had been embroidered. There was a yellow carpet on the floor, the walls were painted the same shade. The fireplace mantel was of white painted wood. Lamps with colorful shades were on every table.

'Please sit down,' she said. 'Relax, Jubal. When you're in my little home, you're not a slave, but a good and kind friend.'

'Thank you,' he said. 'Ain't never been treated this way befo'.'

'I know. If it wasn't for those friends of ours, I'd be on some plantation too, working for a master who might be very kind and who might be very cruel. That's why I know how lucky I am.'

'Yes'm.' Jubal cursed his inability to talk to her.

'Mister Shawn told me you fought a man last week and you refused to kill him, as the crowd called for.'

'Ain't a killin' man,' he said simply.

'I'm very glad of that. I'll see if the water for tea is ready.'

She left him and he could hear her fussing about the kitchen at the rear. Jubal was possessed of a sinking sensation. This girl was so far above him he wondered why she'd bothered to speak to him. She'd prostituted her body to get here, but to Jubal that was of little consequence. She was well-educated. He was too, but he didn't dare reveal that even to her. Women in bed, in the heat of passion, sometimes talk too much. His secret wouldn't be safe with her.

The teacup was lost in his massive hand, but he knew how to drink from it. His mother had taught him that. And he accepted one of the little pink frosted cakes and ate it with a fork. He knew how to do that too.

'Tell me about yourself, Jubal,' she said.

He still found it difficult to address her and, seated across from her, watching her smile, relishing her graceful movements, seeing the rise and fall of her breasts, his maleness began to react. He found it necessary to press his thighs hard against one another lest his desire show. He wanted this unattainable girl more than he'd ever wanted anyone in his life. He wanted to rise up now, take her in his arms, move her to the bedroom which would be close by. He needed her, his passion was all but impossible to control and yet he knew she would never be his.

She was too fragile, too beautiful, too young, and too far above him. He might reach for her, but his arms would never be long enough. He might dream of her and possibly his dreams would be lewd, but he would never lay a hand on her. She belonged to others. She was more his color than she was white, but she'd given herself to the Thibaults, who were his masters. As a slave, he shouldn't be here at all, though Marcy seemed to think it only a friendly gesture. She trusted him – and he didn't think she should – but if Murphy or Shawn found out he'd been here, they'd set him to work in the fields and drive him until he was dead.

He set the cup and saucer down very carefully on the little table beside him. He arose, rather precipitously because he felt smothered, and he wanted to get out of here.

'Gots to go now, Miss Fournet. I thanks you fo' the tea an' the cake. Never tasted anythin' so good in all my whole life. Got to go now. Please . . . you understan'?'

'Yes,' she said. 'I understand. Of course I do. Please come to see me again, and take good care of my friends.'

'Yes'm, Miss Fournet. I takes mighty good care of 'em, I does.' He managed a flash of a smile. 'Fo' you I does.'

She smiled and nodded and held the door for him. He felt like a clumsy fool on his way out. He knew he was bulging in the crotch and he prayed she hadn't noticed. He had a savage need to rid himself of this desire, this overwhelming urge, for fear it might get the better of his judgment and he'd go back.

He tried to walk casually until he was out of her sight and then he began running, but that wasn't good either, because a running slave was apt to be stopped and questioned. He had no time for that.

Back at Congo Square, he sidled up to the first good-looking wench he found. In a matter of minutes, she was holding his hand and pressed against him. He mentioned money, she smiled wider, and led him to a rattrap of a place and a room with nothing but a bed in it.

He hastily removed his pants and shirt while she sat on the edge of the bed watching him with growing interest. When he was naked, he moved up to her. She grasped his testicles with both hands and tugged gently. He pushed her on her back and straddled her. Without preamble or a word spoken, he entered her angrily, forcefully and she cried out. He slapped a hand over her mouth and raised and lowered his body, jamming into her with each savage, raging thrust until he felt his drive sated and his sap run out.

He dressed quickly, threw a dollar on the bed and walked out. He was in a mood to kill someone.

SEVENTEEN

Returning to Briarfield, Jubal found the plantation in the full swing of harvest. Smoke billowed out of the chimneys of the sugar house. Relays of slaves carried wood for the great fires beneath the banks of kettles. Carts, piled high with cane, trundled out of the fields to the sugar house where the load was transferred to the gravity-fed chute which led to the giant rollers.

'A great harvest,' Murphy Thibault boasted to his son. 'You brought back the new hogsheads just in time, and I'm pleased you got plenty of 'em.'

'There's enough.'

'Take charge of the sugar house while I get the niggers hopping in the fields. Night's getting pretty cold and we got to get the crop in before frost.'

Jubal was given the task of supervising one whole area of field work, while Mason took another and Murphy kept moving to oversee it all. No one minded the work. A bumper crop and many filled hogsheads meant time off, free from all work around Christmas time. It meant new clothing for everyone, extra rations of food, maybe seed for the little half-acre farms each family was allowed to plant. And there was always a bonus in cash, sometimes as high as four dollars a head. Dancing was permitted every night and drinking tafia was overlooked.

Jubal appreciated the hard, eighteen-hour-a-day work because it kept him from thinking. He'd been in a continuous turmoil even since he'd walked out of Marcy Fournet's little apartment. He wanted her; he was afraid of her; he dreaded Murphy or Shawn finding out. He kept thinking of running, even though it was a futile idea that would get him nothing but a rope around his neck.

Life on the plantation was no longer pleasant for him. The other slaves were beginning to regard him as a pet of the Thibaults. He'd been given oversee work with power to whip a lazy or rebellious slave if he thought it necessary. Therefore they feared him and mistrusted him. Only Calinda remained constant. She knew he was not a pet, but favored only because he was more capable than the others. She sensed also that there was another woman involved, for Jubal had a habit of talking in his sleep when he was dead tired and he'd been muttering the word Marcy since he'd come back from New Orleans. Calinda knew better than to ask him who Marcy was. He'd never questioned her again about her pleasuring Miss Pauline. If he suspected, he gave no hint of it.

On the third day of the harvest, things were progressing too well. There should have been at least one hitch, according to Shawn.

'Way I figure it,' he told his father, 'we stand to make thirty thousand profit this year. Indigo never paid this well.'

'Neither did rice, and cotton markets are down, so we picked the right one this time, Shawn. If we get it all in. Got the same feeling you have, everything's too good.'

The first hint of trouble came in midmorning of the fourth day. The sky turned very dark in the south. Over the Gulf of Mexico a storm was building. It wasn't unusual at this season. A little rain – even a great deal of it – wouldn't harm this crop. Only frost could ruin it. Rain wasn't frost.

Shawn was growing worried. He and his father were seated on a rail fence eating out of paper sacks, food sent down from the big house.

'Wind's coming up,' he observed. 'Look at the cedars. The tops of 'em.'

Murphy nodded. 'Been watching 'em. Think it'll be a howler?'

'Sky's awful dark, wind ain't dying off and if you notice, it's kinda quiet. You know the kind I mean. Seems like everything just died.'

Murphy nodded. 'Take a mighty big blow to put us out of business, son. Haven't seen one big as that in years. We'll just keep working.'

By four in the afternoon, it was as dark as it usually was at eight. The sky overhead was a deep gray, turning darker. In the south it was black as pitch. The tops of the cedars weren't merely moving, they were bending over, and the wind was whistling wildly. Slaves kept eyeing the sky, fearful of a great lightning storm, but there wasn't even any thunder.

At four-thirty the rain began. Ten minutes later, they knew they were in the edges of a hurricane and it threatened to be a bad one. When the rain became so heavy work was impossible, the slaves were sent to their quarters. Horses, cattle, pigs and sheep were quickly rounded up and confined to the barns. Chicken houses were battened down.

At the mansion, blinds were swung over the windows and fastened. All available pieces of old cloth were gathered up because they knew how this storm, at its peak, would filter rain through any crevice and flood the house out unless the water was promptly mopped up. Plenty of slaves stood ready.

Murphy was worried for the first time. This was no ordinary howler. It was a full-blown hurricane, a tempest that could flatten houses, destroy crops, cause bayous to overflow their banks and flood out everything within their range. Trees could be blown down, roofs torn off. Slave cabins, flimsily built, were sometimes picked up and thrown for yards.

'Reckon we best get ready for trouble,' Murphy said. 'I'll stay here and do what I can about the sugar house. You get back to the main house and help there. Send Jubal to see to the stables and the animals. Have him send all the niggers to their cabins and the barracoons. I want everything nailed down tight as they can get it.'

Murphy made a fast inspection of the sugar house, ordering the fire drenched with water so if the building was damaged there'd be no chance of fire. The wide double doors were closed, though it required four strong bucks to swing them in the teeth of the gale.

There was a bricked archway entrance through which the cane was brought to the press. There was no door on this so Murphy had hogsheads piled up to keep out the rain. The first gust of wind blew them down and back, sending the empty ones rolling about wildly.

Shawn stepped into the open on his way to find Jubal and then go to the main house. The wind took his breath away and he had to turn his back to it so he might breathe again. He hunched his shoulders and plowed through the storm as if it had substance and could check his movements.

He found Jubal herding the field workers toward the cabins. The rain made their thin cotton pants cling limply to their black skins. Their eyes rolled whitely in terror. Some of the newer slaves had never seen anything like this before. Those who had were equally terrified, because they knew what a storm like this could do.

Shawn shouted orders into Jubal's ear. 'Soon as you get the field clear, see to the barns and stables. Keep the animals quiet if you can.'

'Yes, suh,' Jubal replied. 'Goes there right now, suh.'

Shawn left him and sprinted toward the house. On his way, there was another of those strange lulls that sometimes occur before a hurricane is at its fullest fury. The wind died down to a mere gale and the wild shrieking of the trees was reduced to loud wails, as if the limbs and leaves were alive. Shawn was able to breathe normally and his aching lungs gratefully responded to the full supply of oxygen. He slowed down to a trot, looking skyward occasionally, and praying the storm would somehow veer off. He knew, however, that the apex of it had not even been reached, and when it came, this would likely be the worst one ever experienced here.

He was able to see some of the cane fields on his way. The stalks had already been flattened. He knew then that this bumper crop was going to be completely destroyed. A whim of the weather was going to snatch from Briarfield all the profits which should come to it from a season of hard work. He groaned and as the wind picked up, he began running again.

The rain was getting heavier, changing from drops to sheets of wetness because of the wind. He shouted for someone to get the door opened as he neared it, but he couldn't hear his own words.

They'd seen him and Ann Thibault pulled the door open, let him through and then slammed it shut once more. House servants quickly pushed wads of old cloths against the base of the door and jammed additional strips into the crevices around the door.

'Is Murphy all right?' Ann asked.

'He's fine, Mama. Don't worry about him. The sugar house is built like a fort. Better than this house.'

'How bad is it, Shawn?'

'Cane's already busted and lying down. This water will flood the fields, wash most cane out, rot what's left. We got some in the sugar house – maybe ten percent. We'll be lucky if that doesn't get washed out too.'

'It's the evil in this place,' Ann said. 'I've prayed, but prayers do no good when there's this much sin and evil.'

'Don't say things like that,' Shawn begged. 'This is just a storm. Ain't just Briarfield getting lambasted by it, but everything else in this part of Louisiana. Mama, will you take charge upstairs and see the windows are tight with rags, and any water that comes in gets mopped up fast?'

'Yes,' she said. 'Yes, I'll do my best, but I still say the way things have happened here, it's a wonder to me something like this didn't come about long ago.'

'Yes, Mama,' Shawn said, his mind already on something else. He sped into the kitchen where Big and Little Harp were seated on specially constructed low stools. Each had an enormous plate of food in her lap and they were industriously devouring everything on them.

'We dies,' Big Harp said candidly, 'we dies pleasurin' us by eatin', masta, suh.'

'You get your fat tails out of there and see that the doors don't leak and the windows stay tight.'

They lumbered to their feet, grumbling, but obeying. Until he left the kitchen. Then they resumed the stools and the food. Shawn rushed into the ballroom where the tall windows presented the most difficult problem, for they were not equipped with blinds.

Pauline had mustered half a dozen maids and two houseboys and had them carrying furniture out of the ballroom into another part of the house which was less apt to admit the storm. Already the tall glass doors were beginning to hammer and bulge while the drapes fluttered wildly into the room.

'Is everyone all right?' She had to shout, for the wind was now even stronger and louder.

'So far. Pa's in the sugar house. Jubal's down at the stables with the animals. Ma's upstairs. This is a good idea, getting everything out of here because in a couple of minutes those windows are going to cave in.'

'I can manage here,' Pauline said.

Shawn raced to the other side of the house to inspect windows and doors. Pauline stood in the middle of the ballroom. Her face was contorted, not by fear, but by some direct tie with the storm. The wildness outside was matched by that within her. She wanted something. She knew what it was and the urge was growing irresistible. Inspired by the screaming of the storm, fostered by the opportunity it offered, fired by an obsession she seemed unable to resist.

There was a great crash and one of the doors flew open, its glass shattered. Drapes were ripped free to fall in a sodden mass. Another door burst open. Pauline was drenched in seconds. Her carefully coiffed hair was matted and strands were plastered against her face and throat. She began moving forward, slowly at first, toward one of the open windows. At the same time, she took down her hair and let the wind and rain have their way with it.

The force of the gale arched her body back, but she kept advancing in the fury of it. She reached the outside. The limb of a tree sailed through the air and hit the side of the house not far from where she was, but she paid no attention to it. She should have been terrified, but the power that made her go out into this holocaust of wind, rain and confusion was stronger than terror.

She reached the cleared lawn and began to run. There were times when she tried to take a step forward only to be forced to step backwards by the wind She could see the barns now. They appeared dimly out of the haze caused by the gusts. She reached one of them and managed to get the smaller door open. She looked inside. Cattle were milling about, bellowing their terror. She closed the door and went to the next barn.

Here were the horses, reasonably calm so far, because Jubal was there, moving up and down the row of stalls, comforting them, talking to them. When the door opened, he whirled about as if he thought it had been torn from its hinges. He saw Pauline standing there, a slim figure, clothing plastered against her body, revealing every feminine outline. Hair matted, face dripping with moisture.

He couldn't believe it, but there she was, standing before him with her slender arms outstretched. Suddenly the fury of the storm was in his soul too. He advanced toward her, knowing very well what she wanted and what he was going to do. It was a flogging-hanging offense, but he could no more help himself than she could.

There wasn't a word spoken. She reached down, grasped the hem of her skirt and pulled it up over her head. She managed to free herself of it and then she pulled down the white, frilly pantalets and stepped out of them. She moved toward him, slowly at first and then all but launched herself at him.

He met her halfway, his arms went around her as he pulled her to him. She cried out once but the pain of that embrace was ecstasy to her. She could feel his genitals against her nude body, feel them grow and her breathing seemed to match the storm.

His hand slipped between her legs and she spread them to give him more room. She grasped a breast, lifted it and offered it to him. His mouth enclosed it. His hand found a firm purchase on her buttocks He tipped her further back, then lifted her off her feet. She grabbed him around the neck, sank teeth into the flesh behind his ear. He gloried in the pain. He carried her to a mound of straw and laid her down gently. Then he stripped off his wet shirt, pulled down his soaked trousers and got out of them.

He lay down beside her and she stroked him until his maleness was at its hardest and heaviest. His fingers were already investigating the white sweetness of her flesh and the warmth of the orifice she was now offering to him.

She moaned and lay back, with legs outstretched and knees bent. Her eyes beseeched him, her abdomen gyrated, her hips rose and fell, then her body arched high and she rubbed her pubic hair against his chin. His tongue flicked out and plunged deep inside her. She moaned with pleasure, moving her body, pleasuring herself with his tongue, then suddenly pushed her head back. Jubal felt a momentary rage which quickly subsided, for she flipped over and while her hands stroked his testicles, her mouth enclosed his penis. She rolled her tongue around it, teased its fleshy tip and tried to get the entire organ in her mouth, gagging as it started down her throat. Jubal could stand no more. He withdrew his organ, forced her back and mounted her. She was ready, for she guided it inside her. From that instant, they were one. Flesh seeking flesh, passion hungering for the other's passion. Bodies flailing in unison, their shouts and moans drowned out by the storm. With each thrust, she answered with a violence of her own until, finally, they were both spent completely and lay still.

Jubal pulled himself free of her. He was dripping with perspiration. The horses were beginning to move restlessly, and the storm, he suddenly realised, was even worse. He managed to pull on his soggy pants, but he didn't bother with the shirt.

Pauline slipped into her sodden dress, pulled her hair, hanging in a sodden mass, free of it. Her hands moved down, pressed hard against her groin, as if her passion were rising again and she was doing her best to quell it.

She took a deep breath, dropped her hands to her sides, made fists of them. She exhaled slowly and regarded Jubal, who was stroking the muzzle of a horse which was whinnying nervously, whether from their antics or the storm, Jubal didn't know. Pauline walked up to him, raised her right fist and struck him across the face as hard as she could.

Then she walked out, leaving the door open. Jubal closed his eyes and shuddered. He brought both hands to his face. He wanted to lie down and weep. He wanted Calinda to comfort him. He wanted Marcy's tenderness and understanding. He had violated a white woman. That she had come to him, that she had seduced him, had no meaning, no point. He was the one who had entered her. It was his fault, for she could not have raped him. He didn't know if she'd tell anyone. If she did, he was done for.

The horses were nervous again because the door was open. Jubal walked to it, closed it, rolled two big bales of hay in front of it and then went back to his task of calming the animals.

He wished there was some way he could calm himself. The storm in his brain, the fury in his heart, outmatched the storm around him. It was stronger and more terrifying than that gale, because it would never abate. It would stay with him as long as he lived.

He was the clever one, he thought. He was the educated black impounded into slavery, but unworried because he could out-think his oppressors. And here he was, guilty of raping a white woman. Guilty of taking her to his loins and venting his passion upon her.

Where it was going to end he didn't know, but his mind was made up now. He was going to run. There was no help for it. If he remained here, she'd come to him again and again. They were bound to be discovered, and when that happened, she would have but a single recourse – that of accusing him of taking her by force. No matter what he said, no matter how well educated he was, and how loudly he said it, he'd not be believed. He was a dead man now. There was already a noose about his neck. He shuddered and lay down on that same bed of straw and wept in sheer frustration.

EIGHTEEN

Murphy Thibault stood beside the sugar house and surveyed what was left of his plantation. The cane fields were flooded, not a stalk remained standing, and there was no way to salvage the stalks which had sunk into the mud. Part of the sugar house roof had been blown away, the chimneys were down, and the interior was awash. Behind the sugar house, the moist ditch nobody had nerve to call a bayou was a raging torrent of water, floating masses of cane stalks like giant rafts.

Half the slave cabins had been damaged, some severely. In one barracoon the roof had fallen in and a score of slaves were being treated for cuts, bruises and broken bones. Nobody had been killed; none of the whites even scratched. Not physically. Inwardly they'd been torn to shreds.

Shawn, hollow-eyed and gaunt, stumbled up beside his father to survey the desolation. 'Not much left,' he said.

'Nothing left. Not one damn thing worth counting.'

'Got any ideas?'

'One. Just one.'

Shawn nodded. 'I got that one too.'

'There's no way to clean this up without money. No way to make repairs, no way to feed hundreds of slaves, to say nothing of ourselves. No way to get a crop planted. We haven't even got seed cane. Have to buy it. Won't be a crop for more'n a year, and that leaves us high and dry.'

'Jubal?' Shawn asked.

'That's all there is. I stayed awake most of the night, after the damned storm went off, thinking about it. What else is there to do? No bank is going to loan us money on what's left of this plantation. We'll be lucky they don't foreclose on the mortgages they hold now. We have to have money.'

'I know, Pa.'

'Well, why not Jubal? He's just a nigger. A slave! I paid a high price for him. He belongs to me. He does what I say, or I can flog him, or hang him. Work him to death. Makes no difference. If I say he fights Devol's buck, he'll fight him, or I'll kill him.'

'Devol's buck's a mighty powerful fighter, Pa.'

'I know that,' he conceded irritably.

'Likely Jubal gets himself killed and loses the fight.'

'We have to take that chance. There's no betting – yet. The winner simply picks up all the money paid to see the fight. I'd roughly estimate we should get between twenty and thirty thousand dollars.'

'So much?' Shawn marveled.

'Devol often gets as high as a hundred dollars a person. He suggested we hold it at the slave auction yard and that will accommodate several hundred people.'

'Think Jubal will fight?'

'Think? He'll fight or I'll hide him until he'll be worse off than at the hands of Devol's boy. Shawn, he's a slave. He does what he's told.'

'Including dying?'

'Including that. He can live if he fights well. Somebody is going to whip Devol's boy one day. It could be Jubal. You saw how he handled himself at the fight we staged here. The man he fought is still sick. Jubal could have killed him easy if . . . if he'd been allowed to.'

'Drat women,' Shawn said.

'Drat some women,' Murphy corrected him.

'What you want me to do, Pa?'

'I want you to ride to New Orleans today. Put it up to Devol. Don't say anything about what happened here from the storm. If he thinks we need the fight, his terms will get stiffer. Right now he wants the fight because it'll increase his prestige. Goad him into asking you again. Don't be in any hurry, play him along and when you make the deal, be sure as many people as possible hear you do it. Devol will advantage himself under any circumstances, and if he gets the best of me, I'll surely have to kill him.'

'I'll take a fast horse and go alone,' Shawn said.

'I won't tell Jubal until you get back.'

'That's best. Sometimes I think he's got the look of a runner in him, Pa.'

'I know. Seen it too. Go on now. Sooner you get started, the faster we can get this over with.'

Shawn passed Jubal on his way to the house. Jubal greeted him by whipping off his cap and bowing slightly. Then he continued on to face Murphy.

'Masta, suh, don't rightly know whut to do. Gots to clean up 'round heah, but whar does I start, masta, suh?'

'With the fields. Help Mr Mason get all hands working to clean everything up. We can't plant until early next year and I have to get the seed, but it'll take time to get the fields in order.'

'Yes, suh, masta, suh.'

'Is there anything else?' Murphy demanded, when Jubal didn't move.

'Whut you goin' to do, masta, suh? Knows there ain't nothin' lef'. Whut you goin' to do?'

'Start again. That's all I can do. Get busy, will you?'

'Yes, suh, right away, suh.'

Jubal hurried to round up the slaves. He was tired. He hadn't slept well and thought he might never sleep well again. He also had a premonition of something evil. He never questioned but that it had to do with Miss Pauline, because he'd broken no other rules.

He set the men to work. Mason cooperated with him, having accepted him as his first assistant, and happy to be able to pass off the more arduous tasks to him. The hours went by. Jubal knew that Shawn had gone to New Orleans and he wondered if it had anything to do with Marcy Fournet. He decided nothing could have happened there to betray him, and that Shawn was more likely looking for fresh supplies and some seed cane. The journey could be for no other purpose than that.

Twice he'd passed Miss Pauline, each time doffing his cap and bowing. She recognised him with a cool nod and a word or two. He was beginning to think that matter would straighten itself out as if it had never happened. Unless she wanted more. Not that he was averse to satisfying her, but the chances grew more dangerous every time, so he decided to stay out of her way as much as possible and if she was about, make certain he was not alone.

It was five days later when Kip ran down to the slave quarters and pushed open the door to Jubal's and Calinda's cabin.

'Masta say – ' he began.

Jubal grabbed him and lifted him with one hand. 'Nex' time you busts in heah like that, I wrings you scrawny li'l neck, Kip. On'y white masta kin bust in like that an' you knows it.'

'Masta say – ' Kip squirmed hard to free himself and Jubal let go.

'Well, whut he say?'

'You comes runnin' right now, Jubal. He say you come quick or he cuts you balls clean off.'

Calinda raised her big cooking spoon in a threatening gesture. 'Get outen heah, Kip. Talkin' like that. Go 'long. Git!'

Kip left, but he waited for Jubal outside. They walked to the big house together, Kip insisting he didn't know what it was about. Nor did Jubal, and he was deeply worried.

If Miss Pauline had said anything about the incident during the storm, this is how things would happen. He'd be called to the big house first, and questioned. Later he'd be whipped and if it was proven he raped a white woman, he'd be hanged without a further trial.

Murphy and Shawn were alone in the small parlor. Jubal cast a wary eye out for Miss Pauline, but she was not present. Jubal stood before the two men, the old and the young Thibault. He held his cap in both hands.

Murphy said, 'You put on a very good fight here, Jubal. We want you to fight again.'

Jubal shuddered. 'Masta, suh, I ain't a fightin' man. Sweahs I ain't.'

'You looked like one when you beat the ass off Cully,' Shawn said.

'Cully wasn't no bettah'n me, suh. We ain't fightin' men.'

'Jubal, next Saturday you'll be fighting in New Orleans.'

'Cain't, masta, suh.'

'You want a hiding, Jubal?' Murphy asked harshly.

'No, suh, masta, suh, don' want no hidin', but cain't fight. Cully, he busted me good and I hurts inside, I does.'

'You're a liar,' Shawn said. 'I watched you working during the storm. If you were busted inside, you couldn't have swung those fallen trees or toted hogsheads. You're in good shape and you can win the fight if you try real hard.'

'Who I fightin', masta, suh?'

'Mr Devol's buck.'

Jubal shook his head. 'I be daid, sho', masta, suh. You wants po' Jubal to be daid, suh?'

Shawn said, 'Better tell him what this is about, Pa. He's smarter'n most niggers. I think he'll understand.'

'I'm beginning to realise that.' Murphy looked up at Jubal. 'If you win the fight, we can keep the plantation with the money we'll win. If you do not fight, or you lose, there will be no plantation. All the slaves will be put on the vendue table within a month.'

Jubal wrung the cap until he heard the material give. 'Masta, suh, I fight that buck, I loses, and I be daid. Knows he strong an' he always kills. He kill me.'

'Not,' Shawn pointed out, 'if you kill him first.'

'Cain't,' Jubal half sobbed. 'Masta, suh, you whups me an' hangs me it don' make no mind 'cause Devol's boy he kills me I fights him. You wants him to kill me, Masta, suh?'

'If you're not strong enough and brave enough to stand up to him, it's all right with me if he kills you,' Murphy said coldly. 'Now, I'm not talking about this anymore. Friday morning we leave for New Orleans. Shawn goes at once to set this up. Saturday afternoon you fight that buck and you tear him to pieces. I want him killed, Jubal. I want him dead.'

Shawn said, 'If you win, Jubal, we'll write your manumitting papers. You'll be free in two, maybe three months.'

'You can stay right here and be overseer, and you'll get paid every week like Mr Mason. Or you can go off wherever you want. Ain't that worth fighting for?'

Jubal ached to say it wasn't much to promise a man born free that he would be given his papers of freedom. He knew there was nothing he could do to avoid this fight except run. He'd been gravitating toward it anyway. There was the golden girl – Marcy Fournet – whom he had visited and broken all rules, and would sooner or later possess. There was Miss Pauline, who had lain in his arms and received his seed. That was punishable by death, and Miss Pauline would someday talk about it, if for no other reason than to witness his hanging. He remembered the look on her face when the runaway slave was hung. She'd gloried in the whipping and in the hanging.

So he would run because there wasn't anything left for him to do except that. It made no difference now what he agreed to, because he hadn't the slightest intention of carrying out their orders.

'Masta, suh,' he said, 'I fights him.'

'Good,' Murphy exclaimed. 'That's fine. You won't be sorry if you win.'

'That's all, Jubal,' Shawn said.

Jubal bobbed his head. 'Yes, suh, masta, suh.'

He backed out of the room and fled. Shawn lit a cheroot. His hand shook slightly. 'Think he'll do it, Pa?'

'He'll do it or get killed right here.'

'He gets killed either way. Don't give him much of a chance.'

'If he's scared enough, he'll kill that Devol buck. A man fights best when he's scared.'

'You telling Mama about this?'

'Not her nor anybody else. We got troubles enough.'

'Jubal lets that buck kill him, we sure have, Pa. We got troubles, but we ain't got a plantation any more. That's something we can be sure of.'

'What the hell,' Murphy said angrily. 'All we're risking is one nigger. The stakes are worth it. If he gets killed, we're no worse off and there's always a chance he can win.'

'He'll have to be awful lucky, Pa. Seen Devol's buck fight more'n once. I don't think he can be whipped and Jubal sure ain't the one who can do it. If it's even possible.'

NINETEEN

Jubal, in his finery, rode beside Drill as the carriage ate away the miles to New Orleans. Behind them sat Murphy and Shawn, both drinking often enough to keep them from thinking too much. Jubal was, of course, cold sober and coldly planning his moves. During the days up to the time they left the plantation, he'd done nothing but think.

It would be easy if he had a moderate amount of luck on his side. They'd be in New Orleans tomorrow, right after noon. The fight wouldn't take place until evening, when the biggest crowd could be assembled. That meant he'd have from about two or three o'clock until six. Time enough.

He was going to visit Marcy and tell her exactly what was happening. He was going to beg her to go away with him. Getting out of New Orleans wouldn't be difficult. All she'd have to do was dismiss her coachman; Jubal would assume his identity and Marcy would go for a ride which would take them to the outskirts. There Jubal could whip up the horses and place as many miles as possible between the city and himself.

When he was discovered missing, there'd be a great search

begun, and it would be confined to the city itself until they were certain he was no longer there. Afoot, in his flight, he'd have no chance, but in a fast-moving barouche he could make it. Be so far away before the hunt began that they'd never catch up with him. He was rather proud that he'd thought this up. They were not going to get him.

If Marcy refused to go along, he'd beg her to let him use the barouche, to say he'd stolen it. A coachman driving an empty barouche was a commonplace sight. Either way he could make it, but he hoped Marcy would go with him.

But what if either Murphy or Shawn went to visit Marcy? He wouldn't be able to reach her then. However, they were bound to be at the scene of the fight long before it was scheduled. Therefore, he'd have a little time with her.

'Now, listen to me, Jubal,' Murphy said when they reached the city. 'This is an important fight for both of us and I want you in good form. You stay in the stable with Drill until we come for you. Don't eat anything and don't drink. If you touch any tafia or whiskey, you'll get yourself hided good. When it's time, put on an old shirt and pants. You'll have to shuck down for this one. No getting out of that. Be ready now.'

'Yes, suh, masta, suh,' Jubal said unhappily. 'I be's ready, suh.'

'If you win, you'll soon be a free man. Remember that,' Shawn said.

'Sho' will, masta, suh. I remembers.'

Drill drove the carriage to the stable. After the animals had been unhitched, watered and baited, he climbed back into the seat where Jubal had remained.

'When yo' starts runnin', Jubal?' Drill asked.

'Ain't runnin',' Jubal said. 'Ain't no sense runnin'. They fetches me back sure.'

'Whut's worse?' Drill asked. 'Hangin or gettin' yo' arms an' balls ripped off? Me, I runs an' takes my chances.'

'Got to do some thinkin',' Jubal said. 'Goin' to take me a walk.'

'Masta say yo' stay heah, Jubal.'

'Whut the difference? I gets killed anyways. I'm takin' a walk.'

'Don't blame you none. Got me a li'l bottle of tafia you' kin have. Keep you company, you runs.'

'Ain't runnin',' Jubal insisted. He swung down off the carriage and went out into the sunlight. He walked briskly, straight to the area where Marcy lived. He assumed that both Shawn and Murphy would be very busy spreading the word, and making bets, though Shawn should have done a good job of that during the days he'd already been in the city. At these last few hours before the fight, Jubal doubted they'd be visiting

Marcy. Their minds would be on matters more important than pestering her.

Jubal prowled about for many minutes before he risked the open approach to Marcy. There was no other way to do it, so he marched up the outside steps, down along the railed-in gallery and knocked on her door.

She admitted him at once, showing no astonishment, which meant Shawn had been here, likely bedding down with her, these last several days.

'Jubal,' she said, 'I'm very sorry for you. I wish there was some way I could arrange it that you not fight this man.'

'Shawn tol' you 'bout the fight?'

'Yes, he was here several times. Jubal, this man you're to fight – he's never lost. No opponent ever lived after the fight. He's dangerous. Oh, it's all wrong. They've no right to make you fight him.'

'Miss Marcy,' he said, 'I haven't time to beg nor to plead, only to explain. I have one alternative. I can run.'

'They'll catch you,' she warned.

'Yes, there's always that chance, but I have to take it.'

'The plantation – it will be ruined.'

'If I lose the fight, it will be ruined anyway, but I'll be ruined too. I don't believe they think of that. Neither Murphy nor Shawn. . . .'

She stared at him. 'Jubal . . . you're not talking like the Jubal I knew. You're no slave.'

Jubal laughed hollowly. 'Ask Murphy or Shawn Thibault if I'm a slave. It so happens I'm not. I'm a free man. I was shanghaied down here, Marcy. Two white men forced me to come down, with a number of other blacks they'd kidnapped. Some were runaways, some were not. It didn't make any difference. We were put on the block and sold.'

'But can't you prove you're free?'

'Not down here I can't. In St Louis, where I came from, maybe I could. My papa and mama were manumitted. I was born free. I want to go back there and prove it, and then I want to go somewhere so I can live decently, educate myself even further.'

'I don't blame you,' she said. 'I can't help you in this, but I don't blame you and I swear I'll remain silent.'

'Marcy,' he said. 'I want you to come with me.'

She shrank back in the dainty chair she occupied. 'Oh, no, Jubal! Please don't ask that of me. I can't leave here. I . . . just can't.'

'Why won't you come? Because I'm blacker than you are?'

'It isn't that. I'm Negro. I'm reminded of it all the time. I like you, Jubal. I like you very much, but it's simply impossible.'

'It's not impossible, Marcy. I haven't time to be smooth about this, to be glib and fancy. I fell in love with you one night not long ago, when you opened the door to Murphy Thibault. I saw you for a few seconds, and I knew I could never rest until you belonged to me.'

She bowed her head. 'Jubal, please . . . please. . . . '

'I saw you again when you admitted Shawn, and once more I was sure. When you spoke to me at Congo Square, I thought my dismal world had suddenly grown flowers. I was beside myself. I wanted to tell you what I really was, but I didn't dare. Now I have nothing to lose so I can tell you. I can get work. I can make money enough for us. We won't be a slave and his wench. I want to marry you. If you'll just give me the chance.'

'Jubal – no! It can't be.'

'You're scared. I don't blame you for that. But you can send your coachman on an errand. I'll take his place. You can sit in that barouche as bold as brass, and we'll just head out of town. They won't know we're gone for several hours and we can drive the horses fast.'

She got up and walked over to him. She bent and she touched his face and then placed her cheek against his. 'I can't go with you, Jubal. I don't know if I could ever love you. I think I could, but I cannot go. You have to trust me and understand there are reasons. You can use the coach – go by yourself. I don't care if they say I'm implicated in your escape, but I can't go with you. Don't ask me again.'

He jumped up. She was so close to him. He seized her, She wore some sort of sultry perfume and it made his senses reel. He drew her to him. She opened her mouth to protest and he placed a big hand over it. He picked her up, still keeping her from shouting or screaming. He carried her out of the room. He mistakenly began to enter the tiny kitchen, backed out and found the bedroom. He took no heed of its furnishings. All he knew was that she was in his arms, he was going to possess her and after that, she'd go with him. He laid her on the bed. Her eyes were wide in terror and pleading, but she didn't resist. She wasn't fighting him. That was a good sign.

He kept his hand over her mouth while he used his other hand to slip up beneath her dress. She wore under-things. He yanked them down roughly and saw her wince. He was gentle after that.

'Have to do this,' he said. 'I'm so in love with you I can't help myself. I didn't ask you to come into my life. You just did, and from the moment I saw you, I knew this was going to happen.'

She pleaded again with her eyes. She could have bitten his hand, she could have kicked and squirmed, but she was passive. Only her eyes talked to him. He couldn't stand looking into them.

He lowered his pants. There would be no finesse to this, much as he wanted there to be. He didn't have the time and she might elude him if he let go of her to remove his clothes. Afterward, after she'd tasted the sweetness of it all, then she'd be docile and willing. Then he'd strip and so would she, and they'd do it over. Next time she'd relish every last morsel of its wonder.

Her thighs grew hard. That much she resisted. He pried her legs apart, firmly, but without bruising her. He made her lie back. His right hand guided his maleness up to her. She closed her eyes. He mistook that for the beginnings of ecstasy. He entered her. It was difficult for him and he blamed her smallness. She was tiny, dainty and so lovely.

He felt her grow rigid and her face contorted in pain. Then she relaxed. He was inside her all the way, he was drawing in and out, he'd never experienced such astonishing satisfaction. He loved her with all his heart. He grew gentle, undemanding because she was not cooperating. She would next time. She was scared now, not used to him, and he was big. All over big, on top of her, what entered her, just a bigness she would one day enjoy.

He was done. It was over so fast. He removed his hand from her mouth. He lay there, looking at her. He saw two tears well out of the corners of her eyes. He withdrew quickly and got off her.

'Marcy . . . Marcy . . . don't cry. No need to cry. I love you so much I can't describe it. Marcy, we'll be happy together. We. . . .'

He looked down at his hand. It was covered with blood. He backed away, staring at her.

'Marcy . . . it was the first time. For you, the first time. But, Marcy . . . it couldn't be. This is a trick. Murphy was here. You kissed him. Shawn came, he held you in his arms. It can't be that I was first. It . . . just . . . can't be. . . .'

She didn't sit up, she just lay there listlessly.

'Murphy Thibault is my father,' she said. 'Shawn is my brother. They love me very much and I love them. They come to see me every time they're in New Orleans. My mother was Creole, part Negro, of course. She loved Murphy too. She died when I was born. The nuns raised me, but Murphy never neglected me. He is my father. I adore him.'

Jubal stood there, statue-like. He didn't say anything.

'That's why I can't go away with you. It would break his heart, and his heart has been broken enough. When I was born, his wife found out. She lived with him, but never again as a wife, never again without reminding him he was the father of a girl with Negro blood. It has almost killed him. Only Shawn understood, and I love my brother with all my heart.'

'Why . . . didn't you tell me?' he asked in a hushed voice.

'How could I? You never gave me the chance. When you took your hand from my lips, it was too late.'

'Too late,' he said. 'Much too late. For so long I prided myself on being smart and clever. All this time I've been a bigger fool than the most stupid nigger slave. It was there for me to see and understand, but I didn't. I only wanted you. I was an animal. I didn't give you the kind of love a girl like you needs and respects. Two white men slept with you so I had to have you too. That's what I thought in my stupidity.'

'Oh, Jubal, it wasn't your fault. Take my barouche. Go away. Run . . . run as fast as you can. If I could go with you, I would. I cannot, but you must go.'

He shook his head. 'I've deflowered you, a sin that can't be forgiven. I'm a fool. A miserable, stupid fool. In having you, I've also wronged your father and brother. There's only one way I can make up for this awful thing I've done.'

'You can't fight that man. He'll kill you, she said.

'I'm dead already. But he won't kill me, Marcy. I won't let him. Because I have to win the fight. Otherwise, I'm not repaying the wrong I did. I'll fight him and kill him and then I'll go back to the plantation as Jubal, the slave. All I ask of you is silence. It's too much to ask, but I do. Will you help me, Marcy?'

She nodded. 'All I can do is wish you luck. May God go with you, Jubal. I know you must do this thing.'

He touched her hair gently. 'Little Marcy. I spent hours dreaming about you, and you're lovelier than I imagined. What I did is unforgivable, but I ask that you try to understand. Good-bye, Marcy. You won't see me again. Never again.'

He walked out. She turned over on the bed, buried her face in the bloody coverlet and wept.

TWENTY

Murphy and Shawn met him at the entrance to the auction yard. Inside were as many men as could be packed there and others straddled the fence. Two nearby trees were filled with those brave enough to climb the branches. Roof-tops of nearby buildings were filled with men. It was a noisy, bloodthirsty, betting crowd.

'Where you been?' Murphy asked angrily. 'We thought you'd run.'

'No, suh, masta, suh, I din' run. Jubal say he fights this man, he fights him.'

'Pa,' Shawn remonstrated, 'he's here. No sense getting mad at him. Jubal, can you whip this man? Can you beat Rouge?'

'Who?' Jubal asked.

'Devol's boy. His name is Rouge.'

'I whups him.'

'He'll try to kill you if he can. He's very dangerous.' Murphy said. 'The thing is, get him first and as quick as you can. If he ever gets his arms around you, that'll be the finish. He'll break every bone in your body.'

'And then tear your balls off,' Shawn added. 'That's why he's so popular and why most niggers are so afraid of him.'

'Got to get his hands on 'em first, masta, suh. Ain't aimin' to let him.'

'Good. You're a fine boy, Jubal. Go in there now and kill him.'

Devol's boy was already in the roped ring. He had removed his shirt and now flexed his enormous muscles for the benefit of the crowd. When Jubal ducked under the ropes, there were loud laughs and jeers. Jubal paid no heed to them. He divested himself of his shirt, stood there quietly waiting for the signal to begin.

Devol, gold-headed cane in his hand, tall gray hat slightly tilted on his head, his coat and trousers a dove gray, impeccably fitted, smiled confidently at Murphy.

'Like to make a side bet, Mr Thibault? Besides the entire take?'

'There's enough riding now,' Murphy said.

'Fact is, you don't have a dime to your name, do you, Mr Thibault? You're as poor as the poorest nigger on your place. When this is over, I think I'll buy your plantation, suh. If I'm generous, you may have a job as my overseer. Perhaps, I say.'

Murphy wrote out a check for ten thousand dollars. 'This is in the bank,' he said. 'Match it or shut up.'

Devol gulped once, but there was no help for it now. He wrote a check for a similar amount. 'I hope your draft is good, suh,' he said.

Murphy handed both checks to Judge Linder, who stood by and listened. 'If my check isn't good, put me in jail, Judge. If Mr Devol's is worthless, you won't have to jail him because I'll kill him.'

Devol had no further remarks to make and he edged away from Murphy. All he wanted now was to have his boy win, to kill this satin-skinned Jubal. Then Devol could really humble Murphy Thibault. Something he'd wanted to do for years. In a few minutes, half an hour at the most, it would be over.

There'd be a dead nigger lying in the ring and a haughty plantation owner and his son stripped of everything they had.

The auctioneer who seemed to officiate at these fights ordered a shuck-down. Jubal stepped out of his pants. The auctioneer moved back out of the way, ready to duck under the ropes.

'You two niggers fight,' he shouted.

'Ain't got a chance.' Murphy was studying Devol's boy. He seemed huger than ever, built like the trunk of a century-old tree with thick legs, supple arms, a massive chest and slim belly. He was kept in trim all the time, a fighting machine upon whom Devol's fortunes depended.

'Never can tell, Pa,' Shawn said, but without much enthusiasm. 'You got ten thousand to cover that check you gave Devol?'

'No, and I don't know where to get it, but way I figure, if we lose they'll take everything, and if my self-respect goes with it, the hell with that too.'

'Papa, what about Marcy?'

The two fighters were circling one another, getting steamed up, trying to decide on the best method of attack. Murphy watched them a moment before he answered.

'Got a bank account in her name that'll more than take care of her for life. Ain't nobody can touch it, no matter what happens to me.'

'I'm glad of that.'

'We both love that fine girl. She's our responsibility, and don't you ever forget it.'

'Ain't likely to,' Shawn said.

Any further conversation was terminated by the sudden attack of Rouge. From a crouch, he hurled himself upon Jubal. It was so swift that Jubal wasn't prepared. While he did leap nimbly aside, it was a fraction of a second too late and Rouge grabbed him by his left arm, gripped it so that Jubal could have screamed with pain, and then swung him as if he were a sack. Jubal's feet left the ground, he did a complete circumference of the ring, stumbled, and Rouge let go of the arm to try and deliver a kick to the face with a heel as hard as rock.

Jubal's left arm was temporarily useless, but his right was strong. It shot out, grabbed Rouge's ankle, twisted hard, and Rouge came down with a thud that shook the ground. Jubal, had he been able to use both arms, might have ended it then, because Rouge was winded from the force of the fall. But Jubal had to flounder about trying to make his left arm work and all his right could do was pound Rouge's face, which was partially blocked by the big Negro's arm.

The crowd, having paid handsomely for the privilege of seeing one man kill another in a bloody battle, had no favorite even though most of them had bet on Rouge. They cheered either one, cursed either one, and did it loudly and with spirit.

Rouge scrambled to his feet, taking two hard blows to the back of the head in the process, but they didn't seem to bother him. He flew at Jubal again, this time with arms spread wide to envelop Jubal and crush him to death. Jubal stayed away from that one and, as Rouge lumbered by, Jubal leaped on the man's broad back. He wound an arm around his throat, closed the arm at the elbow like a vise and tried to shut off Rouge's wind. It was like trying to choke an iron pipe. Rogue bent down, threw Jubal over his head and before Jubal could get to his feet, Rouge pinned him.

The big buck now showed Jubal two rows of the biggest teeth Jubal had ever seen. Rouge clamped them around Jubal's right ear and bit down. There was a massive crunching sound, excruciating pain, and when Jubal managed to get to his feet again, his hand touched the bleeding spot where his ear had been. Rouge opened his mouth and spat the ear out.

Jubal howled in rage and charged. His right arm, straight out, had the fingers spread. He was aiming at Rouge's eye and his forefinger found it. With the force of the rush behind it, the finger drove deeply into the eye socket, Rouge had his turn of howling in pain.

Both men were maddened to the point of insanity now. Rouge knew the fastest and best way to stop an opponent with the most blood and pain was to mutilate his sex. He made a grab for Jubal's groin, missed and fell in the dirt. He had trouble seeing now, but there was still plenty of fight left in him. He managed to roll over twice as Jubal sought to kick his face in.

He made an ineffectual grab for Jubal's legs, forcing Jubal to retreat. Rouge came up quickly, holding there on one knee, getting his breath back, trying to get used to having only the sight of one eye.

He knew Jubal would leap to the left, as he always did, and Rogue was ready for that. It was the side he could see out of and it helped. He launched himself into a dive, one hand thrust out. Jubal moved as Rouge expected, right into the aim of that extended hand. Fingers closed around Jubal's testicles.

Everything swam for Jubal. This was pain that crippled. If Rouge managed to brace himself and pull, Jubal knew he was a dead man.

He threw himself at Rouge. The big buck, one hand grasping Jubal's sex, the other busy trying to find a purchase in the same vulnerable spot, was wide open. Jubal's teeth clamped around the broad, slightly bleeding nose. He brought his jaws together, felt cartilage crunch. Rouge opened his mouth to scream. Jubal jammed his hand into it. The mouth was big enough. His fingers found Rouge's tongue and yanked at it.

Rouge let go of his hold, brought his hands up to prevent his tongue from being torn from its roots. Jubal yanked harder, bringing Rouge's head down. At the same time, Jubal brought up a knee. He heard jaw bone crack.

Rouge got free somehow, backed away. He was so bloody around the head that he was unrecognisable, and he was half blind as well, but still dangerous. Jubal leaped for Rouge's blind side, grasped his arm at the wrist and elbow, applied pressure and flung the big man to the ground.

Jubal put one foot on Rouge's chest, twisted the arm. Bone broke. Jubal tugged with all the strength he had left. The arm came free of his socket, blood spurted from the shoulder. Jubal didn't tear it off, simply let it hang there, useless for any further purpose.

Jubal had him now. He himself was so badly hurt he doubted he'd ever get over it, but there was a certain grim satisfaction in seeing what he'd done to Rouge – and what he meant to do.

Rouge stumbled forward. He fell, apparently going into unconsciousness. Jubal tried to step back and avoid him, but didn't succeed. Rouge's right arm suddenly clamped a hold at the back of Jubal's neck while Rouge's face was plastered against Jubal's chest. Teeth sought Jubal's left nipple, closed, blood spurted and Jubal yelled in agony.

Now he lost all sense of reasoning. He had to kill this already half-dead monster who didn't know enough to lie down and stop breathing. He had to be stopped, forever.

Blood flowed out of the wound where Jubal's ear had been, more blood poured down over his chest from the open wound where his nipple had been. He knew he was bleeding between his legs. There was an intense numbness there.

Jubal moved slower now. He was at the end of his resources. He had to kill Rouge at once or not at all. He was no longer afraid that Rouge could kill him, because the big buck could only flounder about, growing weaker and weaker.

Jubal was aware that the crowd was yelling in one blast of shrill sound. He approached Rouge, actually feeling sorry for him now. He quietly raised his right arm, closed it around Rouge's head, tucked it down under the arm. His left hand, no longer paralysed, grasped Rouge's chin. Bone scraped as the broken jaw was again displaced. Jubal began to apply pressure.

The crowd had suddenly grown silent. Jubal wasn't aware of this. His world was a spinning top of pain and agony. He suddenly twisted Rouge's head, at the same time applying leverage with his body. Rouge's neck broke with a loud crack.

Jubal let the body fall to the ground. He looked about. Everything was out of focus. But noisy. Painfully noisy! He wished these fool people would stop yelling. Someone approached him. He had no idea who it was.

But he'd won. He was on his feet and Rouge lay dead somewhere back in the ring. Jubal's steps were wooden. He tried again to focus. Something touched the back of his neck. It felt cold. Then there was a sudden and complete blackness from which Jubal would never again emerge.

His body crumpled. That magnificent body. now battered, but still triumphant a second ago, fell limply to the dirt.

Devol backed away, holding the derringer as if it were a weapon worth defying. He screamed his hatred. Murphy came toward him, stepping over Jubal's body. Devol screeched and raised the derringer to use the second and last bullet on Murphy.

Devol never saw Shawn coming at him from the left. Shawn grabbed Devol's right wrist, twisted it, broke it, and the gun fell. Shawn hit him in the face, forced him back into the hands of the maddened crowd.

And it was over.

They buried Jubal in the cemetery Murphy staked out, where the whites of Briarfield Plantation would someday be interred. Jubal led the way for them because, as Murphy said, without Jubal, there'd have been no more Briarfield Plantation. It was the least they could do for him.

Calinda wept quietly. Soon she would bulge with his child.

Pauline wept bitterly and loudly. In her, his seed was also planted and she suspected it.

In New Orleans, Marcy Fournet sat weeping, partly because she could not go to pay her homage to Jubal. Her tears would have been more copious had she known she too would bear Jubal's child.

Jubal was dead, but part of him still lived on in the bellies of three women, one jet black, one pure white, the third a beautiful, child-like girl with a golden skin.

CHILDREN OF KAYWANA

by Edgar Mittelholzer

A sensational and magnificent novel set in the plantations of seventeenth century Guiana – the first of a best-selling trilogy. It is supercharged with the passion and violence of men and women living and working amid the heat, the terrors and the smouldering frenzy of brutalized slaves.

'Full of blood and lust and torture and fighting . . . a magnificent piece of tale-telling.' **Punch**

KAYWANA STOCK

by Edgar Mittelholzer